*Other Bard Books by*
**Jorge Amado**

Dona Flor and Her Two Husbands
Gabriela, Clove and Cinnamon
Jubiabá
Pen, Sword, Camisole: A Fable to Kindle a Hope
Sea of Death
Tereza Batista
Tieta

# HOME IS THE SAILOR

## JORGE AMADO

Translated from
the Portuguese by
HARRIET DE ONÍS

 A BARD BOOK/PUBLISHED BY AVON BOOKS

Originally published in Portuguese by Livraria Martins Editora as "A Completa Verdade Sobre As Discututas Aventuras do Comandante Vasco Moscoso de Aragao, Capitao de Longo Curso" included in the volume entitled *Os Velhos Marineiros*. Copyright © 1961 by Jorge Amado.


AVON BOOKS
A division of
The Hearst Corporation
1790 Broadway
New York, New York 10019

Copyright © 1964 by Alfred A. Knopf, Inc.
Published by arrangement with Alfred A. Knopf, Inc.
Library of Congress Catalog Card Number: 64-12295
ISBN: 0-380-45187-5

First Bard Printing: July 1979

BARD TRADEMARK REG. U.S. PAT. OFF. AND IN OTHER COUNTRIES, MARCA REGISTRADA, HECHO EN U.S.A.

Printed in the U.S.A.

OPM 10 9 8 7 6 5 4 3 2

*But of him, himself, they know not,*
*Nor ever will they know,*
*For he never lived,*
*He neither was nor was not,*
*Like things that exist*
*Only in imagination.*
*Who could invent another!*
          CARLOS PENA FILHO, *Sinister Episode*

*All the winds of the world will*
*meet in congress.*
JOAQUIM CARDOZO, *The Congress of the Winds*

# CONTENTS

*11*

# CONTENTS

# EPISODE THREE:

# CONTENTS

# EPISODE ONE

*Of the arrival of the captain in the suburb of Periperi, in Bahía; of the account of his stirring adventures on the five oceans, seas, and in distant ports, with rough sailors and passionate women; and of the effect of the chronometer and telescope on the placid suburban community*

*Of how the narrator, on the basis of a
certain previous and pleasant experience, prepares to bring up the truth
from the bottom of a well*

MY PURPOSE, my sole purpose—believe me!—is merely to
re-establish the truth. The whole truth, in such a way as to dispel
any lingering doubt concerning Captain Vasco Moscoso de
Aragão and his singular adventures.

"The truth lies at the bottom of a well," I once read, I can't
recall whether in a book or a newspaper. In any case, it was in
print, and who can doubt the printed word? I, at any rate, am not
given to questioning, much less denying, literature or journal-
ism. And if this were not enough, I have heard similar phrases
from the lips of important persons, thus leaving no margin, in
this business of bringing up the truth from a well and putting it in
a safer place, for typographical error, as, for example, *palace*
("the truth is in the royal palace") or *bosom* ("the truth hides in
the bosom of beautiful women") or *pole* ("the truth has fled to
the North Pole") or *people* ("the people are the repository of the
truth"). Phrases, all of them, it seems to me, more elegant, less
coarse, devoid of that vague feeling of neglect and chill inherent
in the word "well."

His Honor, Dr. Siqueira, a retired judge and a respectable,
upright citizen, of shining and erudite baldness, explained to me
that it was a cliché, that is to say, something so self-evident and

19

well known as to be practically a catchword, a commonplace. In his solemn, sententious voice he pointed out a curious detail: not only does truth lie at the bottom of a well, but it is to be found there completely naked, without a veil to cover it, not even its private parts. At the bottom of a well and naked.

Dr. Alberto Siqueira is the pinnacle, the acme of culture in this suburb of Periperi where we live. It is he who makes the Second of July speech in the little public square and that of September Seventh in the primary school, not to mention other less outstanding occasions, and proposes the toasts at anniversaries and christenings. It is to him that I owe much of what I know, acquired during our conversations on nocturnal strolls to his house; I owe him respect and gratitude. When in his solemn voice, with a precise gesture, he clarifies a doubt for me, at the moment everything seems clear and simple; no objection raises its head. But after I leave him and begin to turn matters over in my mind, the simplicity and the proof take their leave, as, for example, in this matter of the truth. Everything becomes confused and difficult again; I try to recall His Honor's explanations, but they elude me. It all becomes a rigmarole. But, how is it possible to doubt the word of such a learned man, with all those shelves crammed with books, legal codes, treatises? Meanwhile, however much he explains to me that it is just a catch phrase, I often find myself thinking about that well, undoubtedly dark and deep, where the truth betook herself to hide her nakedness, leaving us in the worst confusion, arguing over everything or nothing, bringing ruination, despair, and war upon us.

The well isn't a well; the bottom of a well isn't the bottom of a well. According to the proverb, what this means is that the truth is difficult to come by, that she does not show herself in her nakedness in the market place within reach of everybody. But it is our duty, that of all of us, to seek out the truth of every fact, to submerge ourselves in the darkness of the well until we arrive at her divine light.

"Divine light" is the judge's phrase, as is all the preceding paragraph. He is so cultured that whatever he says sounds like a speech, with fancy words, even when he is talking to his worthy spouse, Dona Ernestina. "Truth is the beacon that illuminates my life," His Honor is in the habit of saying to me, when at night, beneath the sky of innumerable stars and scant electric light, we discuss the news of the world and our suburb. Dona Ernestina, monstrous fat, glistening with perspiration, and somewhat retarded mentally, nods her elephantine head in agreement. A shining beacon, casting its rays afar, that is what the truth is for the noble retired judge.

Perhaps for that very reason its light does not find its way into the nearer corners, the side streets, the hidden Alley of the Three Butterflies, which shelters, in the discreet semi-shade of a little house among the trees, beautiful, smiling, brown Dondoca, whose parents sought out His Honor when Zé Canjiquinha disappeared from circulation, traveling south.

He had robbed Dondoca of her greatest treasure, as her distressed father, Pedro Torresmo, picturesquely put it, and had left the girl stripped of her honor and without a penny.

"Destitute, Your Honor, destitute..."

The judge pronounced a moral and moving discourse, and promised to do what he could. And, confronted with the touching sight of the victim smiling through her tears, he came through with a small financial contribution, for under the stiff bosom of the magistrate's starched shirt, there beats—even though it is hard to believe—a tender heart. He promised to issue a search warrant and order of arrest for the "niggardly Don Juan," forgetting, carried away as he was by the cause of outraged virtue, that he was retired, with neither lawyers nor police at his command. He would also bring the case to the attention of his friends in the city. The "cheap seducer" would get what he deserved.

And it was he in person—so zealous of his responsibilities as judge (even though retired) was Dr. Siqueira—who carried the news of the measures taken, to the poor, offended family in its distant domicile. Pedro Torresmo was sleeping off the previous night's hangover; in the backyard Eufrasia, the scrawny mother of the victim, was hard at work washing clothes, and Dondoca was tending the stove. A smile burgeoned on her full lips, timid but expressive; the judge looked at her admonishingly, and took her by the hand.

"I have come to scold you..."

"I didn't want to. It was him..." whimpered the girl.

"It was very wrong," he said, taking hold of her firm young arm.

She burst into tears of contrition, and the judge, the better to reprove and counsel her, seated her on his lap, stroked her cheek, pinched her arm. It was a beautiful sight: the implacable sternness of the judge tempered by the understanding kindness of the man. Dondoca hid her blushing face against the comforting shoulder, her lips innocently tickling the illustrious neck.

The law never caught up with Zé Canjiquinha; but by way of compensation, from the time of that felicitous visit, Dondoca came under the protecting wing of justice, and lives like a queen, dressed to kill, in the little house in the Alley of the Three Butterflies, and Pedro Torresmo has given up work for good. There you have a truth which the beacon of the judge did not illuminate; I had to dive into the well myself to find it. Moreover, in honor of the truth, the whole truth, I should add that it has been a pleasant, a delightful plunge, for at the bottom of that well was the soft, vegetable floss mattress of Dondoca's bed where—after I leave, around ten at night, the erudite conversation of His Honor and his voluminous consort—she tells me intimate details about the distinguished magistrate, which, unfortunately, are unfit to print.

As can be seen, I have some experience in such matters; it is not the first time I have investigated the truth. Therefore, inspired by His Honor—"it is our duty, that of all of us, to seek out the truth of every fact"—I am prepared to unravel the skein of the captain's adventures, clearing up once and for all this much disputed and complicated matter. It is not merely a question of the tangled threads; it is something far more difficult. In the course of it there are knots, sailor's knots, loose ends, threads of different colors, real and imaginary things, and where is the truth of it all? At the time this took place, in 1929, more than thirty years ago, the adventures of the captain, and the captain himself, were the center of Periperi's existence, giving rise to heated arguments, dividing the inhabitants, bringing about enmities and grudges, almost like a religious war. On the one hand were the captain's supporters, his unconditional admirers, and on the other, his detractors, headed by old Chico Pacheco, retired customs inspector, whose memory is still recalled with smiles even today, a slanderer, a harsh, irreverent man, a doubting Thomas.

But we will come to all this in due time; the search for truth calls not only for determination and perseverance, but also for good will and method. At the moment I am still at the curb of the well, considering how best to descend to its mysterious depths. And already old Chico Pacheco has arisen from his grave in the distant cemetery to confuse me, stand over me, upset me. A troublesome fellow, a busybody, a show-off, a maniac in the matter of proof. What he wanted was to be the leading citizen in this flourishing suburban town, where everything is pleasant and gentle, even the sea, a protected gulf where the waves never rise in fury, and a beach without breakers or undertow, where life is quiet and peaceful.

My wish, my one wish, believe me, is to be objective and dispassionate. To seek out the truth amid the controversies, unearth it from the past, without taking sides, stripping from the most contradictory versions all the veils spun by fantasy to hide, even partially, the naked truth. Though I can bear witness in my own flesh, or, to be more exact, the golden flesh of Dondoca, that complete nakedness is not always more seductive than when it plays peekaboo under a sheet or any covering that hides a breast, a thigh, the curve of a hip. But, in the last analysis, the truth we seek with such obstinacy and fury the world over is not something to get into bed with.

## Of the hero's disembarkation in Periperi and his acquaintance with the sea

"LOOK ALIVE, MATES."

It was a voice accustomed to give orders. With a gesture of his hand he set the course, came down the three steps of the platform, and took charge of the crossing, a steady hand at the helm, eyes like a compass.

A kind of small procession formed and marched down the street. At the head walked the captain, resolute and serene. A few yards behind, Caco Podre and Misael, the two porters, with part of his luggage. By that hour of the day Caco Podre had already knocked back his customary load, his gait was somewhat rolling, and the title of "mate" by which the newcomer addressed him was not entirely a misnomer. Then followed the growing group of inquisitive observers, whispering to one another, for the ship's wheel which Misael carried on his head was like the pied piper's flute.

He did not enter the house. He merely pointed it out to the porters, and kept on his way. He made for the beach, walked to the foot of the bluff, measured it with a knowing eye, and began to climb it. It was neither high nor steep, a gentle slope where during the summer days the children clambered up and down, and at night lovers hid from the public gaze. But there was such dignity in the captain's bearing that they all grasped the arduous nature of the undertaking, as though suddenly those modest rocks had been transformed into a sheer stone wall, never scaled by human feet.

When he reached the top, he stood there, his arms folded across his breast, gazing out at the waters. In that silent pose, his face to the sun, his hair fluttering in the wind (that gentle, perpetual breeze of Periperi), he resembled a soldier standing at attention, or, in view of his impressiveness, the bronze statue of a general. He wore an odd coat, not unlike a military tunic, of heavy blue cloth with a broad collar. Only Zequinha Curvelo, a tireless reader of adventure stories, grasped the fact that there before them, in the flesh, was a sea dog, a man whose element was ships and storms. He whispered his discovery to the others: on the cover of a novel about the sea, the story of a little sailing vessel lashed by tempests on the Sargasso Sea, there was a sailor wearing a coat like that.

That motionless pose lasted only a minute, but it was a long one, almost an eternity, stamping the image on the memory of the observers. Then he stretched out his short arm in a long gesture and spoke these words: "Here we are, Sea, together again."

Once more he folded his arms across his breast in a gesture that was at once an affirmation and a challenge. His gaze rested upon the calm waters of the gulf, where the sea and the river met in the hospitable bay. Off in the distance, dark ships rode at anchor, and swift fishing craft skimmed along, their white sails dotting the calm blue of the seascape. That gaze and that immobile posture revealed an acquaintance of long standing with the sea, made up of love and anger, colorful experiences, which even those drab hearts, far removed from adventure and heroism, could sense. But exception must be made of Zequinha Curvelo, for he lived in a different climate, devouring his dime novels about pirates and pioneers. He had the makings of a protoprophet, a St. John the Baptist foretelling the hero who had just arrived.

And so, when the captain descended from the bluff and entered the circle of his observers, murmuring as though to himself: "I cannot live away from the sea," he entered at the same time into the admiration of his new fellow citizens. Yet he seemed not to see them, or to be aware of their presence and their curiosity.

As though each gesture had been carefully calculated, he first measured with his eye the distance between himself and the nearby, isolated house beside the beach, with its windows opening out over the water. He set his course toward the door and prepared to board it. The onlookers followed his every movement, eying him with respect: the round, ruddy face, the thick, silvery hair, the sailor's coat with its shining brass buttons. As the advance began, Zequinha Curvelo interposed himself between the others and the captain; he had found his proper place.

The porters arrived with the rest of the luggage, the captain issued orders, precise, explicit. Suitcases, beds, chests to the bedrooms; crates and boxes to the living room.

Only when these tasks had been carried out did he seem to become aware of the crowd that had gathered and was watching him from the street. He smiled, he bowed, he laid his hand on his breast with a gesture that had something Oriental, exotic about it. A chorus of "Good afternoons" answered his greeting. Zequinha Curvelo, plucking up his courage, took a step toward the door.

From one of the roomy pockets of his coat the captain extracted a surprising object. It looked like a revolver. Zequinha fell back. It wasn't a revolver. What the devil was it? The captain put it in his mouth—it was a pipe, but not any old kind of a pipe, which of itself would have been a novelty in that sedate community. It was of carved meerschaum, the stem in the form of the legs and thighs of a woman; the bowl, of the bust and head. "Oh," murmured Zequinha, who stood rooted to the spot.

When he had recovered from his shock, the new arrival was moving away from the door. Zequinha hurried forward, introduced himself, and asked if he could be of any help.

"Thank you very much," the captain shook his head. He took a visiting card from his wallet, and handed it to Zequinha, adding as he did so: "An old sailor, at your orders."

They watched him in the living room as with hammer, screwdriver, and the help of the porters he opened the boxes. Out of them came strange instruments, a huge telescope, a mariner's compass. The onlookers hung around for a while longer, watching, and then went to spread the news. Zequinha displayed the visiting card, adorned with an anchor, which read:

CAPTAIN VASCO MOSCOSO DE ARAGÃO
*Master Mariner*

And there you have the account of his arrival in Periperi early that infinitely blue afternoon when, with one stroke, he established his fame and cemented his reputation.

*Which deals with retired government
employees and businessmen, women on
the beach and in bed, runaway damsels,
ruin and suicide, and a meerschaum pipe*

A PROPITIOUS CLIMATE, comprised of tragedy and mystery,
anteceded the memorable day of the captain's landing, as
though coming events were casting their shadow before.

Only rarely does anything unforeseen break the monotony of
Periperi's suburban existence. This holds true from March to
November; during the three summer months—December,
January, February—all the suburbs on the Leste Brasileira
Line, of which Periperi is the largest, the most populous, and the
most beautiful, fill up with vacationists. Many of the best
houses, which belong to city residents, are closed most of the
year, opening only in the summer. It is then that Periperi comes
to life, suddenly invaded by gay young people: boys playing
soccer on the beach, girls in bathing suits sunning themselves on
the sand, boats skimming over the water, walks, picnics, parties,
flirtations and love-making under the trees of the square or in
the shadow of the bluffs.

On the memories of these three months, the commentaries on
fancied or real events that took place during the summer, the
year-round residents live for the remaining nine months.
Recalling love affairs, parties, fights between hot-headed,
jealous young athletes, the near-drowning of a child, birthday

27

celebrations, drunken brawls that disturbed the silence of the night.

The year-round population (with the exception of the fishermen and a few storekeepers—the owners of the single bakery, the two bars, and a couple of grocery stores, the drugstore—, several employees of the Leste Brasileira who live near the station) is made up of retired government employees and businessmen and their families, usually consisting of a wife and, occasionally, an old maid sister-in-law. Some of these senior citizens claim they prefer Periperi as the quiet backwater it is before and after the summer season, but the truth is that they all become involved, one way or another, in the turbulent life of the summer visitors. When they are not eying longingly the half-naked girls on the beach—what dishes!—they are making caustic comments about the couples that seek out the dark corners. Mr. Adriano Meira, a retired hardware dealer, goes out every night in summer after nine with a flashlight to check, as he puts it, on the lovers, "to see that they are on the job." He has worked out a complete itinerary of alleys, bluffs, rocks, back yards, doorways, corners where the lovers seek the solitude love demands. The next day Mr. Adriano makes his detailed and spicy report. The old men rub their hands, their eyes aglow.

And this is not merely for summer consumption. Every incident is stored away in memory's mothballs, and brought out, carefully analyzed and broken down, after the vacationists have departed and peace has settled once more on Periperi, when the hours grow long and Mr. Adriano's flashlight picks out nothing in the dark corners but Caco Podre sleeping off a jag or the trysts of cooks and fishermen.

Some summers are exceptional. Not because of the beauty of the weather, or the dazzling splendor of the greens and blues of trees and water, or the cool of the breeze or the star-studded nights. All these things cut little ice with the retired businessmen and government employees. They are the summers when there has been some really juicy scandal on which to feast during the long uneventful months. But these are rare, more's the pity.

Now, the summer that preceded the captain's arrival was lavish beyond measure. Two scandals: one right at the start, in January; the other after Carnival, this one with a tragic ending that made it stand out in the annals of the suburban calendar.

Strictly speaking, it is impossible to establish any real

connection between the case of Lieutenant Colonel Ananias Miranda of the Military Police, and Captain Vasco Moscoso de Aragão. But there is a general tendency to link the two incidents, as though the misfortunes of Ananias were a kind of prelude to the adventures of Vasco.

*Vox populi* would not deserve the respect historians have conferred upon it, nor would it be worth the trouble to narrate here this bloodless scandal of January, were it not for the fact that there is not an event from which some lesson cannot be learned. Thus in the scandalous—and swift—episodes involving the lieutenant colonel, his wife Ruth, and the young third-year law student, Arlindo Paiva, we find at least two valuable teachings. First, even the best and the purest intentions are subject to evil interpretation. Second, one should never trust schedules, however rigid, not even the military.

The intentions in question refer to the student; the schedule, to the mettlesome officer of the Military Police. As for Ruth, hers was the loneliness of the warm afternoons, the slow hours that hung heavy on her hands, the need for moral consolation. What good was it to have a husband, the lusciously ripe beauty with the long-lashed, melancholy eyes fretfully asked herself, as she sunned her neglected body on the beach, if she was always alone during those interminable Periperi afternoons? The lieutenant colonel breakfasted at ten in the morning, sprinted off to catch the train, for the schedule in his division was strict. He didn't come home until seven in the evening, when he changed into pajamas, had supper, and sat dozing in a rocking chair by the door. Was that having a husband, a man in her life, whose duty it was to give her affection and tenderness, to care for her body and her soul, Ruth de Morais Miranda asked herself, listless and lonely on the beach, while the sun burned her body and lack of attention gnawed at her soul.

Touched by the melancholy of the colonel's lady, so in need of moral comfort, of company to assuage her loneliness, young Paiva did not hesitate to sacrifice a few hours of his days, replete though they were with pleasant duties. He gave up his walks, exciting soccer games on the beach, instructive conversations with his fellow students, even a promising flirtation. Generous behavior that bespoke a heart cast in a noble mold, worthy of all encomium. Inasmuch as in Periperi the yearning lady could not fill up her afternoons with trips to the movies, visits with her friends, or shopping excursions in the Rua Chile, he placed his talent, his youth, and his budding and seductive mustache at the service of mitigating her woes.

For his part, the lieutenant colonel one day managed to circumvent the rigidity of the military schedule. What a surprise this would be for his little wife, who was always complaining about his being away! Usually when he returned at nightfall and tried to take her in his arms, she would push him away, vengeful, wounded in her woman's pride: "All day you leave me high and dry here, as though I didn't even exist..."

He bought a kilo of grapes, Ruth's favorite fruit. She loved to sink her teeth into the juicy pulp. He bought a cheese, a jar of marmalade. And, so it would be a real party, a bottle of Portuguese wine. He took the 2:30 afternoon train. Ruth would be alone and sad, the poor thing...

She wasn't alone and she wasn't sad. The minute he crossed the doorsill, the lieutenant colonel got his first surprise: Zefa, the maid, who had been working for them for a long time, no sooner laid eyes on him than she dashed out of the back door, screaming for help. From the bedroom came gay sounds, Ruth's laughter and, my God, someone else's! With the packages dangling from his fingers, the bottle of wine under his arm, Ananias kicked open the door of the bedroom. Limited as he was aesthetically, he was not moved by the sight of two young and naked bodies or by the poetry of the tender exchanges between the gifted student and the colonel's beautiful lady. He was not filled with admiration; he was filled with rage. He got all tangled up in the packages (he had threaded the strings on his fingers), which detracted to a degree from the dignity the situation called for. And this was the salvation of young Paiva. Without a thought for his attire, he leaped from the bed, flung open the window, and made it to the street. As naked as God had sent him into the world, he crossed the square full of people with the speed of a champion of the hundred-yard dash. Finally disentangled from the packages, revolver in hand, the lieutenant colonel of the Military Police came pursuing him with insults and shots. Through the open window, the bolder snoopers could still see the naked and consoled loneliness of Ruth proclaiming its innocence.

The student disappeared, hidden by his family or friends. Long parleys were held behind closed doors between the officer and his wife, suitcases were packed, and they left that same night by the last train. They went off arm in arm and most affectionately, according to the testimony of certain lucky dogs who watched them depart.

To connect these events with the captain would not seem easy. Nevertheless, old Leminhos, retired Post Office and Telegraph employee and the only living witness to these episodes, every time he recalls the history of the captain, never fails to say: "It all began when a major of Briosa caught his wife in bed with a student." There is no way of knowing why Leminhos reduces the lieutenant colonel to the rank of major and establishes a link between Ananias's antlers and the adventures of the captain. Nevertheless, his affirmation is categorical. Leminhos is a man of good sense, and he must have his reasons, which we are bound to respect.

The second scandal was definitely meshed to the captain. Certain things happened in the house where he later came to live, which, if it had not been for the tragedy that befell the Cordeiro family, he would never have had the chance to get at the bargain price he paid for it.

This Cordeiro family consisted of the father, Pedro Cordeiro—who owned a distillery—the mother, and four daughters of marrying age. Pedro Cordeiro would have been in excellent financial shape, except that he was a spendthrift and improvident, and the proof of this was that summer home, large and comfortable, built on a solid stone foundation, almost as fine as his city residence. He spent a fortune building it, and on the house-warming party. He indulged his daughters' every whim; he even bought them a launch with an outboard motor.

The mother was in charge of the campaign to find husbands for the girls. There was always some festivity going on in the house with the green shutters, couples dancing in the big room that looked out over the sea, where later the captain would set up his telescope. The girls went out in the launch, they spent the evening on the reefs, they went to picnics in Paripe, they were on the go every minute, the life of the summer season. One of them, the second, Rosalva, had become engaged the year before to an agronomist, and she did not take the path to the beach at night but sat with her fiancé on the porch, hand in hand. Hand, mouth, and thigh, according to Mr. Adriano Meira, he of the flashlight.

During Carnival there was a dance at Pedro Cordeiro's house that lasted from Saturday until Tuesday. And a few days later came the scandal: Adélia, the youngest of the four, dark and mutinous, disappeared, taking with her her own clothes and the best of her sisters' wardrobe, and, in the bargain, Dr. Aristides Melo, a physician and married. Practically the entire city viewed the spectacle staged by the deserted wife, storming into the shattered home of the Cordeiros, demanding with howls and tears the husband "that trollop of your daughter stole from me." The Cordeiros fled from Periperi, and people were still gossiping about the affair when the shot rang out with which Pedro Cordeiro put an end to 'his troubles in the office of his distillery in Bahía when he was declared bankrupt. The echoes of the shot reached the suburb by train, accompanied by a wave of rumors: all the suicide's property was mortgaged; impatient creditors beleaguered the corpse; the agronomist had broken off the engagement, alleging weighty reasons: a discredited family, a dowerless fiancée. Another daughter, the oldest, had also taken up with a married man, which seemed to be a kind of family failing or fashion. Nobody talked about anything else, and the ladies whispered behind their hands the shocking details of the Cordeiro girls' love affairs.

On one occasion Mr. Adriano Meira caught the oldest of the sisters in the rays of his flashlight, her dress up to her naval, berthed alongside a stranger in the early morning hours on the beach, "showing everything from the waist down." And things of this sort by the dozen. The rains were heavy that year, flooding the sandy streets, stimulating the imagination.

Only the residents of Periperi could fully appreciate a scandal of such dimensions, one girl running away with a married man, another losing her virtue on the beach, and a suicide and bankruptcy for good measure. It filled the rainy days when the vacationers had departed and the suburb lived on memories.

Of the holiday season Periperi preserves only a certain festive air of a summer resort, due perhaps to the color of the houses, which are painted blue, pink, green, yellow, the spreading trees in the square, the beach, and the station. And even more, beyond doubt, to the fact that the bulk of the regular population is made up of people with nothing to do, retired government employees, businessmen, idlers the lot of them. They go to the city once a month to collect their pension, they get out of the habit of wearing a necktie, in the morning they go about in pajamas or an old pair of pants and unbuttoned shirt. They all know one another, they meet every day, their wives discuss domestic problems, exchange slips of plants for the garden, recipes for cakes and preserves, the husbands play backgammon and checkers, lend each other newspapers, some of them go fishing offshore, and they all gather at the station, sitting around on the benches, waiting for the trains to come in. They also meet in the late afternoon in the square. Rocking chairs, armchairs, deck chairs are brought out, in addition to the rustic benches around the trees. They discuss politics, recall things that happened the summer before, and prolong their years far from the hurly-burly of the city, whose lights come on in the distance, indicating that it is time for supper. In the undisturbed peace of this refuge, time moves slowly, and at the torrid hour of the siesta one has the impression that it has come to a full stop.

When the discussion of the Cordeiro tragedy was at its peak, there came a startling piece of news: the house with the green shutters had been sold. How could this have happened unbeknown to them, without anyone getting wind of the negotiations? Nothing there was ever rented or sold without the active participation of the inhabitants, giving suggestions, discussing prices, calling the attention of the interested party to defects and advantages, often arousing the helpless rage of the real-estate agents. And yet this house, so much in the public eye, bespattered, so to speak, with the blood of Pedro Cordeiro, was sold without any participation by them, without their having looked the purchaser over, struck up an acquaintance with him. It was a mystery. There was vague talk of a gentleman of means, retired from business. But what business, what means, what gentleman was this? Nobody knew what his economic status, his civil state, his profession were. They felt cheated.

The mystery could be laid at the door of the rains, there was no other explanation. As a matter of fact, the Magalhães sisters, three old ladies with eyes and ears alert to every sound and movement, whose house was close to the Cordeiros', told about seeing people walking around, two men in raincoats, carrying umbrellas, about a month before. But it was raining so hard they couldn't leave the windows open. Besides, Carminha, the middle sister, had the grippe, and they had to look after her. As it had never entered their minds that the house was for sale, all this undermined their normal vigilance. Two men in raincoats and with umbrellas, the real-estate broker and the buyer, that was all anybody knew.

The arrival of a maid, a dark mulatto in her forties, on the morning train, opened new horizons to the unsatisfied curiosity. She had no more than crossed the threshold of the house when the Magalhães sisters were on hand, offering their help and bombarding her with questions. As the rains had stopped, a crowd of oldsters was gathering in front of the house. They had come out to warm themselves in the sun and they gradually drew near, eager to join in the conversation. But the maid, Balbina, was sullen and grumpy, little given to chitchat. Scrubbing the floor, she answered in monosyllables, turning down all offers of help. But in spite of this, they did manage to find out that the new owner would be arriving in the afternoon.

"With the family?"

"What family?"

They went on duty at the station, having declared a state of alert. This time the new resident would not elude them. The sun had come back, the gentle sun of winter. The days were beautiful; the breeze off the gulf, caressing. They indulged in conjectures: did he play checkers? would he be good at backgammon? Who knows, he might be the long-awaited chess partner for Emilio Fagundes, former section head of the Department of Agriculture, who carried on his matches by correspondence, for in Periperi there was nobody else versed in that scientific and complicated game.

And so, when the captain stepped off the train at half past two, and walked toward the baggage car to supervise the landing of his gear, the majority of the able-bodied men were there waiting for him, raising their eyes from the morning papers or checkerboards to look over the short, stocky arrival, with his ruddy face, his hooked nose, and wearing that extraordinary coat.

"What can that be?" asked Zequinha Curvelo, pointing to the ship's wheel in a crate.

Not even Augusto Ramos, formerly of the Department of the Interior and Justice, and a fervid checker player, who at that moment was setting up a move which would take Liminhos's (of Post Office and Telegraph) queen and three men, could resist the sight of the ship's wheel. He left the game and joined the group. The luggage was spread out over the platform, mysterious boxes with inscriptions in red crayon: "Fragile! Nautical Instruments," a huge globe of the world, a rolled-up rope ladder. The captain was enjoining care upon the porters. Then came the unforgettable scaling of the bluff.

That same afternoon, as the sun was going down and shadow lay over most of the square, Zequinha Curvelo told those who had missed the great scene of the arrival how a shiver had gone down his spine when he saw the captain atop the rocks, undismayed, his face turned to the sun, his eyes fixed on the sea. On the benches and chairs under the tamarind trees, the pensioners and retired businessmen listened with approval. Zequinha was full of enthusiasm: "Even before he went into the house, he went to look at the sea."

The visiting card passed from hand to hand. Old José Paulo, known as Marreco, a retired dealer in pharmaceutical supplies, remarked: "The things that man could tell..."

"Those seafarers, with a woman in every port..." added Emilio Fagundes, with a touch of envy.

"You only have to take a look at him to see that he is a man of action," commented Rui Pessoa, formerly of the Tax Bureau.

Zequinha Curvelo, carrying in his hand a book on whose cover a dauntless sailor was wearing a jacket similar to that of the captain, summed up those first impressions: "Friends, we have a hero living among us."

Night descended, unhurried, slow, like life in Periperi.

"There he comes," someone spoke up.

They all turned in anticipation. At a measured, dignified pace, that of a man in the habit of bestriding the deck in the vast solitude of the sea, the captain came down the street, wearing his pea-jacket, with his pipe in his mouth, and on his tousled hair a cap adorned with an anchor, which they had not seen before. He was looking off into space, undoubtedly accompanied by his memories, his dead sailors, his women left in distant ports. When he came abreast of the group, he raised his hand to his cap in a greeting that was effusively returned. And silence fell, accompanying him on his stroll. Zequinha Curveo could not restrain his impatience: "I'm going to see if I can strike up a conversation..."

"Try to bring him here for a little chat..."

"Let's see what I can do."

He set off at a rapid pace, and caught up with the captain.

"That man must be an encyclopedia," said Marreco.

The captain and Zequinha were coming back toward the group. Zequinha was pointing out the different members, probably giving their names and titles.

"Come over here..."

They got up from the chairs and benches elatedly. Zequinha began to make the introductions; the captain shook hands with each one, saying: "An old sailor, at your service."

They offered him the imposing armchair of old José Paulo. He sat down amidst his neighbors, drew a long puff on his pipe (all eyes were fixed on the carving in the shape of the bare breasts and thighs of a woman, which gave the pipe a suggestion of rare vuluptuousness), and said in his slightly hoarse voice: "I have come here to live because I have never seen two places in the world so much alike as Periperi and Rasmat, an island in the Pacific where I spent several months."

"Were you vacationing there?"

The captain smiled. "Shipwrecked. At that time I was still a second mate aboard a Greek ship..."

"Mr. Captain, please, just a minute. Wait just a minute before you begin," Augusto Ramos interrupted him. "First let me call my wife. She's crazy about stories."

*Of how the voluptuous dancer Soraya and the rude sailor Giovanni participated in the wake and funeral of old Doninha Barata*

NOT EVEN the death—expected, moreover, for months—of Doninha Barata, the widow of Astrogildo Barata, formerly of Acqueducts and Sewers, managed to interrupt the interest aroused by the arrival and installation of the captain. It was as though people could not waste so much time being afraid.

Outwardly, there was no change; wake and funeral followed the usual ritual procedure. Remote relatives from the city made their appearance; Father Justo came from Plataforma to commend the body to its final rest; the women stripped their gardens of flowers, the old men put on shoes and neckties for the funeral. Nevertheless, there was a subtle difference, something you could not put your finger on, as though the presence of death had not made itself so brutally felt, as though it had lingered less time than usual among them. For when death, from time to time, visited Periperi, it did not depart as soon as its macabre task was done. It hung around, even after the funeral, spreading its icy shadow over the retired employees and businessmen, over their stooped wives, and all felt a constriction about the heart, as though the talons of death had closed upon it. The breeze lost its light caress; what they felt upon their shoulders bowed by fear was death's funereal breath. For which of them would it call on its next visit?

No, off there in the city of Bahía, death was not the same thing. It was swift and banal under the wheels of an automobile, in a hospital bed, in pages of the newspaper that recorded crimes and accidents. It was slight and commonplace, often warranting no more than two lines, swallowed up in all the life around it, in the noise and hubbub. There was no room for it in the hasty hearts; its shadow dissolved under the lights, laughter drowned out its rustle. How could women lapped in perfumes, in hot waves of desire, feel its pestilential breath? Death passed unnoticed, once it had accomplished its mission, and disappeared. There was no time to waste on it amidst all the anxiety and eagerness to live.

"So-and-so died," commented the papers, the radios, the conversations. "Poor fellow" "It was about time" "Still so young..." and that was the end of the affair. There were so many things to talk about, so many laughs to be laughed, so many ambitions to be satisfied, so much life to live.

In Periperi it was different. The life of those who lived or vegetated there was not made up of work and struggle, ambition and difficulties, love and hate, hope and despair. There time had no stop, nothing hurried it, events lasted for their full duration. And the longest of all was death, never swift and banal, always lurid and slow, extinguishing by its presence all appearance of life in the town. Hadn't they already begun to die, the retired employees and businessmen, when they disembarked there, moved by the desire to live as long as they could, to stretch out their years far from tumult and desires? It was a population of old people whose only real interest was their own lives, and the death of one of them made them all die a little, left them dejected and melancholy.

The games of checkers and backgammon grew more infrequent. Some of the residents even stopped going out of the house; the ailments of others grew worse; the days were sad and the conversations brief and melancholy. Only little by little was the shadow of death dissipated, driven off by the one desire and love remaining to them: that of not dying. The cracked laughs returned, the small ambition of winning a game of checkers, the vice of gluttony; the conversations at the station, in the square, grew animated once more, and now at night, in the captain's sitting room.

The walls they threw up between themselves and death, to hide them, protect them from its ominous presence, keep the sinister vision from their eyes, were frail.

The captain had been at the wake, wearing his blue-serge reefer with its brass buttons, his pipe and cap. But, perhaps because he had only recently come from the city, he did not enter bent and bowed as if that corpse were the prelude to his own death. He looked down at the shriveled face of Doninha, whom he had never met, and said, almost jovially: "She must have been a beautiful woman when she was young."

It was a lethargic, silent wake. Each was thinking of himself, seeing himself stretched out in a coffin, between smoking candles, with flowers at his feet, everything over for good. Now and then one of them shivered; fear was roweling each of them, the fear of death. They were not thinking of Doninha, of her young days, of her distant and dubious beauty. The captain's phrase aroused them from their torpor. Marreco, who had known the deceased in her youth, searched his memory: "She *was* kind of pretty."

The captain sat down, crossed his legs, lighted his pipe (not the meerschaum, which would have been improper at a wake; this was a black pipe, with a curved stem), looked about him, and encouraged the conversation: "Her face reminds me, I don't know why, of an Arab dancer I knew many years ago, when I was sailing on a Dutch freighter. On account of her my first mate, a Swede by the name of Johann, was ruining his life. But I managed to save him..."

Anyone who has lived a full life is like that: an incident, a scene, a face reminds him of something in the past, a love story, the banks of a river, another face. Was not the captain seeing in the wrinkled, emaciated face of Doninha, where the others saw nothing but death, the brown face and the long blue-black hair of Soraya, the sinful, the voluptuous dancer with the lips of fire? The one for whom Johann, the Swedish mate, driven out of his mind, got into debt, sold things belonging to the ship, tried to kill himself? With a gliding step, Soraya had entered the room as the captain struggled to recall the exotic melody of her hallucinating dance, trying to hum it.

"Music is not my strong point, but I do recall the tune..."

And how could he forget it, when it throbbed like the blood in a man's veins, a music as languorous as a vice? It had corrupted Johann, making him lose his head. Music and dance, Soraya was like a sickness that enters a man's blood, poisoning it. Who wouldn't lose his head over her snakelike arms, her bare legs, the gleam of precious stones upon her breast, a flower on her navel?

All of them understood Johann's predicament, and were moved by the solicitude of the captain for his shipmate, tearing him from the voluptuous and expensive arms of the dancer. Ah, those arms, those legs, those breasts...Each of them saw Soraya there in the room. She danced, and her nakedness of roses and emeralds hid the gaunt corpse of Doninha from their sight, cast out terror and death.

The next morning at the funeral it was once more the captain who broke death's grip on them when he appeared on the scene resplendent in dress uniform. Nobody had yet seen him in full dress, with silver epaulettes, white gloves, a new cap with a golden anchor in his hand. And a decoration on his breast.

"At sea," he remarked, "it would be much quicker. The corpse would be wrapped in a sail, covered with a flag, the bosun would pipe it overboard, and the body would be lowered into the waves. Quicker and nicer, don't you think?"

"Have you ever been present at such a burial, Captain?"

"What a question! Dozens of times...Both present and in charge...Dozens of times."

He half closed his eyes, and those present sensed the parade of memories in that simple gesture.

"I am thinking of poor Giovanni...a sailor who was with me for many years...When I changed ships, he would resign his berth to come with me, for he was devoted to me. But he was an Italian, and as you gentlemen know, the Italians are very superstitious. He was always saying to me: 'Captain, if I die at sea, I want to be buried in my native waters.' According to him, if his body was lowered into another sea, his soul would not find rest."

The funeral procession moved slowly; the captain's voice was unhurried: "When he died, that brave Giovanni, I had the devil's own job."

"What did he die of?"

"Of drink. What else would Giovanni die of? He drank like a man out of his wits—family troubles. So when he died I had to change course for two days. Change course, gentlemen, you can imagine what that was. Just to lower his body into Italian waters. I had promised, I kept my word. I changed course; we traveled forty-eight hours..."

"And the body...?"

"What about it?"

"Could it hold out that long without..."

"We put the body in the ship's freezer. At the hour of the

burial ceremony it was as stiff as salt cod, but in perfect shape. As a result of keeping my word, though, I had a world of trouble with the ship's owners. Don't ask . . ."

But they wanted to know and they did ask. Giovanni, with his drinking and his family troubles, his skin bronzed by the salt spray, moved between them and Doninha's coffin through the streets of Periperi. The captain told about the argument between him and the avaricious owners, his good-natured but firm replies, defending the right of his lads to be lowered into their native sea, their bodies eaten up by fish whose names they knew. Thus, in their final plunge, with their dead eyes they could take in the coasts of their homeland, reach their lifeless arms toward them. But it was a hopeless task to try to convince a brute like Menéndez, who was a scoundrel from the word go, once a petty employee of the firm, who by intrigues and sharp dealing had become the director of the enterprise, leaving his former boss, a good man who understood sailors, almost penniless. A villain, that Menéndez. The captain detested him.

How they would have hid in their rooms, cowered in their beds under blankets, their ills suddenly aggravated, shivering with fear, cornered by death, if the captain had not been in the square that same afternoon, telling about the time he had been shipwrecked off the coast of Peru during a submarine earthquake! Waves like mountains, cleaving the sea in abysses, the sky blacker than the blackest night.

There was a full moon, shedding its light upon the sand and the waters, that night of Doninha Barata's funeral. On another occasion they would not even have noticed the beauty of the sky; they would have been locked in their rooms and in the implacable certainty of their approaching death. But this time the captain invited them to have a drink at his house and observe the sky through his telescope.

## *Of the telescope and its various uses, with Dorothy on deck in the moon-light*

AH, THE TELESCOPE . . . On its wings they set out for the exploration of the moon and the stars, fantastic voyages that broke the barriers of monotony and boredom. As though at the wave of a magic wand, Periperi ceased to be a humdrum suburb on the Leste Brasileira Line, peopled by old folks awaiting death, and became transformed into an interplanetary station from which bold pilots took off on the conquest of space.

The big living room with its windows opening over the waters, where so many gay parties had been held in past summers, with the Cordeiro girls and their friends whirling about in young men's arms, was completely transformed. The vases of flowers had disappeared, the piano on which Adélia had murdered waltzes and fox trots, the victrola, the pretentious furnishings. The room now resembled the deckhouse of a ship, to the point where Leminhos, who had a delicate stomach, felt queasy and a little seasick whenever he went into it. The rope ladder, hanging from a window, led straight to the beach; and Zequinha Curvelo, an aspirant to the post of purser, planned to go in and out by it when his troublesome rheumatism got better.

In the middle of the wall hung the richly framed license and scroll, dating back twenty-three years. One of them, bearing the

42

signature of a former harbor master, testified to the fact that Vasco Moscoso de Aragão had successfully passed all the examinations and tests required for the title of master mariner, which gave him the right to command any type or class of merchant vessel on the seas and oceans. Twenty-three years before, when he was still relatively young, at thirty-seven, he had obtained his captain's license. Young in years, but already an old sea dog, for, as he related, he had begun his career at the age of ten as cabin boy on a slow freighter, and had risen step by step to the rank of chief mate. Time and again he had changed ship, for he loved to see new lands and sail the seven seas, travel under different flags, engage in military and amorous adventures. But when he was thirty-seven and had the qualifications to apply for the post of master mariner, he returned to Bahía, for it was there, at the hands of its port authority, that he wanted to receive the coveted title. He wanted his home port, where his qualifications and abilities were on record, to be the docks of Salvador da Bahía, from which he set out as a boy on his seafaring ventures. He, too, had his superstitions, he added, smiling. Zequinha demurred; that was a noble attitude, which revealed the captain's patriotism, coming from the other side of the world to take his examinations in Bahía. "And, modesty aside, I didn't do too badly," added the master mariner. That had been the enthusiastic opinion of Captain Georges Dias Nadreau, sometime harbor master, and today illustrious admiral of our glorious navy, when he took his examinations.

In another frame hung the scroll of Knight of the Order of Christ, the important Portuguese decoration, with the privilege of wearing medal and chain, conferred on the captain by Carlos I, King of Portugal and the Algarves, for his outstanding service to overseas commerce.

He sat down in a deck chair, with seat and back of oilcloth, beside the ship's wheel, his pipe in his hand, his gaze lost beyond the windows. On a long table stood the huge revolving globe, various instruments of navigation: compass, depth gauge, sextant, hygrometer; the great black spyglass, through which the city of Bahía could be seen close at hand; the callipers to plot the course; and the admired collection of pipes which had captivated them all. The ship's clock was called a chronometer.

On the walls were navigation charts, maps of oceans, bays, and gulfs, of submerged islands. On a cabinet in which the captain kept glasses and bottles of liquor, there was a model of a packet boat in a huge glass case, "My unforgettable *Benedict*," the last of the many in which he had sailed, his last ship. There were framed photographs of other ships, of different sizes and registrations, some of them in color. Each of them represented a part of Captain Vasco Moscoso de Aragão's life, recalled incidents, episodes, joys, and long lonely nights.

And the telescope. It created a sensation when they saw it set up, pointed to the sky. "It magnifies the size of the moon eighty times," announced Zequinha Curvelo, in a growing intimacy with the instruments, the framed photographs, the captain.

That moon-drenched night they forgot the funeral of Doninha Barata, held only that morning, in their eagerness to scan the heavens, to discover the secrets of space, to see the mountains of the moon, its mysterious face, to recognize the constellations whose names they had learned in long-distant classrooms. All of them, with the gaiety of schoolboys, tried to locate the Southern Cross.

Some days later they discovered another and no less fascinating use of the telescope. They focused it in the mornings in the direction of the crowded beach of Plataforma, examining—magnified eighty times—the bodies of the women in bathing suits. Between laughs they argued about whose turn it was to look, whispering salacious remarks to one another, behaving like teen-agers.

They got into the habit of coming to the captain's house to observe the heavens, to listen to stories. The captain prepared a tasty grog from a recipe he had picked up from an old sea dog in the vicinity of Hong Kong. It took him half an hour to prepare it with the help of the mulatto Balbina. It was a veritable rite. They heated water in a teakettle, caramelized sugar in a little frying pan. They peeled an orange and shredded the peel. Then the captain took out some heavy blue glasses (heavy so they would not move with the rolling of the ship), put into each a little of the browned sugar, a jigger of water, another of Portuguese cognac, and garnished it with the orange peel. At first only Adriano Meira and Emilio Fagundes—and, naturally, Zequinha Curvelo—had the courage to drink the strange concoction. But as these insisted that it was tasty and mild—you could use it as medicine, Zequinha guaranteed—they all tried it, smacking their lips, and even old José Paulo, the abstemious Marreco, who never touched liquor, asked to taste it one day, and became a steady customer.

They sat about in deck chairs, sipping the fragrant tipple. Before they knew it, it was past nine, sometimes even half past nine. The rest of the story had to wait for the next day at the station or the square.

It was not long before the captain was the most important and popular citizen of Periperi. His fame had extended to the other suburbs. Everyone praised his manners, his exuberant cordiality, his lack of airs. Important as he was, he was pleasant to everybody, rich or poor; he put on no side.

One night when the sky was heavily overcast and there was rain in the air, Rui Pessoa, formerly of the Tax Bureau, could not contain his curiosity and asked the captain why he had given up his profession while still comparatively young, for he had just turned sixty and had been retired for three or four years. He could not have been following the sea for at least ten years more, why not?

The captain put his glass down on the edge of the table, and sat looking out at the horizon heavy with clouds, and his expression grew serious, almost sad. He did not answer at once. He ran his eyes over the group of friends as though wondering whether they were worthy of his confidence. Zequinha Curvelo felt nervous. Perhaps Rui Pessoa had been tactless. A man like the captain would, of course, have his secrets, buried in the depths of his soul, and it was his friends' duty to respect his silence. He was about to change the subject when the captain got up, took two steps toward the window, and said: "Because of a woman. What other reason could there be?"

He pointed to the *Benedict* in its glass case.

"I was in command of that little ship, bound for Australia. I had never wanted to marry, as I told you. I preferred a woman here, a woman there, whoever took my random fancy in any port of call..." A Frenchwoman in Marseilles, a Turkish woman in Istanbul, a Russian in Odessa, a Chinese in Shanghai, a Hindu in Calcutta. Love in idleness, aching hearts at parting, and the solitude of the ship at night on the high seas. There were so many that he had never wanted to tattoo any name on his chest or arm, as many seamen do. He put their names and addresses in a little notebook, he kept the photographs of many of them, a lock of hair, some intimate garment, the crystalline echo of a laugh, the emotion of a farewell tear rolling down a cheek. But he did not have even these any more, for when he knew and loved her on board the *Benedict*, he offered up as a sacrifice to her the address book—practically a world map—and the specific memories of all the others.

Dorothy was her name, and she was dark, slender, with wind-blown hair falling about her face, long legs, a sulky mouth, and a look of suffering in her eyes. She was of changeable disposition, at times gentle and timid as a child, at times harsh and withdrawn, as though she felt everyone's hand against her. She was traveling with her husband, a colorless being, the owner of factories of some kind, who thought about nothing but business and figures, indifferent to her beauty and the suffering that lived in her eyes. They were taking a trip around the world, he to rest, she, as she confessed later, trying to find her destiny. At night she stood leaning on the deck railing, peering down into the water.

How had the affair begun? He didn't know. As captain, naturally he was thrown with them, and admired her beauty, desired her in silence. But the difference in their ages was great, for she was just twenty-five. They talked a lot together, that is true. He told her about the sea, its storms and calms, his intimacy with the stars. When he came off the bridge, late at night, he would find her alone, beside the rail. They talked of this and that, her eyes fixed on him as though trying to divine what manner of man he was. And one night, without knowing how it had happened, he found her in his arms.

Being captain, he had no right to do that. When he went ashore, a master mariner could indulge himself in the most complete orgy, the most debauched roistering. But while in command of his ship he was supposed to behave like a saint, to be above any temptation...

"And there was no lack of them."

Dorothy strolled into the living room with her slender body, her sulky mouth, her ardent yearning. The retired government employees and businessmen saw her and desired her.

"Captain, did the husband get wise?"

The vulgar phrase offended the captain. It had been love, a love like no other, boundless and irrational, taking possession of him body and soul and driving him mad from the moment he took her in his arms and savored the honey of her mouth. But he was the captain. Never in all his career, in his forty years of service, had he brought the least stain on his name, and he could not, he could not... This was what he said to her with damp eyes, he who had never wept in his whole life.

Had any of the gentlemen ever tried to argue with a woman, to make her understand a situation that was as clear as crystal? Dorothy, even more carried away than he, who needed him, was ready to commit suicide, throw herself into the sea if he did not love her. One morning she went so far as to come to the officers' quarters and knock at the door of his cabin.

She was wearing a transparent lace nightgown which could not hide the eager flesh. In her bare feet, Dorothy ran there amidst them in the living room. Adriano Meira licked his lips.

"And that was too much for you..."

Ah, they did not know him, his inflexibility when it was a question of duty. He did resist. He threw over her bare shoulders (a low-necked nightgown showing the curve of her palpitating breasts—Augusto Ramos heaved a sigh) a raincoat, and led her away almost by main force. That was a dramatic hour for him, torn between love and duty, she half fainting in his arms, as he promised her that he would go ashore at the first port and go away with her forever. To some forgotten corner of the earth. There was a single kiss before the immensity of the sea.

He sent in his resignation by cable. The company replied with pleas, requests, offers to raise his salary. The agents were panic-stricken, for his name carried an aura of respect and fame in the maritime world among seamen and shipowners. He was unmoved; he had given his word and he was in love. At the first port, Makassar, a remote, dirty port in the Far East, he took leave of his crew. Old sailors, gnarled and weather-beaten, wept as they pressed his loyal hand. He had arranged to meet Dorothy in the house of a certain Carol, an opium smuggler, whom he had once done a favor. The husband waited for her in vain, and then continued his travels alone.

Those were two weeks of madness, hidden in a little house on the outskirts of the city, in the tropical jungle, given over to their love with a wild fury, as though they divined...

"The husband showed up?"

What did the husband matter, that nincompoop! His name was Robert; the captain had nothing but contempt for him, he didn't even give him a thought in the whole course of the developments. Vain and fatuous, he thought he could buy Dorothy's love and fidelity with marriage and money... No, the husband had nothing to do with it. It was the fever, that deadly fever of the islands. In two days it finished off Dorothy and the captain's career. How could he ever command a ship again, sail

47

the seas, when there, in that port of Makassar, he could not stop
seeing, not even for a minute, Dorothy's eyes, those agaonized
eyes, glowing with fever, fixed on him as though he could save
her? Her twisted mouth implored him not to let her die now that
she had finally discovered the joy of living. And he could not
even die with her, as he longed to do, and begged Heaven to let
him, for he was immune to that fever, having been exposed to it
since youth. For a time he was out of his mind, he took to
smoking opium. Shipping agents deluged him with offers, but he
returned to his native land. He would never again take the
bridge; for him everything was finished and he swore a solemn
oath to this effect beside Dorothy's grave. For the first and last
time he allowed a woman's name to be tattooed on his arm. He
rolled up his sleeve: there was the name of Dorothy and a heart.

He rolled down his sleeve, and turned to the window, his
back to his friends. It seemed to them that they heard a stifled
sob. They all left together, murmuring a touched "Good night."
Zequinha Curvelo took the captain's hand, and gave it a warm
clasp of solidarity. Each of them carried Dorothy away with
him, her quest for love, her restlessness, her unforgettable
image.

After the others had left, the captain put out the lights in the
sitting room. He would have preferred not to kill Dorothy, not
to have buried her in that filthy port, cut down in the flower of
her youth by fever. He could have put her ashore in some more
civilized spot, but how conclude a love like that, all-consuming
and absolute, except by death? Walking down the hall, where a
glimmer of light shone, he once more saw the restless, tormented
Dorothy barefoot on the deck—what an hour that was!—her
breasts offering themselves through her low-cut nightgown, her
mouth thirsting for love, her body a glowing ember.

Taking Dorothy by the hand, he pushed opened the door of
the maid's room, and the mulatto Balbina, grumbling, moved
over in bed to make room for him. ·

# *In which our narrator reveals himself as something of a scapegrace*

WHO, in this sorry world, can escape the darts of envy? The more outstanding a man is in the opinion of his fellow citizens, the more eminent and respectable his position, the better target does he become for the poisoned shafts of the envious. Oceans of calumny rise to hurl their waves of infamy against him. No reputation, however unblemished and immaculate, no glory, however pure, is above attack.

I have proof of this before my very eyes. His Honor, Dr. Alberto Siqueira, confers honor and status on Periperi by living among us with his degrees, his learning, his starched shirt bosom, his fortune. If he wanted to, he could buy himself a house in Pituba or Itapoa, fashionable summer resorts where the smart set lives and spends the summer. Nevertheless, he prefers our suburb, where there are very few capable of appreciating his ideas, his lofty prose, his speeches with so many dictionary words. We should all take pride in this preference, assuming an attitude of perpetual gratitude in His Honor's presence.

But, instead of this, what happens? They lay him out with the dogs. It does not matter that articles of his have appeared in legal journals, luminous sentences handed down by Dr. Siqueira. I

49

myself have had occasion to go over several leather-bound numbers of the *Bar Review* in which articles that reflect His Honor's wisdom occupy pages and pages. I neither can nor would I venture to pass judgment on these opinions and sentences, written half in Latin, the other half in upper case. But does not another jurist, commenting on an opinion of our judge in the aforesaid publication, call Dr. Siqueira "a luminary of the science of jurisprudence"?

However, not even this printed proof in journals of São Paulo and praise from the capital itself, none of this prevents persons like Telemaco Dorea, a retired City Hall employee, whose head is turned because he published some poems in sprung rhythm in the supplement of a newspaper in Bahía, from saying that His Honor is "nothing but a dolt, a fool (the expressions are that numbskull Dorea's), the biggest horse's ass the law courts of Bahía ever produced." There you have an example of what lack of respect and green-eyed envy can lead to. And the worst of it is that people like Telemaco Dorea find an audience to listen and agree, and that carries fuel to feed his ignoble flames.

There is a whole group of backbiters ready to rip the judge's life to pieces, past and present. Not satisfied with denying his evident merits, applauded in the south of the country, they attack his honor as a magistrate, calling him venal, completely venal. They tell a story, which is not too clear, about two different and contradictory decisions he handed down in one and the same case, the first denying the claims of a large firm of exporters, and a later one, upholding the appeal of the powerful magnates. I see nothing to criticize in the fact that new findings, added to the original brief, should have altered the question greatly, as His Honor points out, reversing the terms of the problem. But according to certain riffraff of Periperi these "new findings" consisted of the sum of five hundred contos, half a million cruzeiros, added to Dr. Siqueira's bank account and not to the brief.

They claim that this is how His Honor built up his fortune, not by inheriting it from rich parents. As far as inheritance is concerned, it was his wife who received it, and if it had not been for that he would never have married her, for even as a girl she was a ball of suet, nicknamed Zeppelin.

And not satisfied with unearthing the past, they mess around in the present, bringing up the matter of poor little Dondoca. As though it were a crime for a distinguished man to seek pleasant surcease to his intellectual lucubrations in the long, dull afternoons of Periperi. Dona Ernestina snored fathoms deep in her siesta, and His Honor took advantage of the situation to indulge the fantasy and sweet delight of love. He confided to me—overwhelming me with the honor of his confidence—that he cherished a protective, almost paternal feeling for the girl. A poor child, deceived and deserted, with so many good qualities, whose sad fate would be that of becoming a member of the oldest profession, if it were not for a protecting arm to uphold and defend her. Moreover, he was entitled to those trifling infractions of strait-laced morality as compensation for his matrimonial obligations, "heavy and hard to bear."

"Heavy and hard to bear," I could well believe, thinking of Dona Ernestina's two hundred and fifty pounds. I could not help calling up the scene evoked by the pathetic adjectives of the judge: to tumble those rolls of fat, free from the restraint of corset and belts, in the hay . . . It must have been a grueling task for His Honor.

But I suppressed my smile; it is not fitting to joke about such things when they involve persons worthy of respect, such as Dr. Siqueira and his fat but virtuous wife. And as far as Dondoca was concerned, what other feeling but gratitude could the judge arouse in me? If it had not been for his generous peccadillo, I would not be enjoying for free the charms of the prettiest and hottest little mulatto in Bahia, and wearing the excellent slippers the judge had left in her house, and eating the chocolates he brought her. But man is vile by nature: there I was, stretched out beside Dondoca in a bed paid for by the judge, eating candy and fruit bought by him, listening to the hussy describing certain idiosyncrasies of her protector, and at the same time imagining His Honor trying them out on the Zeppelin, sweating and panting, in fulfillment of his onerous duty.

I cannot, in all conscience, criticize those who spend their time taking potshots at His Honor's learning and honor. If I, who owe him so many favors and courtesies, laugh and jeer at his little weaknesses; if Dondoca, his protégée, does so, what can one expect of others? Nevertheless, I cannot swallow that Telemaco Dorea, so bumptious and uppity. I took him some sections of the captain's history, the result of patient investigation, of hard work. The rhymster made a number of criticisms: dull, loose style; slow, weak action; clichés by the dozen; characters without inner life. One phrase of which I must confess I was proud, one already mentioned, "oceans of calumny . . . waves of infamy," elicited the sarcastic reproval and scornful laugh of that Dorea, incapable of feeling the power and beauty of the image.

I might add, in this connection, that this very phrase called forth the highest praise from the distinguished and cultured magistrate, a man accustomed to good authors, a reader of Rui Barbosa and Alexander Dumas. Dondoca, too, when I read the passage aloud, more to myself than to her, clapped her hands and exclaimed: "How pretty!" She is not lacking in sensibility, as I had already had occasion to note in bed. Thus, supported by the intellectual elite, represented by the judge, and applauded by the folk, in the sweet person of Dondoca, I relegated to utter contempt the stupid laughter of Telemaco Dorea, a poet for his Negress admirers; henceforth, I promised myself, I would eschew his dull company. Moreover, he is a dead-beat who still owes me a hundred and eighty cruzeiros, which he borrowed last summer to buy fish. "I'll pay you back this afternoon," and I'm still waiting.

To get back to the story of the captain, for when I was making those opening comments about envy I was not really thinking about the judge, or his virtuous wife, or Dondoca, or that ham of a Dorea. The judge came to mind as an example, and like certain boring visitors, I lost all sense of time. I think I wandered off course, too, arguing with that skunk of a Dorea, and lazing about in Dondoca's bed, in her cuddling arms, forgetting the obligation I had assumed: to clear up the tangled history of the captain, make the truth to shine, naked and untrammeled, upon his adventures.

As has been pointed out, nobody escapes the envious. So how could Captain Vasco Moscoso de Aragão, who had been living in Periperi less than a month and was already the most important personality in the suburb, the name most often mentioned, the pride of the town, who was consulted on the most diverse matters, be expected to? His opinion was not only respected, it was law. "The captain says . . ." "Ask the captain . . ." "The captain assured me" were put forward in every discussion, and when he, removing his meerschaum pipe from his mouth, stated his opinion, it was the final, the indisputable word.

The honeymoon of the captain with Periperi, with never a

cloud on the boundless blue sky, lasted a month, more or less. It might have gone on a good while longer if old Chico Pacheco, ex-customs inspector, who had been living there for over ten years and thought he owned the place, had not returned from the city, where he had been visiting his lawyer son.

I have already mentioned the kind of person he was: touchy, troublesome, a backbiter, distrustful and malicious, all sharp edges. He had retired before his time as the result of ill will on the part of his superiors, and because he got mixed up in politics, on the wrong side. He claimed that he was the victim of powerful enemies, and for years he had been involved in a suit against the state. In part he had been successful, securing a considerable increase in his pension; but he kept stubbornly on, for he hoped to be awarded a substantial settlement.

This suit was one of the most discussed topics in Periperi, and a great part of Chico Pacheco's prestige was based on it, on its ups and downs. His return from his frequent trips to Bahía, where he stayed at his son's house to follow the progress of the trial, was a red-letter day for the pensioners and retired businessmen. Chico Pacheco loved to narrate all the details of the question, which was now before the Supreme Court, and he knew how to do it. He blasted the judges, flayed bureaucrats and politicians, knew all the ins and outs of the life of the judges, attorneys, counselors, anybody who for one reason or another had been involved in the case. He was a storehouse of anecdotes, calumnies, and amusing gibes.

His interminable suit really belonged to the whole population of Periperi. In a feeling of solidarity with Chico Pacheco, the pensioners and retired businessmen rose up on their hind legs when an appeal by the defense slowed up the march of the suit, when a request for a new trial delayed the decision. The wife of Augusto Ramos, the one who loved stories, had even made a vow to Our Lord of Bomfin that she would have a mass said in His church if Chico Pacheco won his case. What a pity His Honor Dr. Siqueira was not living there at the time. What a help he would have been, not only to Chico, but to the entire population, with his gifts, his experience. A monumental feast had been planned to celebrate the victory. Chico Pacheco promised to break out champagne when he received the jack pot.

On this occasion he had returned in a bad mood. Just when everything seemed on the verge of a solution, with the trial on the calendar, the state submitted new allegations, and the decision was put off till "the Greek calends," as he told the stationmaster when he got off the train.

He arrived full of tales, anecdotes, scandal about judges and lawyers, a load of news. But he needed the attention and moral support of his friends and neighbors. And he found himself relegated to a secondary plane, which was intolerable to him. The recent and resounding glory of the master mariner filled Periperi from one end to the other, his name was on everybody's lips, his exploits were the talk of the town. How could the petty incidents of a lawsuit dragging on in the courts compare with stories of shipwrecks, storms, love affairs? How compare "subjudice" with Hong Kong or Honolulu? Not to mention the telescope, the ship's wheel, the chronometer.

"Do you know what a chronometer is, Mr. Chico Pacheco?"

"No, and I don't want to . . . I am going to give you the dirt on Judge Pitanga, the one whose wife had seven sons by seven different fathers. That king of cuckolds . . ."

"You ought to see his collection of pipes. You'll even forget about your suit."

And so it went. Chico Pacheco led with his suit, and they trumped it with maps, Arabian dancers, drunken sailors. He talked about an appeal that had been lodged, and they answered with one of the captain's adventures.

That afternoon, as he was narrating the tedious account of the trial to a somewhat less than enthusiastic audience, a sudden animation revealed the approach of the captain. Chico Pacheco looked him over with his mean little eyes—a short, stocky gentleman with thick hair, hooked nose, rolling gait—and spat.

"Him a master mariner? To me he doesn't even look as if he could command a canoe. To me he looks like a storekeeper."

## *Of the drawbacks of not knowing geography and the deplorable tendency to bluff at poker*

"IF I ONLY knew geography!"

Chico Pacheco kept repeating the phrase between clenched teeth, lamenting the wasted days of his youth; he had been a notorious cutter of classes. And all the time he had lost during his life, frittering it away on nonsense, when he could have devoted himself, body and soul, to the intensive study of geography, a science whose utility he had only come to realize!

"I wonder where Marcos Vaz de Toledo would be?" he asked himself, in the hope of seeing his colleague of the Customs Department, whom he had not laid eyes on for more than twenty years, alight in the station of Periperi as if by a miracle.

Marcos Vaz de Toledo, a self-sufficient southerner, was a wizard at geography. You would have thought he had a map of the world in his head: capitals, leading cities, gulfs and islands, lakes and lagoons, mountains and volcanoes, big rivers and little streams, ocean currents, and ports, river and sea. Any port you liked, of Europe and America, Africa and Asia, Oceania, he had them by the dozen on the tip of his tongue. He was a wonder, that Marcos Vaz de Toledo, though something of a bore, a crank about his learning, so that his associates had to flee him, shun his company. You gave him half a chance, and with his long cigarette holder and astounding memory, he began to reel off tongue-twisting names, from Hamburg to Shanghai, from New York to Buenos Aires. Chico Pacheco, who was fond of talking and averse to listening, had given him the nickname of "tramp freighter," the kind that can't pass any port, however miserable, without entering.

All too late, Chico Pacheco recognized his mistake in underestimating that storehouse of geographical knowledge. He had looked upon Marcos Vaz de Toledo as a nuisance, a bore, had slipped around the corner to avoid him. What he wouldn't give now to have him in Periperi, with his inland seas, his tributaries and meridians, those hundreds of precious ports! Of all that farrago of anchorages he could recall only the most familiar, the easiest names, which were of no use whatever to a person trying to expose an impostor. For he was sure they were dealing with an impostor who was trading on the good faith of the simple-minded senility of Periperi, of those credulous half-wits ready to believe any charlatan, to swallow the tallest tales. Why, he himself, time and again, had fed them the biggest kind of lies, and they had never even suspected.

Nowhere in the world was there such a good market for a liar to display his wares as in Periperi. He received in payment the coin of respect and consideration. The proof of this was he, Chico Pacheco. They respected him more for the stories he invented about judges and lawyers, for the exaggerated accounts of tricks and makeshifts of the law than because of the injustice of which he was the victim. The trouble was that his lies were trivial and limited, his range of action did not go beyond the city of Bahía, dealt with people everybody knew, on a stage half an hour away by train.

How could he compete with a Munchausen who knew no bounds, standing on the deck of ships in the midst of distant seas and oceans, defying the tempest, shipwreck, sharks, battered by the four winds, and with more women than he knew what to do with, most of them impassioned and wanton, regular cows?

Chico Pacheco squinted his little eyes; he had never seen such bold-faced impudence. Not even Romeu das Dores, who made a business of giving false testimony in court (payment in advance), a depraved old drunk, was so cynical. The captain had no sense of fitness (captain, my foot). He would butt in anywhere and begin talking, interlarding his tales with highfaultin and complicated names of ports and topographical features, with nautical terms, and he sold his cock and bull stories very well, at the highest price. Those jackasses of Periperi drooled over them, that pack of dolts. The only thing left for them to do was to kiss the captain's (captain in a pig's eye) ass. The nitwits!

But he'd never pull the wool over his eyes. What he had to do was expose the impostor, unmask the charlatan. Ah, if he only knew geography he would throw down a few ocean currents at his feet, some latitudes and longitudes, mix up his ports of call, and quickly force him to come down from the bridge and go ashore for good. "I'll have to send to Bahía for some textbooks."

Ever since he got back he had been chewing the bitter cud of a hideous spite. And it was affecting his liver; his normal pallor took on a yellowish tinge. The figure of Vasco Moscoso de Aragão, his pipes, his nautical instruments, his framed charts and ships, spyglass and telescope, his pompous cap, ruled Periperi from one end to the other, from the station to the beach, leaving no room for another person of consequence, another celebrity, another hero. Puffing at his straw cigarette of rope tobacco (how could a straw cigarette that stank compare with a meerschaum pipe, perfumed tobacco?), Chico Pacheco ruminated spite and plans of revenge.

And all the while, he thought to himself, it was as plain as the nose on your face, except to one who refused to look or those poor gaping devils with one foot in the grave, heading for the last roundup. Like that fool of a Zequinha Curvelo, so lost in admiration, who had become a seaman second-class, following the charlatan around like an orderly, carrying the spyglass for him in that grotesque ceremony of inspecting the bay for incoming ships from the top of the bluff. People gathered to watch, as though the port of Bahía were now under the supervision and management of the inhabitants of Periperi. As he climbed down, Vasco announced: "It's a Dutch steamer. A perfect landfall..."

Or he revealed confidentially: "A freighter from Panama. Probably carrying contraband."

They exchanged knowing glances, feeling themselves involved in daring enterprises, all of them with a touch of the smuggler about them, especially Zequinha Curvelo. "What a bunch of clowns," muttered Chico Pacheco, yellower than ever, the bitter taste of envy in his mouth with its decayed teeth. He looked at the smiling, cordial face of the captain (captain, hell), his air of a storekeeper, and he was more than ever convinced that if that character had ever gone to sea it had been aboard some coastwise tramp, and his knowledge did not extend beyond the ports of Ilhéus, Aracajú and Belmonte.

He went about sowing his suspicions as though he didn't mean anything by it. They rubbed his nose in the license, signed and sealed, in plain sight of everyone in its gilded frame in the sitting room. Yes, the license was something it was hard to deny. But what did it prove, except maybe the command of one of those cockleshells of the Bahian Line on which, during the short trip from Caravelas to Salvador, the passengers puked up their guts? Maybe not even that. Who knows but what the captain (captain, my ass) had never gone beyond the São Francisco River, in some sidewheeler, from Joazeiro to Pirapora, from Pirapora to Joazeiro, in his whole life. Only fools could be taken in by that peddler's mug, that seller on the installment plan; not he, Chico Pacheco, accustomed to hold his own with wily lawyers, aces of the courtroom, scoundrels of every sort. Those stories about ports of Asia, islands of the Indian Ocean, women of Ceylon, Greek sailors—Vasco had either read them somewhere, or heard them, or simply made them up. A side-wheeler on the São Francisco River was the most Chico Pacheco would allow him.

He lost the first round to the license, but he was not discouraged. After all, he had been tempered in the fire of ten years of litigation with the state. While he waited for the textbook he had asked his son to get him (he would spend the rest of his life studying geography if he had to), he decided to feel out the enemy's weak spots, details that might arouse doubt and win him allies.

He took note of Emilio Fagundes's letdown. When he had been with the Department of Agriculture, Emilio Fagundes's name had appeared in the papers, thanks to his skill at chess. He had even taken part in a tournament in Rio, and had come out in fourth place, which was no small triumph. Now, retired, he had only one complaint about Periperi: the lack of a good chess player there. Nobody went beyond checkers, backgammon, and dominoes. He had been full of hope on the arrival of the captain (captain, shit), but all in vain; the man hardly knew the difference between a rook and a bishop, a knight and a king. He would have to go on playing by correspondence with partners in the city, solve the problems published in the special sections of magazines and newspapers. It was a great disappointment.

"I would have thought that a seafaring man surely knew how to play chess," he confided one day to Chico Pacheco.

For the first time in his life, the ex-customs inspector managed to work up an enthusiasm for the complications of chess. Until then, he had looked upon it as the most tiresome of games, and on Emilio Fagundes as a lunatic. It really was odd that a seafarer should be devoid of interest in a game that was so useful to kill time. For the long hours of smooth sailing there could hardly be a better pastime. He chose to hurl the gauntlet of the chessboard on the deck at a most dramatic moment, when the captain (captain, balls) was trying to avoid a fatal crash between his ship and an immense iceberg in the North Sea one cold, foggy night. The fog was so thick you could have cut it with a knife, like cheese; the passengers were in a panic when the white mass of ice showed up off the port bow, a floating mountain...

"Mr. Vasco, could you tell me one thing..."

"Captain Vasco Moscoso de Aragão, at your orders."

He insisted upon the use of the title, for, as he said, he owned no fortune nor honor beyond his captain's license. By a supreme effort, Chico Pacheco controlled himself and gave him his title: "Captain, would you mind telling me something that I can't help wondering about. How is it that you, a man of the sea, with so much time to kill, don't play chess? I have heard it said that it is a favorite game aboard ship."

"Well, you have been misinformed, my dear friend. A seaman's game is dice or cards, games of chance. A good game of poker, for instance. I have spent nights without sleeping, until sunup, at the poker table..."

And taking his cue from this, he proceeded, without turning a hair: "That time I was shipwrecked off Rasmat, the island that resembles Peripepi, all we had in the lifeboat with us were some ship's biscuits, a little water, and a deck of cards. And even then, surrounded by danger on all sides, we enjoyed a good game of poker. There were five of us, and while one took the helm, the other four played. We bet our biscuits and the swallows of water we were entitled to. It was fun. Two days and two nights..."

Now, Chico Pacheco was good at poker. "Poker? Hooray! We can get up a game, I've been wanting to play for a long time. Marreco is a confirmed gambler."

"Not a confirmed gambler. But I like a hand or two..."

"Leminhos, too—not to mention Augusto Ramos."

Who knows but what that story of playing poker was another of Vasco's impostures? Ah, if he didn't know the rules, how to bet, when to bluff...

"We could get us a game right now."

"Sorry. Not now. I must finish my story," parried Vasco, returning to his interrupted narration.

"Leave the end till later," Chico Pacheco insisted.

"He was at the most interesting part," Rui Pessoa reminded him.

"I could feel cold shivers up my back," confessed Zequinha.

Chico Pacheco looked contemptuously at the group around Vasco. The fools! Couldn't they see that they were being bamboozled? He'd be willing to bet the imposter did not even know how many cards you dealt, the value of a straight or three of a kind. He smiled in anticipation. The voice of the captain was sonorously reeling off the dramatic tale. The mountain of ice was on the point of ramming the ship, the passengers were screaming, the crew had lost their heads, when he, snatching the wheel from the helmsman's hands...

"As soon as you get through, I'm going to call Augusto Ramos... We could play at your house, couldn't we, Marreco?"

"I only play if we keep the stakes low. Not over a nickel." Marreco had to keep an eye on expenses, for he helped out a widowed daughter-in-law and her children in Bahia.

The iceberg missed the ship by a cat's whisker, Chico went off to get Augusto Ramos and the deck of cards. With firm hands on the wheel, Vasco watched triumphantly as the iceberg slowly drifted away, drawn by the polar currents.

There was no lack of decks of cards. Nearly everybody played solitaire in the long afternoon hours before gathering for their chat in the square. Decks of thick cards, greasy from handling.

"Come on, let's go," Chico Pacheco urged impatiently.

"The kibitzers are to keep quiet," warned Leminhos, for everyone was gathering around for the coming match.

"I'd already heard that story about the iceberg."

"Don't you remember the sinking of the *Titanic*? It struck one of those things. They're very dangerous."

Vasco, smiling, came over and picked up the deck. Chico Pacheco's face lighted up when the captain (captain, screw me), at the sight of the greasy cards, threw them back on the table and shook his head.

"Not with that deck. Impossible."

"Now, sir, don't be so pernickety. For a penny-ante game like this they're all right. Let's sit down." Chico Pacheco pulled up a chair.

Zequinha Curvelo was still seeing the iceberg: "I would throw myself into the water if I saw one of those things bearing down on me."

"No, I won't play with that deck, it's no fun."

"Or would it be maybe that you don't know how a game of poker goes?" Chico Pacheco brought out triumphantly.

Vasco Moscoso de Aragão looked at him in surprise: "And why wouldn't I know?"

"How should I know?"

Vasco turned and walked away quickly. Chico crowed: "That customer never sat in on a game of poker in his life. Who ever heard of playing in a lifeboat? He must think we are blithering idiots. One lie on top of another..."

"Lie?"

"Come now, Leminhos, haven't you got eyes in your head? You just have to show him you weren't born yesterday and he pulls in his horns. Didn't you just see what happened with this business of the game of poker? Playing for biscuits, swallows of water... I get the cards, the players, and he ducks out... Just because the deck is a little worn. What a lame excuse! Show me the sailor, no matter how worthless, who doesn't know how to play a little poker."

Zequinha got down from the iceberg, still shivering, and came to the defense of his idol: "Who told you he didn't know how? Did he tell you that?"

"There you go, toadying to that nincompoop."

"Toadying, hell. But I'm not envious."

"And who is? Envious of what?"

"Take it easy, gentlemen," interrupted Marreco. "What goes on here? Two old friends arguing over nothing."

"I won't have doubt thrown on the word of an honest man."

"What I doubt is his poker."

"The fact is that he took it on the lam," Rui Pessoa pointed out.

But Vasco was already on his way back, bringing two decks and a box of chips. Handsome, new, shining cards, with a picture of a transatlantic liner stamped on the back, the blue smoke rising from the funnel. Those were decks of cards! They were passed around from hand to hand.

Nor was Chico Pacheco's defeat that afternoon limited to this detail. A good poker player, but nervous and irritable, trying to bluff all the time, he was not a foeman worthy of the steel of Vasco Moscoso de Aragão, infectiously good-humored, playing with knowledge, assurance, and nautical terms. Knowing when to stay in and when to quit, knowing exactly when to bluff, quickly learning to read each player's face. Chico Pacheco could deny everything except his skill at poker. He was a past master.

Zequinha Curvelo was following the game from a chair beside his hero. The iceberg had long since disappeared, melting away in the southern waters, and now the steady hand and clear eye of Vasco were proving themselves at the gaming table. From time to time Zequinha cast a disdainful glance at the slanderous ex-customs inspector. And when Vasco, with a pair of queens, called Chico Pacheco, who had been betting on nothing but a pair of sevens, Zequinha could not hold his tongue: "Envy can kill, Mr. Chico Pacheco."

It really could. Chico Pacheco felt pains in his liver. He had to buy another five milreis worth of chips.

That memorable game of poker launched a new custom in Periperi. Every Thursday evening old José Paulo, Augusto Ramos, and Leminhos, besides the inevitable kibitzers, gathered at Vasco's house for a hotly contested game. Zequinha Curvelo began to fathom the secrets of the game; it's a sailor's duty to understand and love poker. Chico Pacheco refused to form part of the group. He would not set foot in the house of the captain (as much a captain as the whore who bore him).

## Of the celebration of St. John's day, with liquor, hominy pudding, and sharks, or the envious discomfited

JUNE CAME in with its attendant showers, flooding the sandy streets. The ears of corn were piled high in the kitchen for hominy cakes, hominy pudding, and fresh corn cakes. It was a month of gluttony, when the retired officials and businessmen forgot their diets, swigging genipap wine, wallowing in delicious dishes. They would pay for these excesses, of course; some of them would have to give up salt or sugar as their various ailments, diabetes or rheumatism, got worse. In many homes, prayers were said to St. Anthony for thirteen days straight, first those which were sung in front of the improvised altar of the matchmaking saint, then the dances to the accompaniment of the harmonica. In the square a pole was raised high with St. John's banner, and the bonfires were being readied for the holy night. At the end of the month, widows and widowers would honor St. Peter, their patron saint. A whole month of festivities, with the children shooting off firecrackers and squibs, with budding love affairs thanks to the prayers to St. Anthony, and the girls leaning over magic basins of water to see in them the faces of their future husbands. The post of sponsor of the feast of Saint Peter was an honor sought by all the male inhabitants of Periperi.

The feast of St. John was celebrated in every home, for even in the poorest a bottle of genipap wine was opened, and there was hominy pudding, corn or manioc cake, tapioca couscous, and tamales wrapped in corn husk. But the feast of St. Peter was held in the square, with amusements for the poor children of the fishermen and the railroad workers of the Leste Line, pupils of the primary schools. Father Justo came from Plataforma, said mass in the morning in the little church, had lunch with one of the bigwigs, and attended the afternoon merrymaking. At night the bonfires were lighted, corn and sweet potatoes were roasted in the embers, the sparks crackled in the air, balloons drifted skyward, the innumerable stars were multiplied.

The matter of the sponsor of the feast taxed Father Justo's tact to the utmost. To be sure, his cassock hid the frock coat of a diplomat; he knew how to win over the most recalcitrant, smooth ruffled feelings, taking coffee with this one, having lunch with that one, tea with another, a sip of genipap wine and a taste of hominy pudding in dozens of houses. He returned to Plataforma at peace with the faithful of Periperi, but with a terrible attack of indigestion.

Every year the aspirants to the sponsorship were many. They all felt that they had the right to preside over the afternoon festivities, when the children competed at sack races, picking up an egg with a spoon, and climbing the greased pole with a five-milreis bill fastened to the top. True, it involved certain expenses, but nothing worth mentioning, compared with the honor of sitting beside Father Justo in the square and listening to the high-flown speech of one of the school children, written by the teacher and learned by heart by the orator with the aid of threats, anguished effort, and the ferule.

As early as April, Father Justo began to receive at his presbytery in Plataforma hints, messages, and visits from the candidates and their relatives. Candles were lighted in the church; there were even those who ordered a mass said.

The oldest inhabitants, nearly all of them, had already been honored with the supreme annual dignity of Periperi. Old José Paulo had been chosen three times; now he was not even in the running, as he avoided all unnecessary expense. Adriano Meira, Augusto Ramos, Rui Pessoa had all been sponsors. Even Leminhos, a relative newcomer, who had retired at the age of forty-five because of his health, had been awarded the honor. Chico Pacheco, too. Four years before, he had presided with luster and solemnity at the festivities of St. John. Then why, in that year of the captain's arrival, had he decided to seek the coveted post for himself? If anyone had a right to it, it was Zequinha Curvelo, who had been living there for five years, and who up to then had been overlooked by the priest. Nevertheless, it was Zequinha himself who, before anyone else, had suggested to His Reverence the name of Vasco Moscoso de Aragão. In his opinion, there was no question as to who should be the sponsor of the feast of St. John that year. It was simple justice to select the distinguished mariner who enhanced the fame of Periperi with his presence. Father Justo agreed. He cultivated the new inhabitants, he liked to win their confidence and friendship. It seemed a choice that would arouse no resentment; the most important citizens, such as old Marreco, Adriano Meira, and Emilio Fagundes, all approved it. Not to mention the lesser fry, who adored the captain, always ready to help them out in a pinch with a small loan or stand them a drink. This was, he explained, a custom of his seafaring days, of his dealings with sailors and their problems, their binges. He liked to help his fellow men, give them advice, listen to their confidences. This time Father Justo thought nobody's feelings would be hurt, no jealousy aroused by a choice so generally applauded.

But he was wrong. When the news reached Periperi, Chico Pacheco flew into a rage. He had informed the priest over a month before that he was a candidate, he had sent him a capon and a bottle of *jurubeba* wine, Lion of the North brand, a veritable nectar. And without warning, he had been stabbed in the back, shamefully betrayed. As though the delays in his suit and the disillusionments suffered in Periperi were not enough, now the church had sabotaged his candidacy and allied itself with the impostor, the charlatan. Chico Pacheco was seized by a sudden and violent anti-clericalism; he developed a warm sympathy for the Masons, called the clergy in general and Father Justo in particular everything he could lay his tongue to, imputing to him mistresses and bastards.

If the choice had fallen on anyone else, he could have borne the humiliation in silence. He could even have put up with Zequinha Curvelo, in spite of the fact that he had presented himself as a candidate just to keep Vasco's "orderly" from obtaining the postponed honor. He wanted to prevent the victory of the bootlicker, and the result was a horrendous defeat for himself, the worst he had ever suffered. The truth of the matter was that ever since that poker game he had been in such a state that he seemed to have forgotten his pending suit in the courts of Bahía, as though the greatest enemy he had in the world was Captain Vasco Moscoso de Aragão.

Ever since that afternoon of the iceberg and the new decks of cards, he had given up insinuations and had taken to direct accusations. He went from one person to another, analyzing Vasco's stories, bringing out supposed contradictions, calling attention to details which in his opinion were spurious.

It cannot be said that he was successful in his attempt to demoralize and destroy his rival. But there is no denying that his persistence managed to instill a grain of doubt in people's minds, a vague mistrust as to whether the captain was really so heroic and his career so adventurous, so full of perils and loves. Could so many extraordinary things happen to one man, one life be so rich when all theirs were so poor and drab?

Adriano Meira, an irreverent old sport, went so far as to risk a joke that was in poor taste, once when the captain was relating one of his most sensational exploits, that story about the nineteen sailors who were devoured by sharks in the Red Sea. He, Vasco, had escaped thanks to divine grace and his skillful use of the knife with which he had slit the bellies of three ravenous sharks, three of them.

"Scale it down, captain. That's a couple of sharks too many."

Vasco looked at him with his clear eyes, like those of a child: "What was that you said, friend?"

Adriano became embarrassed, so calm was the voice, so limpid the gaze of the captain. But as he had just been talking with Chico Pacheco, he made an effort and followed up the wisecrack: "Too many sharks, Captain..."

"And what do you know about sharks, sir? Have you ever sailed the Red Sea? Your remark has no foundation, I can assure you of that. There is no place in the world where you'll find so many sharks."

No, he could not be a liar. He had not even noticed the irony and doubt in the joke, nor the bantering tone. If he was a charlatan, as Chico Pacheco claimed, he would have taken offense and given him an angry answer. Adriano Meira was ashamed of himself.

"You're right, Captain. People should not talk about things they don't know."

"Neither talk nor take charge of..."

For he had not known *El Gamil*, an Egyptian freighter carrying a cargo of cement, when he accepted its command on that slow and monotonous trip from Suez to Aden. And he did not realize his mistake until it was too late; the ship was in terrible shape, not even the intercommunication system worked. And the crew was a shady-looking lot of customers, with faces that would frighten you. Fortunately, he had with him the faithful Giovanni, that seaman on whose account he had got into trouble years later with the European shipowners. And when *El Gamil* sank, with a hole in its hull, only he and Giovanni were saved, picked up by a Norwegian ship after that holocaust of men and sharks. He still kept that lucky knife, and he would show it to them one of those evenings when they came up to have a drink with him.

The effects of Chico Pacheco's relentless campaign did not go beyond such passing doubts, momentary misgivings. Adriano Meira had a bone to pick with him the next time he met him.

"You and your talk . . . The man is a liar, the man is a liar, that's all you can say. I tried to catch him out and made a fool of myself. The captain even showed me the knife he killed the sharks with."

"God, what morons you are."

He got on the outs first with one and then with the other, more bitter and biting all the time, his mouth running over with dirty words, encompassing in his contempt and rage the whole population of Periperi, the senior citizens and their wives, all of them rapt auditors of the captain's adventures.

The choice of Vasco as sponsor of the festival of St. John instead of himself was the straw that broke the camel's back. Even after it was announced, he tried to exert pressure on the priest, reminding him of previous gifts, and holding out to him the prospect of substantial donations when he won his suit against the state. Afterwards he lashed out against His Reverence, calling him a rake and a trimmer, which was an obvious exaggeration, for all Father Justo was trying to do was to keep peace in his flock, and not even the most viperine tongues could say anything about women in his life, aside from the girl who took care of the rectory, and was of a sweet, gentle beauty, looking like the image of a saint.

Chico Pacheco, at one time the most sought-out inhabitant of Periperi, almost as highly respected as old Marreco, missed by everybody when he wasn't around, could not bear so much humiliation, such disloyalty. He could not stand it to see the charlatan with his foolish face, the face of a storekeeper, alongside the ingrate of a priest (who, if he had one iota of dignity, at least ought to return the capon and the *jurubeba* wine), presiding at the feast of St. John. He made up his mind to go away. But, not wanting to give comfort to the enemy, he fabricated a story about his suit coming up and being on the point of settlement. Not even this news, which at any other time would have been sensational, caused a ripple in the indifference that surrounded him now, all because of a contemptible liar wearing a ridiculous pea-jacket. The station was empty as he left in a pouring rain. He seemed like a fugitive, wrapped in his impotent rage.

## In which Dondoca is untrue in thought
## to the narrator

I MUST CONFESS that the malicious campaign, born of envy
and spite, unleashed against the captain by Chico Pacheco,
shook my once unconditional admiration for the remarkable
figure of the hero a little. Examined in the light of the scathing
criticism of the ex-customs inspector, some of the captain's
adventures did seem slightly exaggerated. I don't say this to
influence anyone's opinion. I am taking the position of an
impartial historian and, if I bring up the matter, it is because it
surprised me somewhat that the retired government employees
and businessmen attached so little importance to the comments
and observations of Chico Pacheco, that they should have
maintained such a solid front with the captain.

In a work of investigation such as this I have undertaken (to
while away the time and also with the idea of submitting it in the
literary-historical contest sponsored by the Public Archives),
which attempts to reconstruct the truth, certain details have to
be exposed, if not to public debate, at least to the consideration
of persons of authority, qualified to pass judgment upon them.

For that reason I have consulted His Honor, Dr. Alberto
Siqueira, whose importance in Periperi today equals that of

Captain Vasco Moscoso de Aragão in the past, on the matter. The judge is a man of vast learning, there is no branch of human knowledge that does not interest him, from law to philosophy, from economics to the controversial problems of sex behavior. He even knows a little medicine, or perhaps I should say a good deal, and it is he who looks after Dondoca with skill and devotion when she suffers from the heavy and frequent colds to which she is subject. I had occasion to see him (for of late, as further proof of confidence and consideration, he opened to me, in the middle of the afternoon, the door of his "home away from home," which I enter only at night and on the sly) with his shirt sleeves rolled up, bathing the delicate feet of Dondoca in a basin of hot water, and then wrapping them in a towel. According to His Honor, there is no better treatment for colds and grippe. It is a good treatment both for the patient and for the doctor *ad hoc*, it seems to me, for on the pretext of bathing Dondoca's feet the judge's bold hands moved up to her knees and adjacent areas, making her writhe on the bed, shamelessly laughing with pleasure, and winking at me with the air of an accomplice. And all the time he was murmuring sweet talk, tender words: "My little pussy cat, she's not feeling well . . ."

It was a touching sight to see this distinguished man, the glory of Bahian jurisprudence, squatting beside a tin basin, washing, drying, kissing the feet of a poor mulatto girl, who is not too bright and does not have a penny to bless herself with. Further proof of his noble sentiments, which I take this opportunity to proclaim.

When I consulted him about my doubt, he answered that it did not surprise him that the captain's audience should have been so credulous, for they were confronted with concrete proofs of his statements: the framed license, the Order of Christ—highly important—the compass, the telescope. How were they to doubt, and give credence to the calumnies of Chico Pacheco, a forerunner of the backbiters who still plague our quiet suburb, gossiping about their fellow residents, casting aspersions on their neighbors' honor?

His Honor had been considerably offended of late because of word that reached his ears about a discussion that arose in connection with his career. I don't know who carried the echoes of this debate to him, and I don't want to mention names, for our small community is full of mischief-makers and tale-bearers. Besides, I owe thanks to this particular scandalmonger and his scandalmongering for, as a result of this story, my credit with

His Honor was strengthened. It is to it that I even owe the invitation to accompany him to Dondoca's house, a satisfying proof of friendship, even intimacy. We know that a married man has no hesitation about taking an acquaintance to his home and introducing him to his wife; what is unusual is for him to take him into the home and presence of his mistress. Only the closest friends, those who are like brothers, are worthy of such trust.

This was because I defended him when Otoniel Mendonça, one of Telemaco Dorea's bootlickers, went about shooting off his mouth to the effect that Dr. Siqueira had retired after his application for the post of judge of the Court of Appeals had been turned down for the third time. The head of the government had stated the last time the position fell vacant that if he had to choose between a sewer rat and His Honor, he would appoint the rat—it robbed less and stank less. Can you imagine!

In indignation, I vehemently defended the outraged honor of my master. I had old scores to settle with this Otoniel Mendonça and I was just waiting for the chance. He was still fairly young, and he had played me a dirty trick when the two of us were trying to make time with a hustler who had turned up in Periperi at fair time from God knows where. The memory of that painted Manon filled me with anger and eloquence. I vented my contempt and some severe adjectives on the head of the imbecile and won the approval of the listeners. Otoniel himself, frightened at seeing me so worked up, backtracked, said he was an admirer of the judge, that he was only repeating stories that were going around in Bahía... As you can see, not only a slanderer but a coward.

But coming back to the affairs of the captain—the sole reason for these reflections of mine—I laid the problem before Telemaco Dorea, the modernist poet. Our relations, which of late had been strained, had improved. He sought me out, all smiles and affability, to compliment me on a sonnet I had written—alexandrines of the proper length, thank God—published in a little review that belongs to a friend of mine, an intelligent and enterprising young man. There are those who call him a dead-beat, accusing him of getting money out of the hard-working Spanish colony, of publishing diatribes against the businessmen who refuse to advertise in his paper. I think this is nothing but intrigues and calumny, I prefer to take no notice of it. Telemaco really liked the sonnet, he was lavish in his praise. He compared me to Pethion de Vilar and Artur de Sales; I was touched by his spontaneous recognition of my poetic gifts. I was so moved I embraced him. He's not a bad fellow; just a little boisterous, with a rough side to his tongue at times, but might not that bitterness be the result of his financial difficulties? He receives a miserable allowance, barely enough to live on. There is no question but that he has talent, and if he didn't go overboard about futurism, he could write good poetry.

I explained to him my concern over the attitude the inhabitants of Periperi had assumed in the first phase of the struggle between the captain and Chico Pacheco.

Telemaco did not agree with His Honor—"what does that animal understand about human behavior?" According to him, it was not the concrete and material proofs—license, charts, chronometer—that were the basic reason for the support given to the captain. It was not so simple and easy, nor do people attach so much value to material proofs. The reason they had sided with the captain, and braved Chico Pacheco and his terrible tongue, was the need they all felt, those unassuming and timid pensioners and retired businessmen, of their ration of adventure, their dose of heroism. No matter how down-to-earth a man may be, however humdrum his life, deep inside him there is a flame, at times barely a spark, but capable of turning into a blaze if the propitious occasion arises. This is what makes it necessary to flee mediocrity, the tediousness of the drab days, all so petty, all alike, if only on the words of a tale heard or a book read. In the adventures of the captain, in his daring, hazardous life, they encountered the dangers they had never undergone, the fights and battles they had never taken part in, the glamorous and sinful love affairs they, alas, had not enjoyed.

What could Chico Pacheco offer them? The pettifoggery of a suit against the state? That was very little. If it had even been a criminal case, with an adulterous wife, a scoundrel of a lover, shots, stabbings, a tense jury, a prosecuting attorney, the lawyer for the defense, jealousy, hate, love, he might have had a chance. But this litigation about a pension was as nothing compared to what they needed, their lack of a more meaningful, deeper life. The captain was the generous donor of human greatness. There you have the secret of his success.

I must confess that all this seemed to me complicated, confused, and a little highfalutin. Telemaco Dorea is like that, but, at bottom, he's not a bad fellow. He paid me several more compliments, borrowed two hundred cruzeiros to be returned two days later, and left.

I finally laid the question before Dondoca in the warm bed

where at night I take the place of His Honor. True, I am devoid of his lofty intellectual attainments, but I have certain physical advantages. The hussy laughed her ingratiating laugh: "Even though he's old, that captain has his charm. I like his voice, his pretty eyes, his hair. It would be nice to lie and listen to him tell his adventures. There's not a woman who doesn't like a man like that."

"Just to listen to him, or...?"

Dondoca laughed fit to kill: "Who knows? Maybe..."

As though the judge were not enough, the slut! Pulling me by the hair and with her mouth against mine, she said: "Tell me another of his stories, one with a woman in it and the sea all around, go on, sugar..."

I swear she was thinking of the captain, the trollop!

## Of how the Second of July celebration unleashed the storm, or the return of the desperado accusing the youth

AND SUDDENLY, one of those perfect winter days with a bright and cloudless sky, an unruffled sea, nature at peace with man, the storm broke.

It was not long after the Second of July, celebrated that year with exceptional pomp in Periperi. Previously the observation of Bahía's national holiday had been limited to a ceremony in the primary school: a speech by the teacher and anthems sung in shrill, off-key voices by the children. Aside from this, it was a dull day, everyone recalling other Seconds of July in the city, the parade of groups dressed like Indians, the ceremonies in Sé Square and in Campo Grande, the fireworks.

That year, however, the captain, an undisputed authority on civic affairs, took charge of the celebration. He had already revolutionized the festival of St. John by tying a brand-new twenty-milreis note—out of all reason!—at the top of the greased pole; multiplying the number of children's contests, with prizes for the winners; financing a feast for the poor in the house of Esmeraldina, a seamstress who was something of a screwball, who loved to sing and dance, make matches and undo marriages, a kind of *femme fatale* to workers and fishermen, with a long record of fights, knife play, and threats of death to her credit. The rum flowed freely, the harmonica and guitar wailed far into the night, the uproar was deafening, when at eleven o'clock the captain appeared, wearing his dress uniform, accompanied by Zequinha Curvelo (who now smoked a pipe, too), to see how the party was going.

The Second of July found him in dress uniform from early morning; his soul, too, decked out in patriotic ardor. How he had discovered that Caco Podre in his salad days had been a private first-class, nobody knew. Perhaps from his habit of talking with all and sundry, of listening patiently to their confidences and memories, of discussing their problems. The result was that the population of Periperi awoke at daybreak that Second of July to the martial sound of the bugle. It was Caco Podre in the square, playing reveille with all the enthusiasm of one who recaptures the lost years of his youth, while the captain hoisted the flags of Brazil and Bahia on the greased pole converted into a flagstaff. There may have been a few false notes, for Caco Podre's musical memory was a little rusty, but who noticed such trifling details? The retired officials and businessmen started from their beds, half asleep. What the devil was that, what was going on? They pricked up their ears. The bugle call broke the morning silence. They recalled the sun of the Second of July, which, as the well-known anthem affirms, "on that day is Brazilian, Shines brighter than on the first."

Could it be something having to do with the armed forces, the frightened inhabitants wondered? Maybe it was a revolution; the papers had been full of rumors. That's what it was, a revolution, without doubt, for immediately afterward a mighty bombardment shook Periperi to its foundations. Rockets bursting in air, bombs booming salvos under the competent control of the captain issuing orders to Misael, the other railway porter: "Twenty-one. That will do!"

Faces still heavy with sleep appeared at the windows. Children went running to the square, where fishermen and workers of the Leste Line had gathered. The captain was making a speech to them for the first time on that memorable day. In a little while Old José Paulo, Adriano, Emilio Fagundes, Rui Pessoa, and the others arrived in pajamas. Zequinha Curvelo, standing at attention beside the flagpole, wore a ribbon displaying the national colors in his lapel.

At ten o'clock there was the customary ceremony in the school, but greatly amplified, with the declamation of Castro

Alves's *Ode to the Second of July*, and another address by the captain, an elegant discourse, with magnificent figures of speech. Accompanied by Labatut, Maria Quiteria, Periquitão, Vasco Moscoso de Aragão came from the fields of Cabrito and Pirajá, from the battles of Itaparica and Cachoeira, entering the city of Salvador by the Lapinha and Soledade Road, bending with emotion over the body of Joana Angélica fallen at the door of the convent for fallen women in Lapa, driving out once and for all the Portuguese colonizers. The captain was transfigured, fuming with indignation against the Lusitanian oppressors, extolling the memory of the brave Bahians, the liberators of the Fatherland. For it was on the Second of July that independence was really achieved, the blood of the Bahians giving reality to the call to arms of Ipiranga.[1]

After the hymns, he led the two porters, the teachers and the pupils, Zequinha Curvelo, and the rest of the population in a parade down the main street to the square, his martial voice issuing orders: "Forward, march!" "Right, march!" "Attention! Halt!" The buttons of his uniform gleamed in the sun, the silvery dust of a light shower accompanied the paraders.

In the square, children and teachers, Zequinha, the porters (Caco Podre was now a little unsteady on his legs, for he had begun to drink before daylight) stood at salute, and all swore allegiance to the flag. At the end of the afternoon the captain said a few more words to the people who had gathered to see the lowering of the flags. This final ceremony was somewhat marred by a lamentable occurrence: by this time Caco Podre was practically in a coma, and could not sound a note on the bugle. A student with a trumpet took his place, but it wasn't the same. However, this did not dim the splendor of the celebration; the firecrackers, skyrockets, Roman candles made up for it. Misael stayed comparatively sober.

---

[1] When Brazil proclaimed its independence on September 7, 1822, the Portuguese troops in Bahía refused to recognize it. Dom Pedro I, Emperor of Brazil, dispatched Brazilian troops to the city under the command of the French general, Labatut. Labatut arrived in Bahía in October, 1822, organized the famous battalions of Brazilian volunteers—one of which Maria Quiteria, a national heroine, joined—and besieged the city. The Portuguese attempted to fight their way out, but on November 8 were defeated in the battles of Pirajá and Cabrito. After these victories, Labatut tightened the siege, and on July 2, 1823, the Brazilian troops entered the city, driving out the last of the Portuguese and establishing Brazil's independence. (Translator's Note)

76

"Yes, sir," commented old Marreco when it was over, "captain had to come here to live so we could have a dece¹ celebration of the Second of July... What a fellow!"

The captain's reputation was really established; it stood, so to speak, like a statue on the pedestal of affection and admiration of his fellow citizens of Periperi, definitive and charismatic. Nobody there had ever been so highly regarded, so unanimously sought out and respected. The news of that Second of July celebration carried his fame to the outer limits of the suburbs of the Leste Brasileira Line. Not a move was made in all those environs without consulting the captain.

And then suddenly, after all that splendor of the Second of July, on a bright day made for tranquil pleasure, the tempest broke. Chico Pacheco arrived at the station, noisy, happy, and in a hurry.

"He's won his suit," thought Rui Pessoa when he saw him alight.

He had no more than set foot on the platform than he began boasting to Rui, to the stationmaster, the employees, the trackwalkers, Caco Podre and Misael:

"Didn't I tell you? Didn't I warn you? I warned every one of you. Nobody ever pulls the wool over my eyes... A faker, that's what he is. He never set foot on a ship, never."

He went from house to house, seeking everybody out, one by one. Even Zequinha Curvelo received a visit from him. Being triumphant and in the right, he could afford to be generous. He carried in his pocket a little black notebook which he consulted from time to time. He repeated his grotesque tale, interlarded with guffaws and insults against the captain: "That son-of-a-bitch of a charlatan..."

There were those who believed every word he said and began to look contemptuously at the captain, laughing as he went by; others thought both sides had exaggerated, that Vasco was not the hero he made himself out to be, nor was Chico Pacheco's tale as true as he claimed, but these were in a minority; the third group did not believe one word of the ex-customs inspector's tale, and remained unconditionally on the side of the redoubtable master mariner. Adriano Meira was in the first group, Zequinha Curvelo in the last, and somewhere between them, trying to conciliate them, was old José Paulo, the respected Marreco.

Conciliation was difficult, perhaps impossible, for the

on an asperity hitherto unknown in Periperi.
cited, refused to yield an inch, old friends stopped
one another, Chico Pacheco and Zequinha Curvelo
to blows. The suburb was divided, its former peace,
even in the newspapers of the capital, had come to an
end. Passions, like a whirlwind, swept Periperi.

With his notebook in hand, Chico Pacheco went about
repeating his findings, his horrendous tale. It dated back to the
beginning of the century, to the time when Dr. José Marcelino
was governor of Bahía.

# EPISODE TWO

*Complete and faithful reproduction of Chico Pacheco's narrative, presenting a trustworthy picture of the customs and life of the City of Salvador da Bahía at the beginning of the century, with illustrious members of the government, rich businessmen, haughty damsels, and strumpets with hearts of gold*

# EPISODE TWO

*Complete and faithful reproduction of Chico Pacheco's narrative, presenting a trustworthy picture of the customs and life of the City of Salvador da Bahía at the beginning of the century, with illustrious members of the government, rich businessmen, haughty damsels, and strumpets with hearts of gold*

## Of the pension Monte Carlo and five important gentlemen

GLITTERING WITH jewels, rings on her fingers, necklaces at her throat, a tiara on her head, earrings in her ears, the train of her evening gown swishing behind her, her full bosom rising out of her bodice, her lips parted in a smile, Carol hurried forward as she saw them at the head of the stairs: "At last . . . I thought you weren't coming today."

She carried her fifty-six well-spent years and the flesh against which she carried on a losing battle gracefully. The flesh had come with age and the savings wisely invested in stocks and real estate. A triumphant career, compounded of work and sorrows, forty years in brothels, first as an inmate, afterwards as a madam, ever since that far-off day when she ran away with a traveling salesman who was passing through Garanhuns, and took her in with his gab and his city ways, promising her the world with a fence around it. A week later, he left her high and dry in Recife, a girl of sixteen, without a cent, not knowing a soul, utterly inexperienced. She went wandering from bridge to bridge, looking down into the waters of the river as though seeking a way out.

On certain quiet afternoons, stretched out in a rocking chair that was like a throne in the dining room, her jewel box on her plump thighs, Carol recalled that hideous night: little Carolina, dishonored, deserted, a lump in her throat and a tremor in her knees, lost in the streets and the terror of the city, tempted by the waters of Capibaribe. She let the diamond rings, the necklace of real pearls, pins, brooches, and bracelets, emeralds and topazes slip through her fingers, and remembered that night when all the weariness and all the fear in the world were hers. Later on, she became Carol, and now she could smile at the memory of those suicidal hours and the traveling salesman. He had seemed to her like the prince in a fairy story when he appeared in Garanhuns with his sample cases and his line of talk when he was nothing but a poor devil, without money or charm. Princes were those men now coming up the stairs of the Pension Monte Carlo, on the Praça do Teatro, the most elegant and luxurious sporting house in the city of Bahía, the sole and exclusive property of Carolina da Silva Medeiros, better known as Carol, the Golden-Tongued.

The five men, all dressed in white duck, wearing elegant straw hats, spats, and curled mustaches, carrying elegant canes, enthusiastic and noisy, encircled her in an effusion of hugs and kisses, jests and gallantries.

"Hail to Our Queen and Lady!" A tall man, a well-preserved forty, with tanned skin and cropped hair, bowed over her hand.

"What an honor, Colonel. Come in, the house is yours."

A strong, attractive gentleman, very blond, with mocking blue eyes, bent low before her, in an exaggerated bow: "Here I am at your feet, lady of my heart."

"Don't lie, Captain. I know who the lady of your heart is."

"More beautiful than ever," said a third as he kissed her hand, covered with rings and skilled at caresses.

It was she, however, who leaned over to greet and then embrace him: "Dr. Jerónimo, welcome, I am your humble servant, yours to command."

And she turned to a young man with cheeks like a girl's, a silent pretty boy: "The lieutenant is impatiently awaited."

And finally she embraced with real friendship the last of the group, with his hooked nose, his romantic locks, and a certain melancholy in his affectionate eyes: "Mr. Aragão. Aragãozinho! What a sight for sore eyes!"

Aragãozinho's eyes became even sadder, in spite of the indubitable affection in Carol's voice, and her enthusiastic greeting. She noticed this, and knowing the reason, she whispered in the youth's ear: "You just keep on, and you'll win out. I know what I am saying." And then louder: "I hear secrets and sighs."

The colonel remarked with a laugh: "Nobody can do anything with this Aragão of ours. Neither epaulettes nor titles help..."

It was to him, too, that the waiter spoke in a fluty voice and with effeminate gestures: "I saved the corner table for you, Mr. Aragão, the usual one."

They walked over to it, and Carol accompanied them as a token of utmost deference. The women at the other tables stirred, ready to leave their chance clients at the first call from the madam or one of the new arrivals. The lieutenant threw his arms around a little blonde who was alone, hidden behind the orchestra.

Aragão ran his eyes about the room until he met those of Dorothy. There she was, her hands in the hands of Roberto, who had her clasped against his fat chest in a hold that went a little too far even for those surroundings. His swinish snout was nuzzling the nape of her neck. Dorothy's eyes, uneasy and almost pleading, came to rest on Aragão's, and a timid smile flowered on her lips. A warmth of springtime rose in Aragão's breast. That Dr. Roberto Veiga Lima, the vain, fatuous, wastrel son of a rich father, was unworthy of the fragile, sullen beauty of Dorothy, her frightened eyes, that need of love that burned in her cheeks like a fever.

All that demonstration of esteem on the part of Carol was neither fortuitous nor gratuitous: those five gentlemen sitting at the table, ordering drinks, honored and protected her house. They were the cream of Bahía, the playboys most sought after among those who frequented cafés, gambling tables, bordellos, and houses of assignation. They formed the center of a large, lavish circle made up of the best people of the city. But these five were inseparable, they met every day toward the end of the afternoon, to play billiards, drink beer, or at poker sessions that lasted far into the night, or suppers at cabarets.

"Those five own the state," people would say when they saw them enter the State House, a government bureau, a bar, the Pension Monte Carlo, and they were not far from the truth.

Carol whispered something in the ear of the colonel, and pointed to a tall, striking brunette.

"She arrived today from Recife... Out of this world."

"You only look after the army. What about the navy?" asked the one with blue eyes who looked like a gringo.

"I've got something special for you, Captain. Just what you like, well-toasted."

A guffaw went up from the table. The dark-skinned woman came over, a *femme fatale*. The orchestra struck up an Argentine tango, Roberto got up to dance with Dorothy. In his ten years at the university he had not learned medicine (gossip had it that he had finally been awarded his degree on the basis of seniority), but he certainly had learned the waltz, the tango, the maxixe, and was a first-class dancer in spite of his weight. He put on a beautiful exhibition as he led Dorothy through the steps of the tango. She took advantage of the opportunity to kindle Aragão's breast with long looks and timid smiles. The waiter brought drinks, women circled about the table in the hope of being called over. The little brown girl Mucu sat on the blond captain's lap, tickling him under the chin. Carol was in her glory, proud of her house, her orchestra, her hand-picked girls, her respectful waiters, her stock of liquor, her high prices, her first-class clientele. Especially those five.

Colonel Pedro de Alencar, of Rio, a widower without children, commanded the 19th Battalion of Riflemen stationed in the city. Captain Georges Dias Nadreau, harbor master, whose father was French and whose mother was from Minas Gerais, was crazy about poker, good-looking Negro women, and amusing escapades. He spent his time playing jokes on his friends, but he was the most loyal of comrades when the chips were down. It was he who had designed, framed, and hung in the Pension Monte Carlo a sign reading: THE CABARET AND HEARTH OF THE BOHEMIANS. Dr. Jerónimo de Paiva, some thirty-odd years old, a lawyer without clients and an obscure journalist in Rio, had been brought to Bahía by the governor, who was a relative of his, to write his speeches. He was the head of the cabinet, and enjoyed great prestige. He was planning to enter politics and run for the federal legislature in the next election. Lieutenant Lidio Marinho, aide-de-camp to the governor, and son of Colonel Américo Marinho, feudal lord of the uplands of the São Francisco and state senator, was the match all the marriageable girls in the city dreamed about. They watched him behind the window curtains, sighing as he walked past in his elegant uniform; they dreamed of dancing with him at balls and surprise parties. Pugnacious and romantic, Lidio was also the darling of the women of the sporting houses, where his adventures took place.

And finally, Mr. Vasco Moscoso de Aragão, or Aragãozinho, head of the firm of Moscoso & Company, Ltd., one of the richest in the city, wholesale dealers in jerked beef, codfish, wines, butter, Portuguese cheese, potatoes, and assorted products to all the area around Bahía, the south and the backlands, as far as Sergipe and Alagoas, employing a whole force of traveling salesmen. Vasco Moscoso de Aragão's was considered one of the tidiest fortunes in the Bahian business world, and his firm, one of the most solid and well established.

The liquor flowed freely at the table, for those clients paid no thought to expenses. They lacked neither position nor money. When she was with them, Carol, too, had a sense of power, as though she belonged to government circles and big business, was at home in the State House and the banks, with a finger in the political pie. Didn't Dr. Jerónimo, who even as a young man had been attracted by women like her, mature, experienced, well-fleshed, frequent her sagacious bed? When Georges teased him, the head of the cabinet answered: "I'm no dog to be gnawing bones. I don't like green fruit, either. Carol has her secret charms..."

Her secret charms! The wisdom of her vast experience. And her prestige. Hadn't she already got an appointment in the Government Printing Office for a nephew of hers, the son of a younger sister in Garanhuns whose husband did nothing but insult his fallen sister-in-law? Just a word in the ear of Jerónimo, one delirious night, and it was done. She had privates promoted to corporals, got her protégés, the sons of poor folk, her godchildren, into the Naval Training Academy. She could count on Aragãozinho's endorsement whenever she needed to borrow money from the bank to invest in another piece of property. For the dances at the State House, when the cream of Bahian society gathered there, it was Carol who planned the menu, supplied the liquor; the waiters of the Pension Monte Carlo were hired to serve the guests, the upright gentlemen and virtuous ladies. Discreetly she gave and countermanded orders; even upstate politicians came to do her homage and seek her support. That same little Carolina from Garanhuns, who was on the point of committing suicide one night on the bridges of Recife and who today displays her jewels in her house on the Praça do Teatro of Salvador da Bahía. Smiling at the five gentlemen around the table.

## Of the firm of Moscoso & Company, Ltd., a commercial interlude with a note of sadness

THE FIRM was founded by old Moscoso, the maternal grandfather of Vasco, and quickly rose to prosperity and standing. José Moscoso was a Portuguese with an instinct for business and stern principles, whose word was as good as his bond. For fifty years he lived exclusively for his firm, drudging away like the lowliest of his employees, "setting an example," indifferent to comfort and amusements, sober in eating, dress, and love. He had only one daughter by his wife, and when he became a widower, he satisfied his rare urges with the colored cook.

Vasco succeeded him as head of the firm which in those fifty years had grown from a modest office to a building that occupied three blocks at the foot of Ladeira da Montanha. The top floor housed the employees, and there were better rooms for the good customers from the interior who visited the capital on business. They ate on the premises, too; there was no set work week, no Sundays or holidays.

Vasco lost his father when he was three years old, and soon afterwards his mother, who was unable to live without that faithless, passionate husband. Vasco was brought up by his grandfather, who put him into the business when he was ten years old, just out of primary school. He began at the bottom, sweeping out the rooms and the warehouse, and then loading merchandise like any other porter. He slept with the other employees on the third floor and took his meals with them, in the morning and evening, at the patriarchal table presided over by old Moscoso. Like them, the first woman he knew was the colored cook, the same one his grandfather utilized, and those nights with black Rosa, in her stifling, windowless room, were his only joy. His grandfather never allowed him any special privileges, except to kiss his hand at the morning blessing.

While he lived, old Moscoso watched his grandson and shook his head in discouragement. The boy showed no inclination or gift for business; he was careless and absent-minded, without the least sense of responsibility. As a young man, he was sent to Jequié and Sergipe as a salesman, and the results were deplorable. The gloomiest forebodings of old Moscoso and Rafael Menéndez, the firm's number one employee, efficiency personified, were fulfilled.

Vasco's connection with the illustrious corporation of traveling salesmen, a much sought-after employment in those days, was brief but dazzling. His dealings were governed by his likes or dislikes; he extended credit to storekeepers who were on the verge of bankruptcy, whose establishments the other drummers carefully avoided. As he was incapable of collecting a bill, he granted the most absurd terms. In the city of Estancia in Sergipe, territory that could be covered in one day, he spent a week, enchanted by its shady streets, the liveliness of the town, the bathing in the Piautinga River, the pretty girls in the windows or at the piano, the languishing looks of Otalia, the boardinghouse keeper, who was crazy about the new salesman. Never had one of José Moscoso's salesmen embarked on so slow a journey or one that had such disastrous results. They had to send an experienced salesman to that territory, considered the easiest of all, to restore the reputation of the firm, which was seriously damaged by that novice who seemed bent on revolutionizing the profession. However, Vasco left the reputation of the firm and his own high and unforgettable in every whorehouse to be found in the cities he visited. He took a complete course in women, making up for his years of abstention in the warehouse at the foot of Ladeira da Montanha, where the rigid principles of old Moscoso imposed impossible hours and reduced lasciviousness to the limited charms of black Rosa, which, notwithstanding, were in great demand and forbidden.

Shaking his head gloomily, old Moscoso put him back in the office, where he continued to be more or less useless. He was only good for accompanying the upstate customers, who stayed at the warehouse, on their visits to the city. At this he could not have been better, with his agreeable manners, his pleasant conversation, an excellent companion for a night on the town. Though "night on the town" is a figure of speech, for if old Moscoso, with his big watch hanging from his fingers, could not apply to the customers the established schedule—"To bed at eight, not one minute later"—he applied it to his grandson with a rigor unattenuated by the fact that the down on the boy's sensual lip was turning into a heavy mustache. Not to mention the fact that the allowance made Vasco for his expenses was limited to the cost of transportation.

Old Moscoso exerted a certain amount of pressure even over the customers as regards hours, money spent on loose living and women, repeatedly mentioning how little credit in his opinion men of irregular habits, who frequented bars and whorehouses, merited. "What confidence can one have in a man given to drinking and whores?" The question clipped the wings of the plans caressed for months by upstate businessmen, waiting for their visit to the capital to sate the flesh. But even so, the customers went, and Vasco, taking advantage of every opportunity, sabotaged the counseled visit to historic sites, substituting for it the cordial atmosphere of the sporting houses, where the young heir apparent was beginning to establish firm connections.

Old Moscoso, his eyeglasses hooked on his nose, wearing a black alpaca coat, bent over the letter books of the firm, watched his grandson sitting motionless in front of the letter he had started, his eyes staring through the window, dreaming. His discouraged glance met the censorious gaze of Rafael Menéndez. The old man shook his head, the head clerk gave him a pitying look. The fact was that José Moscoso loved his firm better than his family, which now, moreover, was reduced to that lazy grandson, as fantastical as his father, that prater, that faker of an Aragão, with a well-established, fully deserved reputation as a liar, who had turned the head of his only daughter, and had lived at his expense for five years. He had even cost him a pretty penny after he died, for that imbecile widow of his had demanded a first-class funeral and a marble mausoleum for her "adored spouse." In the opinion of the relieved father-in-law, seven feet of plain ground would have been too much honor for that worthless son-in-law, known among his friends as Limber-Tongued Aragão, so many and such whoppers did he tell. A more cynical and brazen character old Moscoso felt had never walked the face of the earth. Hints and suggestions rolled off him like water off a duck; after a seemingly endless honeymoon, he laughed in the old man's face when the latter suggested that he go to work in the office of the company. Who did his father-in-law take him for? he asked, half amused, half offended. For a dolt, a poor devil fit for nothing but the degradation of a business office, handling groceries, codfish, potatoes? To whom did he think he had married his daughter? Apparently he was not aware of his talents, his abilities, his connections, his plans. His honorable father-in-law could dismiss from his mind the idea of fixing him up with a job. His future was assured, and if he had not yet gone to work, it was because the crux of the problem lay precisely in choosing between five or six possibilities, each more desirable than the other, which had been offered him by his friends, men of outstanding prestige. Mr. Moscoso himself would benefit by the friendships of his son-in-law, who would secure for the firm government or private contracts, which would be like picking up money in the street. What would Mr. Moscoso say, for example, to a contract to supply the Military Police with dried beef and codfish for a year? He, Aragão, had only to whisper a word into the ear of the quartermaster general, and the thing was settled. Mr. Moscoso could count on the contract, like money in the bank. And the full amount, for he, son-in-law and friend, would accept no commission.

For the five years of his marriage he remained in the same state of indecision, unable to make up his mind about any of the five or six magnificent possibilities, and the new offers from his friends, who were filthy rich. Nor did he secure any government contract for the firm; he was always going to take up the matter the next day. However, he was adamant in his refusal of a job as employee of his father-in-law, considering the repeated offer almost an offense and an affront. He was a character of such integrity of purpose that he never set foot in the three-story building, knowing it only by sight when he chanced to pass by the Ladeira da Montanha.

On his sudden death—nobody ever dreamed he had a bad heart—the moneylenders turned up with overdue notes, miscellaneous loans, penciled I.O.U.'s—a fortune it added up to—which old José Moscoso, who was also a character, refused to do anything about. One could say that Limber-Tongued Aragão was mourned by his wife, his many barfly friends, and his manifold creditors, who were shocked by the flinty indifference of the departed's father-in-law.

The widow could not endure the loss of her adored spouse, and months later she was buried in the same marble mausoleum. She had never for one instant doubted her husband, his gifts, his fidelity, his devoted love. And from one point of view, Limber-Tongued Aragão was an excellent husband. He spent almost every afternoon with his wife, petting her, babying her, with a great show of affection, and making love to her with constancy and skill. But after dinner he was a free man for the night, always taking pains to explain to his wife that he had weighty political and business matters to attend to. He would come home at dawn, smelling of rum and women, with his invariable cigar, his invariable satisfied smile. Not even the birth of a son, which linked him even closer to his wife, modified the regularity of his irregular habits (in old Moscoso's opinion). He got up at noon, ate and drank like a lord, devoted the afternoon to his wife and son, leaving his night free for bars and sporting houses, for shooting the breeze with his friends. His father-in-law recognized that he had one single virtue: nobody had ever seen him drunk. His resistance to alcohol was fantastic.

Bent over his desk, old Moscoso looked at his grandson and saw in him the son-in-law of execrated memory. What good had it done to bring him into the business when he was ten years old, to train him in his responsibilities? The same dreamy eyes of the father, the same satisfied smile, the same absolute indifference to the problems of running the enterprise—in a word, a calamity. He would have to take measures, and serious ones, if he did not want to see the powerful and highly reputed firm, the work of a lifetime, crumble to bits in the hands of his grandson.

Therefore, when he felt that death could not be far off, he converted what had been a private business into a corporation, making some of his oldest and most able employees stockholders. The head clerk, that Spaniard Rafael Menéndez, was made director, and by the terms of old Moscoso's will, the complete management of the business and its future was left in his hands. Vasco received his grandfather's holdings, which gave him a major share of the profits—in a word, a considerable fortune and no responsibility.

Thus he found himself free of duties, fixed hours, obligations, and with plenty of money. He left all decisions to Menéndez. Only once did he disagree with him and impose his own will, which was when the Spaniard decided to fire old Giovanni, a porter who had been with the firm almost from the start. For over forty years he had carried on his head load after load, from the warehouse to the wagons, never taking a day off, with never a word of complaint, acting as watchman at night, sleeping on the bales in the warehouse, opening the door for the customers who came in late, those who ventured to transgress old Moscoso's schedule. Vasco was grateful to him, for the Negro Giovanni had always taken his part, from the first hard days when he had come to work in the business at the age of ten. He told him stories at night; he had been a sailor when he was young, and he talked to him of seas and ports. Born João and a slave, he had run away to the freedom of the sea, where the Italian crew of a ship had metamorphosed him into Giovanni. He was the only one who showed affection for the child, a prisoner on the gloomy top floor, where the smell of spices was so strong it made the head swim. He had grown old with the firm; now he was seventy and not as strong as he had once been, and he could not handle all the work. Menéndez decided to fire him and hire another porter.

Even after his grandfather's death, and in his new position as nominal head of the firm, Vasco was still a little in awe of Menéndez. The Spaniard was one of those smooth, two-faced persons, who kowtowed to his superiors and was overbearing with those who were subject to his orders or inferior to him in rank and importance. He had taken over the management of the business with an iron hand, and everything ran on greased wheels. But the employees complained that it was even worse than in the days of old Moscoso. Vasco was afraid of the cold and critical eye of the Spaniard, his way of talking without raising his voice, without getting excited, but with unalterable firmness. When he was a child and then a young man in the office, Menéndez had not dressed him down as he did the others. But, as Vasco well knew, every mistake he made, every infraction of the rules of the establishment was brought to his grandfather's knowledge. Including his rare nocturnal escapades, when the Negro Giovanni covered up for him. Now Menéndez bowed and scraped to him, showing him a consideration and respect formerly reserved for old Moscoso. Nevertheless, he attempted to stand by his decision when Vasco, upset and indignant, came to discuss the matter of the Negro's dismissal. Giovanni had been to see him the night before to tell him what had happened. Menéndez had paid him his pittance of a wage and discharged him without even a word of explanation.

He found Vasco in a bar with his friends, and told him what had happened, his tired eyes blinking to keep back the tears, his voice quavering: "The company ate my flesh, now it wants to throw away the bones..."

"That is not going to happen," Vasco assured him.

The old Negro showed his gratitude with a piece of advice: "That gringo's no good, Mr. Aragãozinho. Watch out for him, or he will still do you a bad turn."

The next day Vasco appeared in the office bright and early, which was a rare event. He sent for Menéndez, he was serious and stiff, and the employees began to whisper among themselves. From old Moscoso's office, now used by Vasco, came the angry voice of the head of the firm. Menéndez's voice was inaudible; never a shout or a loud word fell from his stern lips, even when he was insulting in the most scathing terms an employee who was at fault.

It was not easy for Vasco to get his way. He raised his voice, he said it was an inhuman thing to fire old Giovanni, that they had no right to turn him into a beggar at the end of his days, a man whose whole life had been devoted to the work, the prosperity of the firm. Menéndez smiled his cold smile, nodded his head in agreement, but stuck to his guns: on principle, when an employee couldn't do his work any more, the only thing to do was to get rid of him and hire another. This was the rule of the game; he merely applied it. If he made an exception in the case of Giovanni, if he continued to pay him his salary, the other employees would demand the same treatment. Could Mr. Vasco (now Menéndez always prefaced the name of the new head of the firm with this respectful handle, whereas for more than twenty years he had addressed him as Aragãozinho) imagine where a policy of that sort would lead to? No, no, he could not act differently.

Vasco was not interested in principles or policy; all he knew was that it was cruel, downright heartless to fire Giovanni.

Menéndez washed his hands: Mr. Vasco was the head of the firm, what he decided would be done. He should, however, think twice before abrogating a rule that affected every aspect of their business existence. It was the very foundation of the firm that he was endangering, without taking into consideration the fact that he, Vasco, would not be the only sufferer thereby, but all the other stockholders. He was not speaking for himself; what he was doing was defending a principle, not a few insignificant milreis.

Vasco lost his head and began to shout. When all was said and done, over fifty per cent of the shares belonged to him and he could decide the matter himself. Even more mealymouthed, the Spaniard agreed. And seeing the rage Vasco was in, he proposed an arrangement which would take care of everything. Giovanni had been discharged, and would continue so. But they, the two of them, Mr. Vasco and Menéndez, would guarantee him a living, giving him a sum each month to cover his expenses. This proposal was the beginning of prolonged negotiations, for the old Negro would not hear of leaving the warehouse and moving somewhere else, not even to Vasco's house. Finally they reached an agreement: Giovanni would continue as night watchman, with half his former salary, and Vasco would pay the other half out of his own pocket. As he thanked him, the Negro repeated his warning: "Boss, watch out for that Spaniard. He's a mean bugger."

Menéndez represented for Vasco freedom from all responsibility. He went to the office to relieve his conscience, exchanged a few words with the Spaniard, listened with one ear to his remarks about business, and went to see Giovanni in the warehouse. He did not stay long. He always had an appointment with one of his many friends in the group to which he now belonged, or in one of the houses a new woman was waiting for him, some recent conquest.

A bachelor, he fell in love at the drop of a hat. Openhanded, lavish, almost a wastrel where money was concerned, always picking up the check in bars and cabarets, he was popular with women, and when one of them took his fancy, he went all out, setting her up in a house, loading her with gifts. His latest passion was Dorothy, a girl who was being kept in Carol's establishment by Dr. Roberto Veiga Lima, a wealthy, non-practicing physician, who was famous in the circles of harlotry for his violent jealousy and his brutality. He was, one might say, the opposite of Vasco: women avoided him in spite of his money. For some mere trifle he would beat a girl up, and there were those who said his mania for whipping his bed companions was a vice. He had brought Dorothy back from the country after a trip to Feira de Sant'Ana. He kept her a virtual prisoner, threatening her every minute, and Carol regretted having agreed to keep her in the Pension Monte Carlo. She had not been able to refuse; Roberto was a steady customer, a lavish spender, his family was one of standing. Nevertheless, she regretted it. Poor Dorothy lived more confined than a nun in a convent. Roberto turned up at the most unexpected hours, threatening the poor thing with a thrashing. At night, in the ballroom, grappling Dorothy to him, he would put on an exhibition of the tango or the maxixe, ready to start a fight if one of the other clients gave the poor girl a look or a smile. Carol, who was everybody's confidante, knew that Vasco was interested in her, and she also knew that Dorothy was crazy about him. In those months in the Pension Monte Carlo the girl had learned a lot. She was no longer the simple farmer's daughter the doctor had discovered in Feira. The only thing she wanted now was to escape the clutches of her violent patron and throw herself into the arms of the good-natured and generous businessman.

It was to this complicated and trying passion that Carol and Jerónimo ascribed the melancholy expression in Vasco's eyes. The harbor master thought there might be another reason—a young virgin, a love affair with matrimony as its object, a state of madness for which Dorothy would be a good cure, an infallible remedy. The colonel disagreed with all of them, diagnosing it as a deep-seated, incurable sadness, going far back. Lieutenant Lidio Marinho had no preconceived ideas, he merely stated a fact: that brute of a Vasco, in spite of being so gay, was given to spells of hypochondria. Maybe it was his liver, but anyway it did not make sense in a man with all his money. They were all in agreement on one point: they had to find the reason for that secret sorrow that gnawed at the breast of Vasco Moscoso de Aragão.

A good talker and pleasant company, rich and young, with the health of an ox, why, then, did he give the impression of hiding some secret sorrow, an incurable wound? His friends were worried, especially Captain Georges Dias Nadreau, who was gay by nature, and to whom sadness and suffering were in the nature of a personal affront.

*Of the harbor master, his Negro and
mulatto women, and Madalena Pontes
Mendes, a stuck-up damsel*

THE HARBOR MASTER, Georges Dias Nadreau, liked to see
merry faces around him, lips parted in a smile. That was his
climate; he could not bear glum people, which may explain his
dislike for his home, where his wife was the perfect image of
sadness and piety, dedicated to the church, to good works,
devoted to the sick and the suffering, to orphans and widows,
completely happy during Easter Week with the scenes of the
Passion—the Meeting Between Christ and His Mother, the
Crucifixion—the washing of the feet of the poor, the candles, the
images draped in black, the funereal sound of ratchets taking the
place of the gay pealing of the bells.

How had he, that lighthearted navy lieutenant, come to
marry a girl so different from him in temperament? When he
first knew and fell in love with Gracinha in the Navy Club in Rio,
there was nothing melancholy about her. She was all youthful
laughter; she found the lieutenant's jokes wonderfully
exciting—a feeling the admirals did not always share. It was the
death of her ten-months-old baby that had brought about that
aversion to life, that renunciation of the fallacious happiness of
this world. The child, whom the mother idolized, had taken sick
suddenly, running a temperature for no apparent reason; they

had not called a doctor. The baby died while Gracinha and her husband were at a party aboard a warship. She was dancing with Georges when the news reached them. She felt herself responsible for the child's death; she put on mourning for the rest of her life, and renounced all pleasures and amusements, turning to Heaven, where the babe surely was, and to the church, in the hope that God might forgive her and she would be reunited with her child after death, for which she prayed every day. Her rejection of the things of this world included her husband, at least as far as any physical relationship was concerned. Georges felt the death of the child deeply, "Sailor Boy," he had called him, and had dreamed of a brilliant career for him. But he did not succumb to his sorrow, as his wife did. He tried to convince her that they should have other children to fill the void left by "Sailor Boy." She repulsed him with horror, begging him in tears never again to seek her out for such a sinful purpose. Such things were over for her forever. She wanted a room of her own, apart from him, and she advised Georges, too, to renounce the deceitful pleasures of this world, to return to God and hope that He in His mercy would forgive him his past sins. Georges's jaw dropped; he was defeated. He had understood and shared his wife's initial despair, but he thought it would be of brief duration, two or three months. She, however, locked herself up definitively in her sorrow, a ghost wandering about the house, her wasted lips murmuring prayers, hiding her beauty, which had only begun to unfold, in black dresses and endless tears. She moved into the child's room, turning it into a kind of votive chapel. For a time Georges did his best to break down the barriers of sorrow and despair, but to no avail. He obtained a transfer to another city, but Gracinha continued indifferent to everything that was not the memory of her child and the life eternal. Whereupon he washed his hands of her, and began to live his own life.

He spent as little time as he could at home. He busied himself with the problems of the Port Authority and the Naval Training Academy, with the little park that encircled the house facing the sea of Bahía. After hours, he would take off his uniform, put on civilian clothes, and set out to find Jerónimo in the State House, the colonel at the headquarters of the 19th Riflemen, or go directly to Barris, where Vasco Moscoso de Aragão lived in the house he had inherited from his grandfather, and in which he had spent his infancy. They went out to play billiards, they tossed to see who would pay for the drinks, dined together, and then it was time for women or poker.

Vasco's friendship with that group of distinguished men had begun some time before, as a matter of fact, through Captain Georges, in a cabaret. Dressed in mufti, with his blue eyes and fair hair, Georges looked like a foreign visitor. Nobody would have guessed that he was a captain of the Brazilian Navy. Vasco was sitting alone at a carefully chosen table, near the stage where Soraya, a dancer who was on tour in the city, would soon be doing her turn. He had heard about her and her dances from his friend Johann, a Swede, a buyer of tobacco, piassava fiber, and cacao, who had an office downtown, and a last name it was impossible to write or pronounce. At the table next to his sat the harbor master, whom Vasco took for a European. For a while he amused himself trying to figure out his nationality: Italian, French, German, Dutch? As though his wheat-colored hair and light blue eyes were not enough, the fact that the gentleman was accompanied by a luscious, dark mulatto confirmed the fact that he was a gringo. Vasco turned the matter over in his mind. Curious, the charm Negro and mulatto women had for foreigners. The sight of a dark-skinned girl sent them off their rocker. Whereas he, a Brazilian of mixed blood, was crazy about blondes. What was the reason for this difference in tastes? But before he could come up with an answer, three scowling characters walked into the cabaret, and as they went by his table they gave his chair a rough push. It was apparent that this was all part of a plan; it was clear from their violent behavior. Their objective, Vasco quickly realized, was to beat up the gringo and take the girl from him. But it turned out that the foreigner was no pushover. What had looked like a certain massacre turned into a bloody battle, for the European stood there, slugging it out. Bottles and chairs flew through the air. Vasco could not restrain himself. He found that business of three to one all wrong, and stepped into the fight, backing up the stranger. The woman let out a scream; one of the troublemakers had given her a couple of resounding slaps. Vasco was strong; he had grown up carrying bales, and Giovanni had taught him how to fight *capoeira* fashion.

The fight was hot and heavy, and ended with the intruders being thrown out. The owner of the cabaret, who knew who Georges was, took a hand in it, too. And along with him, the waiters, and they got the three under control. Later they found out who they were. One was the lover of the mulatto; the others, two friends of his who had come to avenge the treachery of which the first had been the victim, and cure the unbearable suffering of the horns that had been put on him. Georges after his victory refused to send for the police, as Vasco suggested. The mulatto, her lip split, seemed touched by the devotion of her lover, the ardor of his sentiments, which could induce him to organize and carry out an attack on the harbor master, the authority over sailors and seafarers. The exploit won her back, and she left the victors in the cabaret, to follow love's call, at the heels of the defeated champion.

Vasco accepted Georges's invitation to sit down at his table, they exchanged cards, the businessman's face lighted up when he discovered who it was he had helped out in that difficult moment: "Captain, this is a great pleasure! Would the gentleman believe that I thought he was a foreigner!"

"My father was French, but I am from Vila Rica in Minas."

"This is an honor for me. I am at the gentleman's orders."

"Let's forget this 'gentleman' business. We are friends."

They wound up fraternizing with Soraya at the end of the evening. Johann put in an appearance, joined them, they applauded the dancer, the daughter of an Arab of São Paulo, they bought her champagne, and took her and two other women to a hotel some distance off which the captain frequented. The next day Vasco was introduced to the colonel, to the lieutenant, and to Dr. Jerónimo. Before long, Jerónimo had asked him for a loan, thus definitively sealing the friendship and the admission of Vasco into the distinguished circle.

And into high society. He began to be invited to festivities at the State House, receptions, dances, to watch the Second of July and Seventh of September parades from the official box, beside the governor, the higher authorities, the superior officers. Jerónimo took a great liking to him, and always wanted him around. Moreover, all four had a high regard for him, as did the others—majors, captains, judges, congressmen, cabinet officers—who joined the circle from time to time for a chat, a hand of poker, a binge. Other drawing rooms were open to him, the close friend of the governor's cabinet secretary, of his aide-de-camp, of the commander of the regiment, the harbor master. Vasco gave up his former associates, businessmen, merchants, dull, narrow-minded beings. Only Johann, whom Georges had taken a liking to, still enjoyed Vasco's friendship.

He turned up once in a while, still crazy about Soraya, and talking about taking her away from the cabaret. A knockout of a woman, a ball of fire in bed, but the worst dancer Johann had ever seen perform in public. And he had seen a good bit of the world before he settled down in Bahía.

Vasco Moscoso de Aragão had everything a man needs to make him happy. Money and social recognition, health and good friends, an abundance of women, luck at cards, no worries to fret him. Then why the devil that touch of melancholy that clouded his clear eyes, cut short his gay laugh?

Captain Georges Dias Nadreau liked to see happy faces around him. He made up his mind to investigate the secret cause of that inexplicable sorrow and, at the same time, discover the cure. For a while he thought it was love sickness, jealousy, a wound that time would heal with a new passion; Dorothy, for example. Of late, Vasco had been showing interest in a young society girl he had met at a party at the governor's mansion, the daughter of a judge, as snobbish as they come, by the name of Madalena Pontes Mendes. Georges was worried: how could an affected, stuck-up girl, stiff as a poker, and with an expression on her face as though she were continually smelling a bad smell, have that effect on a sensible man, to whom women were no novelty, taking the joy of living out of him? It was crazy, but the longer one lives, the more convinced one becomes that the world is full of crazy things.

"That Madalena makes me feel like vomiting," said the harbor master to the colonel of the 19th Riflemen. "What a pain in the ass..."

His hope for Vasco's cure rested with Dorothy, in those burning eyes, those kissable lips, a woman thirsting for love ("You only have to look at her to see it"), who needed a man to ride her through the fields of night and gallop to the frontier of the dawn, past sleep and fatigue.

"Now that one is worth a headache... But to worry over a conceited snip who thinks of nothing but herself is a mug's game."

It was Georges's considered opinion that Vasco had to settle matters once and for all with Dorothy. And he discussed the problem at length with Carol.

*Of reality and dreams in connection
with titles and commissions*

YES, Madaléna Pontes Mendes and her supercilious nose had
a lot to do with Vasco Moscoso de Aragão's secret sorrow.
However, it was not the pangs of love, a successful rival,
unrequited passion, as Captain Nadreau imagined. If the
merchant cherished certain matrimonial intentions toward the
sour damsel, her snobbishness and scrawniness had never made
his heart miss a beat. He never closed his eyes to evoke her naked
image, and he devoted more time and respect to her asthmatic
father, the judge, and her mother, the descendant of barons,
than to the haughty daughter.

Any thought of marriage, if he had one, would have occurred
to him as part of a plan to completely integrate with the Four
Hundred of Bahian Society, that embattled social redoubt, with
their coats of arms and titles. But if this really passed through his
head, a little turned perhaps by his new associates, by the lights
of the governor's mansion, his contact with the governor, the
elegance of the wives of the honorable members of the cabinet, it
never got as far as a definite plan. It was all vague and of brief
duration, a fleeting idea, a bitter chagrin.

He may have thought about a distinguished marriage that
would link his honorable and plebian name, smelling of codfish

and dried beef, with a high-sounding patronymic of the local nobility, redolent of recent slaveholdings and a little come down in the world because of abolition. An inexperienced calculator, he had fixed his eyes on Madalena Pontes Mendes, who could boast a baron on the distaff side, and letters from Pedro II in the archives of her paternal grandfather, a learned legislator, long in pride and short in worldly goods. Vasco launched his campaign by dancing attendance on the parents and courting the daughter.

In a fatal waltz came the disillusionment. He had asked Madalena to dance, and chatting of one thing and another, they came around to the subject of engagement and marriage in connection with another girl. Madalena informed him that her one stipulation for whoever hoped to lead her—that bag of bones!—to the altar was a title or a commission. She did not insist on a title of nobility; naturally, a count or marquis or baron would be the ideal, though this was now difficult under the Republic, since that miserable betrayal of the poor Emperor, a friend of her grandfather's, with whom he even corresponded. She referred to democratic university titles, a doctor's diploma, the commission of an officer of the army or navy. She was not going to marry just anybody, she, the granddaughter of a baron, the daughter of a judge, and become the insignificant wife of a plain Mr. So-and-so. She wanted to be Senhora Doctor or Senhora Captain or Senhora Commander; money did not mean so much to her, but family and name did. This she insisted upon.

Vasco missed a step, turned pale, and shriveled inwardly. He had brought the conversation around to that subject with the idea of getting himself into her good graces, and the vain broomstick had thrown in his face the fact that he was a nobody, one of those Misters to whom she referred in a tone of utter contempt. He didn't get to the point of entering his candidacy; he became abashed, tongue-tied, and moved silently through the rest of the dance. His depression mounted.

For that depression of his was due to a single reason: the fact that he did not possess a title to precede his name. Why didn't he go ahead and take Dorothy away from Roberto, whose only hold over her was the money he gave her? Vasco could assure her much more money, more comforts, a house of her own, in addition to a pleasant life, with parties, outings, gay nights, champagne. Not to mention the horror of her having to put up with a swine like Roberto nuzzling her neck, squeezing her up against him, wallowing in her bed. Vasco sighed for Dorothy, his heart thudded sadly because of her and at night he thought of her, naked, with her turgid breasts, her firm thighs, her rounded buttocks, her velvet belly. Why didn't he snatch her out of Roberto's arms? Fear? Yes, fear of Roberto. Not physical fear; he was not afraid of that tub of lard, and a man who beats a woman is always a coward, incapable of standing up to another man. Anyway, who would venture to stand up to Vasco Moscoso de Aragão, friend of Dr. Jerónimo, with authority over the police, with soldiers and sailors at his orders, if he needed them? He only had to say the word to the colonel or the commander.

It was a different kind of fear, born of the respect of the merchant for the university graduate, with his sheepskin, his class ring, his doctor's thesis. Vasco could never span the gap that separated him from them. He felt humiliated in their presence; he was not their equal.

This was the real cause of that melancholy expression, of the sorrow that gnawed at his happiness and worried his friends. In Vasco's opinion, men who had a title or a commission formed a separate caste, elevated above other mortals, superior beings.

There was not a moment when Vasco did not feel his inferiority. When he entered the Pension Monte Carlo and Carol greeted him tenderly as Mr. Aragãozinho, after hailing the other four as Colonel, Doctor, Captain, Lieutenant. When a new woman was discovered and brought to join their circle at the table of a cabaret or the parlor of a sporting house, after being informed of the station of the others, she would ask what his title was or propose that she try to guess it: "Let me think . . . The gentleman is a major, I would swear it."

In the governor's reviewing stand, when the chief of state was introducing them to some important dignitary, after the sonorous syllables of the titles of the others had rolled off his tongue, and his turn came: "Mr. Vasco Moscoso de Aragão, one of our prominent businessmen."

Mr. Vasco . . . All day long he kept hearing the hateful prefix, as humiliating as a slap in the face, a deliberate insult. It mortified him to the depths of his soul, he could feel himself redden, he hung his head, his pleasure in the celebration gone. His day was ruined. What difference did all his money make, the liking so many people had for him, the friendship of important persons, when he was not really one of them, when something separated him from them, creating a gulf between them? There were those who envied Vasco, looking on him as one of fortune's favorites, with everything he needed to make him happy. It wasn't true. He lacked a title to take the place of that humiliating "Mister," anonymous, vulgar, making him one with the mob, the riffraff, hoi polloi.

In the silence of his bachelor's home, after the merry nights on the town, how often he thought about the matter, his good-natured face gloomy. What he wouldn't give for a title, even that of dentist or druggist, which would make it possible for him to wear an identifying graduation ring and use "Doctor" before his name!

He even thought of buying a commission in the national guard, the kind that in the early days of the Republic were sold by the thousands to ranchers of the back country for a few contos de reis. So many commissions were scattered about the backlands that the term "Colonel" became the generic designation of a rich planter, losing its martial connotation, its professional dignity. Moreover, military honors were no longer shown these colonels, not even the salute, nor were they allowed to wear a uniform. It would accomplish nothing, it would be ridiculous.

He dreamed, for dreams are free, of a papal title, but it did not get beyond the stage of imagination, a momentary consolation, toppling to earth at the harsh breath of reality. The title of "Count" conferred by the Vatican would cost a fortune, completely beyond his means; everything he owned would not pay for it. There was only one papal nobleman in Bahía, one of the Magalhães, a member of a firm in comparison with which the house of Moscoso & Company, Ltd., was a country store. That Magalhães had built a church out of his own pocket; he had sent the Pope an image of Christ in gold, he supported priests and religious brotherhoods; he had spent two hundred contos de reis to be made a count, he had made a trip to Rome, and yet all he got out of all this was the title of "Commander." It was not only a matter of money; one had to have rendered outstanding services to the Church, give evidence of a religious fervor and an intimacy with the cloisters that was definitely not Vasco Moscoso de Aragão's strong point. His name was unknown in the bishop's palace.

Lying in bed, sunk in thought, sometimes with a tired, satisfied woman breathing deep in sleep beside him, Vasco cursed the memory of his grandfather, that narrow-minded old

Portuguese, for whom the only thing in the world was money. Why, instead of putting him in the warehouse on Ladeira da Montanha while he was still a child, to sweep floors, run errands, carry bundles, hadn't he sent him to school, and then to the university, to the School of Medicine or Law, thus assuring him a higher social status? Oh, no, nothing like that. All old Moscoso thought about was the business, and training his grandson to take his place one day.

He brushed aside the image of his grandfather, of whom he had no memories pleasant enough to be worth keeping. He gave his imagination free rein, and for a few minutes he was happy, blissfully happy, putting the longed-for, impossible titles before his name.

"Dr. Vasco Moscoso de Aragão, Attorney." He saw himself in the courtroom, in legal robes, addressing the jury, pointing a finger at the prosecuting attorney in a withering aside, or, at the moment of the defense, telling, in a tremulous voice, the history of the accused, a victim and not a criminal, helpless in the hands of fate. A good, hard-working man, fulfilling all his duties, a devoted father, a loving husband, crazy about his wife, and the flighty thing had put a set of horns on him ... No, that wasn't the right expression to use before the jury ... And the flighty thing, without taking into account the love of her husband, her innocent children, the decency of her home, had dragged the honorable name of her husband through the bed of betrayal ... That was it. He liked the phrase, it moved even him. His name was famous among the greatest lawyers of the state, mentioned in conversation, praised to the sky: "What talent! What eloquence! He could melt a heart of stone! He can make any jury eat out of his hand!"

After getting the murderer off, he saw himself in his shirt sleeves, in the operating room, wearing rubber gloves, a gauze mask over his face. It was Dr. Vasco Moscoso de Aragão, who had received his training in the hospitals of Paris and Vienna, the famous surgeon (he refused to consider any other branch of medicine), opening with his steady, delicate hands the abdomen of the governor, under the tense, anxious gaze of relatives, Jerónimo, politicians, students, and nurses. The sudden illness, the public alarm, the danger of death if the operation was not performed immediately. But an operation of this sort (Vasco did not know exactly what he was operating for, which was the affected viscera or organ, which part of the gubernatorial abdomen he was going to open and sew up, but these were minor details), which had never before been attempted in Bahía, filled the doctors with apprehension at the thought of the responsibility involved. The celebrated professor of the School of Medicine had refused to undertake it. And meanwhile the life of the governor in danger, the affairs of state neglected, the political situation at the boil, and the opposition hopefully rubbing its hands. Jerónimo's dramatic appeal to his friendship and skill. The tense atmosphere of the operating room, the smile on the doctor's lips, his dexterity, his assurance, his imperturbability, his fund of knowledge... He extracted from the illustrious abdomen a... What was it he extracted? A huge stone. He had heard of kidney stones, a mortal, incurable ailment. The students could not contain themselves; they burst into applause and cheers, the members of the faculty came over to congratulate him.

A man saved from prison, the governor's life saved, he next transferred his activities to the field of engineering. Dr. Vasco Moscoso de Aragão, civil engineer, with advanced and specialized studies in Germany, cutting through the barren backlands to bring progress on the steel tracks of the railroad. Under the blazing sun, amidst the gnarled forest, at the head of work gangs, the perspiration running down his thoughtful forehead—so many obstacles to overcome, and the discouragement and weariness. And that mountain, a little out of place in that flat, arid landscape, barring the path of progress! The tunnel, an immortal creation, one of the longest in the world, mentioned in geography books. The day of the opening: the locomotive driver yields him his place. It was fitting that the great engineer, the man who had conquered the desert, the mountains, and the river, should drive the first locomotive, draped with flowers. Dorothy had come, suddenly converted into the wife of the disagreeable Secretary of Transport, a conceited jackass, who looked down his nose at the businessman Aragãozinho, the friend of Jerónimo and Lieutenant Lidio Marinho, barely extending two fingers to him in a cool, formal greeting; Dorothy had come, breath-takingly beautiful, and as she broke a bottle of champagne against the engine, her eyes met those of the engineer who was being honored and a timid flirtation ensued between him and the unexpected wife of the Secretary.

Major Vasco Moscoso de Aragão, of the cavalry, for the

cavalry is the most gallant branch of the army, rode before his troops, with his authoritative voice, his aristocratic air, his martial bearing, his breast covered with medals. And as the war could not be avoided, with the Argentine armies treacherously invading the frontiers of Rio Grande do Sul, the parade of the Seventh of September was transformed into the embarkation of troops for the south, en route to duty, glory, death. The entire population of the city thronged the streets, the women weeping as they embraced the soldiers, the girls strewing the way with rose petals. On his white-faced horse, his glittering sword in hand, his eyes blazing, Major Vasco Moscoso de Aragão was the very image of war and victory. His career on the battlefields would be swift, one deed of valor after another, promotion following promotion, attaining the rank of general after a few months and several battles, dying gloriously the end of the war. As he entered Buenos Aires amidst a hail of bullets and cannonballs, a stray bullet struck him in the breast. Not even then did he fall from his white-faced horse. Bent over in his saddle, his breast shattered, his inflexible will carried him to the government palace. His name became a legend, known to every school child.

But as that war took place both on land and on sea, especially on sea, the ship under the command of Admiral Vasco Moscoso de Aragão, the youngest of his rank in the navy (he had begun as lieutenant commander at the outbreak of hostilities), ran the blockade of the Argentine fleet, and single-handed bombarded Buenos Aires, silencing the batteries of the enemy city, and entered the port aboard his cruiser, flying the flag of the young Brazilian Republic. From the bridge, leaning against a cannon, the admiral issued his orders: "Each man at his post, ready to die for Brazil." The phrase had a pessimistic ring. It was better to change it to: "Each man at his post, ready to give his life for Brazil's victory!" That was better, more inspiring. He took up his binoculars, examining the Argentinian positions. In a firm voice he ordered: "Fire!" and the cannon belched death over the proud city. In swift and incredibly daring maneuvers, he sank the ships in the harbor one by one. He destroyed the forts, ripped apart the defenses, and amidst the smoke and the blaze of the fires, in the turret of his ship, Admiral Vasco Moscoso de Aragão entered the conquered port, bringing the war to an end.

The woman stirred, opened her sleepy eyes, recognized the room and the bed. By good luck the choice had fallen on her the night before; she must show her gratitude, maybe he would even take a fancy to her. She held out her arms, her voice coy and soft with sleep: "Mr. Aragãozinho..."

That broke and shattered the dream, the dream which is man's freedom, that which can never be tamed, oppressed, or stolen, his last and lasting prized possession. Those words tumbled Admiral Vasco Moscoso de Aragão from the turret of his ship.

## In which the oaf of a narrator reappears, trying to foist a book on us

ALLOW ME to interrupt the account of the captain's adventures, according to the version of Chico Pacheco, destined to have such serious consequences in Periperi, to solemnly state, on the basis of personal experience, that this business of titles and commissions is no joke. Even today, when times have changed, it is one thing to be a doctor or an officer, and something very different to be a poor devil without a diploma. For the first, all privileges and prerogatives; for the others, the harsh letter of the law. The diploma holders even have the right to a special prison, not to mention the officers, confined to the casino of their quarters, a mere formality.

There are those today who make fun of doctors, laugh at lawyers, taking the attitude that the graduation ring is no proof of competence. I have even read an article in a newspaper, adducing all sorts of arguments to prove, firstly, secondly, thirdly, that all the ills from which Brazil suffers stem from the university graduates. It may very well be; I think so myself, but I do not discuss the matter, for I respect freedom of opinion. Nevertheless, I could swear that the author of the article holds a doctor's degree in something, or is an officer on active duty, for otherwise how would he have the courage to make such assertions? To compete with a doctor is folly, utter madness, and I am proof thereof.

That is why I completely agree with the captain (until Chico Pacheco's version is proved beyond the shadow of a doubt, I shall continue to use the title; a historian cannot jump to conclusions). The cause of his depression seems to me more than justified. Rich though he was and free from worry, he must have suffered humiliations and vexations for lack of a "Doctor" or "Major" before his name, for not having gone to a university, even if he had barely scraped through, like that loafer Otoniel Mendonça, that friend of Telemaco Dorea, from whose calumnies I defended the eminent jurist, Dr. Alberto Siqueira. Would you believe that illiterate Mendonça is a Bachelor of Law? He spent his college years hanging around the red-light district and ripping people up the back in the Civilizacão Bookstore in the Rua Chile. The professors hardly ever laid eyes on him, by which, incidentally, the venerated masters lost nothing. Nevertheless, repeating courses, taking examinations over again, scraping through by a cat's whisker, he got his sheepskin, and equipped with it, chiseled a political job (one of those good ones where you don't have to do a lick of work), and hung out in the Rua Chile, slandering his fellow men. His services to the state did not add up to one hour a day. Nevertheless, even this seemed too much to him, and he claimed he had developed a lesion in his upper left lung. Without hesitation, they gave him sick leave, and he is still on it to this day, fat and sassy, sullying the landscape of Periperi with his presence.

Now see the difference: just because I do not have a university degree, I went through particular hell to secure a six months' leave in the bureau where I work. The doctors were adamant, they couldn't praise my vision enough, they said they had never examined such perfect eyes. A friend had assured me that the claim of eye trouble never fails to work, that the doctors, out of sympathy, sign the papers without questions or examinations. Hogwash! If they didn't examine his eyes, it was out of consideration for his dentist's diploma. Even though a dentist is a kind of second-class doctor, he still had advantages. I managed to wangle my leave only through the accidental discovery that one of the doctors was the nephew of an intimate friend of mine. I sicked his uncle on him, and the joker then discovered that I had cataracts so advanced that I was threatened with imminent blindness. I was given six months' leave, and when this was up, it was renewed. In this way I could devote myself, at the expense of the state, to carrying out my work on *The Vice-Presidents of the Republic*. I don't know if you are acquainted with this work of mine; if you have not read it, it would be worth your while to do so, for, modesty aside, it was received with approval and esteem.

However, what happened with this book is further proof of the importance of having a university degree. I wrote it to fill a gap and repair an injustice. A great deal has been written about the presidents of the Republic, especially when they were in office, a deluge of praise. But the vice-presidents were completely ignored, unless they happened to take over the reins of government. Who can recite by heart the complete list of vice-presidents of the Republic? Who remembers, for example, the name of the vice-president during the term of office of Prudente de Morais or Hermes da Fonseca? I doubt that anyone does. That in itself proves how timely my book was.

I was also encouraged to undertake this arduous assignment by the contest for historical monographs sponsored by the distinguished Institute of History and Geography, which carried a modest prize in money and the printing of the winning entry at the Institute's expense. Tempted by this honorable distinction, I managed to find the time, thanks to my cataracts and my friend, and I took on the vice-presidents. I compiled a valuable work, if you will forgive the vanity, in which the reader will find the full name, parentage, date and place of birth and death, schools and universities attended, positions held, outstanding accomplishments, noteworthy facts regarding each of the vice-presidents. I did not overlook the wives and children, and, in some cases, even the grandchildren are mentioned. It involved a brutal amount of work and gave me a miserable cold because of the dust in the State Library.

Well and good; I submitted my work for the prize, sure that I was going to land it, and I suffered the deception of seeing it awarded to the only other contestant, Dr. Epaminondas Torres, for a work on the Sabinada.[1] Even in the number of typewritten

---

[1] During the Regency there were various revolts, the most important of which was the Sabinada. It began on November 7, 1837, and was led by Sabino Alvares de Rocha Vieira, professor of the School of Medicine, journalist and politician

pages, his work was inferior to mine: forty miserable sheets, exactly half the number of mine. And why was he awarded the prize in such a flagrant act of injustice? You shall know at once. Offended in my pride, I went to the Institute to talk with the secretary. He looked at me under his glasses, and answered: "Who are you to come here talking about an injustice? Don't you know who Dr. Epaminondas Torres is? Don't you know that he is one of our most distinguished lawyers? May I ask what titles you hold?"

You see? My mistake was to have competed with a university graduate. What titles did I hold? None, unless you want to count a few sonnets published as fillers in newspapers and magazines. I swallowed the insult; I tried to get the Institute at least to pay for the printing of the book, inasmuch as they had done me out of the prize. I found them well disposed; the noble historians were probably suffering twinges of conscience. But the director of the Government Printing Office, where the volumes were to be printed, mine and the prize-winning one, neatly hoodwinked the old fellows of the Institute, never sending the originals to the press. Some months later he resigned his post and the new director would not even discuss the matter. Thus the work of Dr. Epaminondas never saw the light, so there was no way of comparing it with mine, which makes me think there must have been dirty work at the crossroads in this whole affair.

As for *The Vice-Presidents of the Republic*, I published the book at my own expense in the Graphic Arts print shop of Mr. Zitelmann Oliva, who charged me a price that was out of all reason, but arranged credit terms, taking my signed notes. I sweated to meet the payments, but it turned out a nice volume, ninety-two pages of "useful information," to use the words of the erudite author of *The History of Bahía*, Dr. Luiz Henrique Dias Tavarez, who wrote me as follows: "Dear Colleague: Thank you for sending me your book, *The Vice-Presidents of the Republic*, a repository of useful information. Cordially yours, Luiz Henrique."

If I transcribe the full text of the flattering letter of the

---

who had taken part in the fight for independence. He and his companions proclaimed a Bahian Republic, which was to be independent of Rio de Janeiro until Pedro II came of age. Badly organized and poorly carried out, it was completely defeated by March 16 of the following year. (Translator's Note) distinguished Bahian, it is so that yellow journalist, Wilson Lins, can read it. Hidden behind the pseudonym of Rubião Braz, this cheap lampooner tried to humiliate me in an article in *A Tarde*, to make me look ridiculous. If I had had a university title, he would have been pleasanter and more cordial. He and all the critics. Instead of insulting me, they would have sung my praises.

These jumped-up critics should take note of a reference to my work on the part of an eminent historian of São Paulo, Dr. Sérgio Buarque de Holanda, to whom I had not even sent a copy of the book, because, I must confess, I was unaware of his existence and his glory. In the *Estado de São Paulo*, in an article having to do with a certain Worthy and Venerable Order of the Blue Hippopotamus, he alludes to *The Vice-Presidents of the Republic*, listing it as one of the reference works of that learned organization, a volume, he adds, which is "a joy, a veritable delight." In his manifest admiration for the work, he even proposed my candidacy for the Venerable Order, on whose roster of members my unworthy name seemed to him indispensable. All I know about the Order is what Dr. Holanda wrote about it, in somewhat esoteric and obscure language, such as that of a real historian should be. I managed to gather, nevertheless, that it was an organization with lofty qualifications and objectives, founded in the Church of St. Peter of the Clerks in Recife, by representative figures of our intellectual life. Unfortunately, I have had no further notice either of the Order or of my candidacy, so generously put forward by Dr. Sérgio de Holanda. Undoubtedly, they began investigations, and when they found out I was not a doctor, they dropped me like a hot potato.

The book also warranted words of unstinted praise, most gratifying, from our retired judge, Dr. Alberto Siqueira. He pointed out two or three insignificant grammatical oversights, adding that such slips were of no importance whatever in so valuable and patriotic a work. I shall correct them in the second edition, which will appear soon, for the five hundred copies of the first edition are practically sold out, in spite of the lack of co-operation on the part of the booksellers—I lack the prestige of a title—who did not display the book in their windows, hiding it on the shelves. I sold it myself to friends and acquaintances, a copy here, a copy there, adjusting the price to the pocket of the purchaser.

All this proves to satiety that Captain Vasco Moscoso de

Aragão did not want for reasons to be melancholy and worried. A title dresses up a name, gives it standing, opens doors and arms, assures consideration. This is so true that even the most ordinary people are aware of the problem. Only a few days ago Dondoca, that linnet whose warbling brightens the existence of His Honor and this your humble servant, informed me, between kisses, of her impending and solemn graduation, complete with cap and gown. She had kept her studies a secret to surprise me. And surprise me she certainly did, for our amorous Dondoca (our: that is to say, mine and the judge's) can barely sign her name and count on her long supple fingers.

"Graduation, star of the night of my life? Graduate of what? In which Faculty did you study?"

"In the Academy of Dressmaking and Design of Dona Ermelinda in Plataforma, Mr. Dumb Ox. See that you treat me with respect, for now I am Doctor..."

"With respect, for now I am Doctor..." You see? Am I right or wrong? Doctor of the needle and scissors, our sweet Dondoca, not satisfied with being Doctor, *honoris causa, magister inter pares*, in the science of love.

Today the captain would not have this problem to vex him. In four or six months, and with the outlay of a modest sum, he would be a Doctor of Public Relations, of Hair Styling, of Administration, or Publicity.

Not long ago I was introduced in the capital to a well-spoken young chap, self-satisfied beyond belief. "Doctor of Publicity," he condescendingly informed me, making a hundred and twenty thousand cruzeiros a month—so help me God!—trained in São Paulo and New York. He convinced me that it was he who directed my life, my buying habits, my tastes, through the science and art of publicity, the marvel of the age. The most exalted of present-day professions, which lies at the root of a country's production, consumption, progress. The highest form of literature, art, and, in the last analysis, poetry is advertising, commercial *réclame*. Homer and Goethe, Dante and Byron, Castro Alves and Drummond de Andrade are slobs compared to a youthful bard who specializes in jingles about soap, toothpaste, refrigerators, kitchen equipment, plastic towels. In the emphatic opinion of the Doctor of Publicity, the greatest poem of our time, the masterpiece, the Mt. Everest of poetic genius was written by that specialist who promoted the sales of Jovial Anus Suppositories. A sublime poem by reason of its inspiration, its perfect form, the force of emotion it transmitted; the sales of the suppositories had increased by 178 per cent, thanks to this modern muse.

If it were today, the captain could become a Doctor of Publicity just by taking a correspondence course.

## *Of the abduction of Dorothy, and a judge in small clothes*

THE ABDUCTION of Dorothy was planned by the armed forces, Colonel Pedro de Alencar, and Captain Georges Dias Nadreau, with the active collaboration of the state, represented in the complot by the head of the cabinet and the aide-de-camp of the governor. Carol was commander-in-chief of the complicated operation, and not one of the outstanding strategists whose name History records could have surpassed her in the perfection of organization, the knowledge of logistics, the painstaking study of all the details, the choice of men to carry out each phase of the secret and difficult undertaking. Even though the idea was conceived by Captain Georges, it was Carol who, beyond the shadow of a doubt, was responsible for its complete success. They toasted the outcome and Carol with champagne in a spree that almost made history in the cabaret and sporting-house circles of Salvador da Bahía, for Captain Georges, in view of the splendid result of Dorothy's abduction, wanted to enlarge the plan, taking advantage of their experience and enthusiasm to stage anew the "rape of the Sabines" that night.

Number 96 Ladeira da Montanha was the site of the Castelo de Sabina, a house that specialized in foreign women: French,

Polish, German, mysterious Russians, and one Egyptian. Some of them had been born in the vast confines of Brazil, but others dropped anchor in Sabina's bay after long careers begun in the ports of Europe, with layovers in Argentina and Uruguay. And among them one stood out, not because of her beauty, but because of her highly specialized knowledge of her métier, the famous Madame Lulu, indisputably French, with more than thirty years' experience, so famous and sought after that she had a permanent waiting list of clients. And no matter how expeditiously she worked, there were always some who had to wait until the next day. They tell of a colonel from the back country, a rancher over Amargosa way, that he came to Bahía especially for a tête-à-tête with this solicited and competent courtesan, planning to spend only two days in the capital. He had to stay a week, for the time of the distinguished Parisian, who contributed more than anyone else in Bahía to the influence of the culture and civilization of the Eternal France on Brazilian customs, was completely booked. The rancher spent a week and almost a conto, which at that time was a fortune, on fare, hotel, meals, and other expenses; but as he himself said when he took the boat for home: "It was cheap at the price; it would be worth another week and another conto." Such testimony makes further praise of Madame Lulu's abilities and the Castelo de Sabina superfluous.

What the harbor master proposed was nothing less than the invasion, by the volunteer and victorious abductors of Dorothy, of the Castelo de Sabina, a fortress defended from public curiosity by hermetically closed windows, whose door opened only to admit customers, friends, and acquaintances, or persons especially recommended. After the boarding, the battle, and the victory, the entire seraglio, including Madame Lulu, would be transported to the Pension Monte Carlo, and that foreign, industrious population would be handed over to Carol for her to utilize like prisoners of war. Carol deserved this and much more, Captain Georges proclaimed, as he raised his glass in a toast to the heart and mettle of the serene hostess, smiling satisfaction in her rocker.

Not without some difficulty did his friends manage to dissuade Captain Georges from his martial plans. They could not, however, prevent him from washing Carol's feet in champagne as an act of supreme homage.

While the friends were thus celebrating the success of the

abduction, in a far-off little house on the outskirts of Amaralina, which had been rented several days before, fanned by the ocean breezes, illuminated by the full moon that had been especially arranged for by the romantic Lieutenant Lidio Marinho, listening to the waves breaking against the rocks and breathing in the aphrodisiac smell of the ebb tide, Vasco Moscoso de Aragão took in his arms, like an impatient lover on his wedding night, Dorothy's fragile body. The tender chicken, the English ham, the cold tenderloin, the apples and pears, the Malaga grapes remained untouched; they barely moistened their lips in champagne. It was a different thirst and hunger, of long standing and that brooked no delay, that devoured them, that was not to be slaked with bread and wine. It was thirst of kisses and caresses, hunger of yielding and possessing, of living and dying in each other's arms.

At that same hour, still trembling, locked in under seven keys in his paternal home in Nazaré, Dr. Roberto Veiga Lima was asking himself the reason for that terrifying experience: those men wearing black masks who had invaded the Pension Monte Carlo in broad daylight, armed to the teeth, shouting threats and curses, and had jerked him out of Dorothy's bed. He had looked on the face of death that day; he could still feel the chill in his heart.

It had happened in the quiet hour of mid-afternoon, when the house was filled with silence and peace. The women were out in the streets, shopping, strolling, or at the movies, because it was Thursday, matinee day. The waiters didn't arrive until five. Carol herself often took advantage of the lull to go to the bank or visit her tenants and colleot the rent for her houses. Only Dorothy never went out, for all walks or amusements were strictly off limits for her, except in Roberto's company. For that reason he felt himself under the obligation to come at that time every day: he stretched out in bed with Dorothy to get his money's worth. Sometimes he took her out to dinner, and they came back later in the evening to dance and drink. He did not leave her until dawn, when he returned to the home of his parents, with whom he lived. That was how he handled a woman he kept: a tight rein and her time occupied.

That day Carol had stayed at home, resting in her rocking chair in the parlor. And one of the girls—that minx of a Mimi, still in her teens—was busy in one of the rooms. It was Judge Rufino's day, an elderly customer, in his seventies. He came

invariably and punctually every other Thursday, at three
o'clock. He could be heard puffing up the stairs as the cuckoo
clock in the parlor began to call the hour. The judge paid well,
but he demanded young girls like Mimi, more or less the age of
his granddaughter. He carried a package of cakes and candy,
and he kissed Carol's hand.

The judge had no more than locked himself in the room, and
had not even finished undressing—he was just unlacing his high
shoes so he could get off his underdrawers—when the hubbub of
the invasion stopped him cold.

"What's the racket?"

Mimi did not know. Naked in the bed, she was nibbling cakes
and candy. A desperate scream came from the parlor; it was
Carol, calling for help. Mimi jumped out of bed, opened the
door, the judge behind her, not realizing the state he was in: one
shoe off, one shoe on, his bony chest bare, his tottering legs in his
long underdrawers.

Carol was sitting in the rocking chair, a gag in her mouth,
while one of the masked men stood over her with a pistol.
Confused sounds came from Dorothy's room. Still holding the
pistol to Carol's breast, the masked man turned to Mimi and the
terrified judge: "You two . . . Quiet there, don't make a move . . ."

"I've done nothing," whimpered the old man. "Let me go
right away, my son is a congressman, for the love of God . . ."

"Don't take a step, or I'll drill you . . ."

"My God, what a mess I've got into . . . What will people say
when they hear about it . . . For the love of God, let me go . . ."

Through the wide-open door of Dorothy's room came the
pleading voice of Roberto: "Don't kill me . . . I've done nothing
to her. I was not the first, she can tell you herself. When I got
hold of her, she had already been cracked. Just ask her . . ."

For Roberto had taken the abductors for outraged kinsmen
of Dorothy, vengeful backlanders, who had come from Feira de
Sant'Ana to cleanse the honor of the girl in blood. In the blood
of her seducer, and they were surely thinking he was the one who
had led her astray and had set her feet on the downward path. He
was trying to explain that when he ran into her she had already
lost her cherry, and was nearly starving to death on the street
corner. Covering him with their guns, the bandits reduced him
to silence. One of them brought a coil of rope, and being a
master in the tying of knots, he soon had Roberto's arms and
legs trussed up. Another, in a hoarse voice, ordered Dorothy to

get dressed and pack her suitcase. They went off with her, leaving Roberto with his eyes popping out of his head and the perspiration dripping down his neck, giving him one final warning: "Don't try to find her, if you value your life."

In the parlor the other bandit sat down in a chair, across from Carol, the more comfortably to keep her covered, and ordered Mimi: "Come here... Over here by me, don't be afraid."

The voice reminded her of another voice, so familiar she almost recognized it. But that was silly; how could Lieutenant Lidio be that masked man? She obeyed the order and went over. Running his free hand along her bare flesh, the bandit lifted her onto his lap. The judge felt as though he were about to faint, his stomach all upset, seized by sudden, uncontrollable cramps.

Out of Dorothy's room came the others, one of them carrying her suitcase. The courteous bandit put Mimi down (how funny, Lieutenant Lidio Marinho used the same perfume!), and the invaders backed out of the room, their guns aimed at the demoralized judge, reached the stairs, and ran down them. Judge Rufino was muttering: "I need a bath..."

The first thing Carol did when she had removed the gag from her mouth was to tend to the old man. In her well-mapped plans she had forgotten that it was the third Thursday of the month, the judge's day. She sent him off to the bathroom, accompanied by Mimi, with a fresh cake of soap and a clean towel. Then she went to set Roberto free, and had a long talk with the young doctor. It would be better for the tranquillity of them all if he didn't come back to the Pension Monte Carlo, and gave up Dorothy for good. Otherwise those ruffians, come from God knows where ("They're her relatives..."—Roberto's mind was made up on this point), might return, kill him right there or in the ballroom, and ruin her business and her reputation for good, when there had never been a scandal, or a fight, or a crime in her house.

"I am leaving for Rio by the first boat."

"And while you wait, it would be best if you didn't go out of the house."

Roberto left her what money he had with him, which wasn't much, but it was something. After all, he was responsible for that invasion, for the fright of the judge—a fine mess he'd made of himself, the poor thing—for the moral damage the Pension Monte Carlo had suffered. When the news got around, who would run the risk of visiting such a dangerous place? Roberto promised to send her a further sum before he embarked. All he asked of Carol was that she go out and look around to make sure none of the bandits was lying in wait for him. She came back assuring him that the coast was clear, and he left.

Carol was still laughing in her rocking chair when the judge emerged from the bathroom. He, too, was longing to leave those dangerous surroundings as quickly as he could, but how could he go without his underdrawers? If he put his pants on over his bare skin, he would probably get a bad cold, or—who knows?—pneumonia. Carol lent him a pair of lace-trimmed panties of one of the girls, a thin one with long legs. She and Mimi laughed heartily to see him thus attired, and even the judge laughed. He accepted the offer of a cordial after he got dressed, even though he refused to stay on that afternoon—what good would it be after that fright?—but he promised to come back the following Thursday, after Carol convinced him that a scandal of that sort would not happen again. She explained to him that what had taken place was the result of old enmities of Roberto, whom she had forbidden to set foot in the Pension Monte Carlo ever again. Roberto was a bad egg, the judge agreed, paying Mimi for her time and the bath, kissing Carol's hand, and begging them both to keep his malodorous participation in the afternoon's happenings a secret.

These happenings were celebrated well into the dawn, noisily, by the friends, the four habitual ones and five or six more whose participation in the abduction had been needed to make the *mise en scène* more brilliant, to suit Captain Georges Dias Nadreau. It was hard to persuade him to give up the idea of the "rape of the Sabines," with Madame Lulu toiling up the Ladeira da Montanha to the Praça do Teatro, in chains, Carol's slave. The harbor master was in high spirits; he thought he had eliminated, for good and all, the cause of that expression of sadness which darkened the loyal face of Vasco Moscoso de Aragão. Now, without a tinge of melancholy, the merchant could enjoy the blessings Providence and his grandfather had conferred upon him: wealth, bachelorhood, luck at cards, charm for women, innate attractiveness.

"I would trade my commission for his luck at poker," said the captain.

"And I mine for his luck with women," sighed the colonel.

"With my eyes shut, I would trade my lawyer's diploma for one fifth of his shares in the firm..." laughed Dr. Jerónimo, adding: "And throw in my future seat in congress for good measure."

"Your seat in congress? Really?" exclaimed Carol in wonder, for she was aware of the journalist's ambitions.

"What good are titles and commissions, dear Carol, compared with money? If you have money, you can have anything you want: commissions, diplomas, a seat in congress, in the senate, the most beautiful women . . . With money you can buy anything, my child."

For the time being, Vasco Moscoso de Aragão had Dorothy in the moonlight, in the perfume of the sea, in the song of the waves, rocked by the winds, dying in sighs, coming back to life in moans of love, her face feverish, her mouth insatiable, an indecipherable rose of purple. When their strength finally gave out, and she fell asleep, Vasco lay stretched out beside her, weary and grateful, and dreamed with his eyes open, a smile on his lips, hearing in the distance the siren of a ship. In the tempest-tossed night he saved the ship in distress, bringing it safe to port through the driving rain, where, numb with fear and anxiety, Dorothy awaited her lover, Captain Vasco Moscoso de Aragão.

*Of how, during a monumental binge,
Vasco wept on Georges's shoulder, and
the result of these confidences*

THE MONTHS went by. Roberto took a trip to Rio, and when
he came back he brought among his luggage a Peruvian Indian
girl, meek and quiet. Lidio Marinho had four or five new affairs
in divers sporting houses, including one with Mimi, to whom he
revealed the mystery of the abduction and the masked bandits.
Judge Rufino died in a whorehouse, scandalizing the city. In
spite of his promises to Carol, he never returned to the Pension
Monte Carlo, horrified at the prospect of another assault. He
took to patronizing more inconspicuous establishments, and he
died at Laura's place, where he had discovered a certain Arlete,
who was not quite fifteen. The poor child, when she heard the
death rattle in the throat of the old man aboard her, began to
scream at the top of her lungs, weeping and carrying on,
arousing the whole neighborhood, including a civil guard who
was playing the numbers nearby. Thus the matter came to the
attention of the public, and a veritable crowd of onlookers had
collected in front of the brothel on Ladeira de São Miguel when
the body was carried out. Shameless wisecracks provoked loud
guffaws; the dead man's son, who was a member of congress,
was pointed out. Arlete and Laura were taken to the police
station, where they underwent all sorts of annoyances. The only

one who benefited from the scandalous episode was the civil guard. He resumed his play, putting 500 reis on the number 7015, a combination of the ages of the deceased and Arlete. An intelligent and lucky hunch; the numbers game calls for perspicacity, close watch over the forces of destiny, the ability to draw lessons (and hunches) from events.

So many things took place, including Vasco and Dorothy's love affair, so intense and feverish, so impetuous and absorbing for a time. To the point where he had her name tattooed on his right arm, her beloved name and a heart, a skillfully executed job performed by a Chinaman with a wispy beard who turned up in Bahía, nobody knew from where. Their mad passion began to cool off, naturally, little by little, as happens in the daily course of living. Vasco began to cast languishing looks at other women, to sleep around a bit here and there, even though Dorothy spent the whole summer, with him footing the bills, in the little house of Amaralina, and he took her dancing and to the Pension Monte Carlo. When winter came, she returned for good to the Pension, and Carol, who understood human nature and the fragility of infatuations, advised her to smile at the other customers, and encourage them. Vasco maintained certain rights of priority, and a certain responsibility for her expenses, but the idyll was over.

Only that old sadness, the melancholy that veiled his eyes and tinged his smile, persisted and deepened. His friends began seriously to suspect some secret ailment, that Vasco was condemned to death within a brief space of time and was keeping it to himself. Perhaps a heart ailment, known only to him and his doctor. Hadn't his father died of a heart attack while still young? According to Colonel Alencar, who passionately upheld this hypothesis, that would explain many things: his not getting married, the way he threw his money around, his eagerness to live fast, as though he wanted to enjoy as many of the good things of life as he could in the little time left to him. That had to be the reason.

Menandro Guimarães, a well-known doctor and, moreover, a heart specialist, to whom Vasco had taken Dorothy several times because of the continual colds from which she suffered, soon disabused them of the idea.

"He's as strong as an ox," was the doctor's answer to the group of friends. "He's got a heart like a horse. He'll die of old age, like his grandfather. Where in the world did you get such a crazy idea?"

"Hell!" said Captain Georges Dias Nadreau. "I am going to find out what is eating him. And what do you want to bet I will?"

"Vasco is like that, it's part of his make-up, why do you worry about it?" philosophized the doctor, for whom only the ills of the body existed.

"Because I can't bear to see people sad. And least of all a friend of mine."

This marked the beginning of the "phase of the great interrogatory," as Jerónimo called it. Whenever they were with Vasco, Captain Georges began to probe, to turn the conversation to the most diverse subjects, trying to get confessions out of him. He rummaged about in Vasco's infancy, adolescence, his years in the office, his trip as traveling salesman, his first love affairs, his plans. The harbor master was not content to draw out Vasco. He talked with Menéndez, with the Swede Johann, who was still crazy about Soraya and was now living with her. He even had a long talk with the Negro Giovanni. Fruitless sessions, which turned up nothing. Never had Georges come across a man with so many reasons to be happy, completely, totally happy. Why the devil, then, that sadness?

But everything in the world finally comes out, even the most carefully kept secret. Everything becomes known, every mystery is one day cleared up. It was the night of the great spree, in celebration of Lieutenant Lidio Marinho's birthday and engagement. The lieutenant's engagement to the daughter of a planter from the south of the state had been announced that afternoon at an intimate gathering, and the marriage was set for December.

They began to drink early, before the formal announcement was made. They kept on during the dinner given by the future father-in-law at his mansion in Campo Grande Square, drinking Portuguese wines and French champagne. When they arrived at the Pension Monte Carlo, a whole troop of friends and women, they found the parlor decorated with tissue-paper flags, the girls dressed fit to kill, the waiters and the orchestra in their places, and not a single customer. In a touching proof of friendship, Carol had closed her doors to all the other customers that night and had reserved the Pension exclusively for them.

The group had increased in number for such an important celebration. There were officers of the 19th, of the Port Authority, of the Military Police, colleagues from the State House. Captain Nadreau had gone from brothel to brothel, from sporting house to sporting house, collecting all the lieutenant's known lights-of-love, to surprise him. He had arranged for all of them to be at the Pension Monte Carlo, along with several others, including Madame Lulu, who was to make the welcoming address to Lidio in the purest French of the *maisons closes* of Paris. Georges and Vasco had taken charge of preparations for the celebration; they wanted it to be something extraordinary, the like of which had never been seen. When they got to the bachelor's dinner, they were already a little high, the captain laughing hilariously, the businessman moody, as he always was when he drank too much. At every sporting house they visited they tossed off a drink; it would have shown a lack of consideration for the madam and the girls to refuse.

It really was a celebration the like of which had never been seen, a memorable spree, a carousal that went down in the annals of the city, for in the early morning hours, the men in underdrawers, the women in chemises, they paraded through the Praça do Teatro to the rejoicing of the nighthawks passing by, and under the impotent gaze of guards and policemen, who would have had to be crazy to try to interfere with this highly original exhibition. For at the head of the cortege, carrying a bottle of champagne and singing in a hoarse voice, went Dr. Jerónimo Paiva, the governor's nephew.

In the midst of the celebration, when the fun was at its peak, after a performance of the cancan by Madame Lulu, Georges announced to Colonel Pedro de Alencar, pointing to Vasco, whose melancholy increased with every drink: "I am taking the bull by the horns. That gloomy Gus is going to tell me what ails him."

He lifted the mulatto, Clarice, off his knees, took Vasco by the arm, and led him over to a deserted corner of the room: "Mr. Aragãozinho, right now and without further delay you're going to tell me what is the shit you've got stuck in your craw. Open your mouth and cough it up."

"Cough what up?"

"Whatever it is—a woman, sickness, remorse over some crime...I want to know what the hell is the reason for this sadness of yours."

Vasco looked at his friend, sensed his loyalty, his genuine interest. The harbor master was a good man.

"What's got me down is something that, when you stop to think about it, is sheer nonsense. I know it, but I can't help its

125

bothering me, and I keep thinking about it..."

"Thinking about what?" This was the moment of truth. Georges was absolutely sober, his head clear as if by magic.

"I am not the equal of the rest of you, I am not..."

"What is it you're not?"

"Your equal, don't you understand?"

"No."

"Look, you are the harbor master, an officer of the navy, a captain. Pedro is a colonel; Jerónimo, a doctor; Lidio, a lieutenant. And I? I am nothing, a shit-face, Mr. Vasco, Mr. Aragãozinho, without a title of any kind."

Looking the captain in the face, he opened his heart and gave vent to his pent-up emotion: "Mr. Vasco . . . Mr. Aragãozinho...Every time I hear someone call me that, something happens inside of me, a humiliation..."

"Of all the idiotic nonsense! That never crossed my mind. I thought of everything, even that you had committed a crime, how should I know? But not that you were suffering because you didn't have a title...For God's sake..."

"But you don't know..."

"What a laugh! Just the other day all of us were saying that we'd trade our titles, our positions, to have what you've got...It certainly takes all kinds of people..."

"You don't know what it's like to go around all the time with colonels, captains, doctors, and not be anybody."

The captain suddenly burst out laughing as though he were feeling the effects of liquor again, as though Vasco's sorrows were the greatest joke, and he went on laughing. Vasco took offense: "If it was to laugh at me, why did you ask?" and he got to his feet.

The captain grabbed him by the sleeve: "Sit down, you big dope," and he managed to choke back his laugh. "You mean to tell me that if you had a title that would be the end of this gloominess, of this doleful face?"

"How am I going to get a title at my age?"

"I'm going to fix you up with one."

"You?" asked Aragão suspiciously, knowing Georges's fondness for jokes.

"Yes, I. Your worries are over."

"Look, Georges, I am going to ask you to do me a favor. Joke about anything you like, play any kind of trick on me, but not in connection with this. I ask it of you as a favor."

He spoke solemnly and with deep emotion. The harbor master shook his head, and fixed his blue eyes on Vasco: "Don't be crazy. Do you think I am a person to joke about the sufferings of a friend? I told you I'd fix you up with a title, and you can leave it to me. I'm in earnest. Today is a day to be jolly, let's have a drink. Tomorrow we'll talk about this again. I'll take care of everything."

The next day, early in the afternoon, the captain sent a sailor to Vasco's house with a message: the captain was waiting for him at the Port Authority. The merchant was still sleeping off the effects of the night's celebration. Only Georges had that incredible resistance: he could go to bed at dawn and yet be at his desk exactly on time, shaved, smiling, as though he had had twelve hours' sleep.

Vasco got ready quickly. There came to his mind the talk they had had the night before in the midst of that memorable carousal. What kind of a title was this that Georges was so solemnly promising him? He was still afraid it might be a farce, but his friend had seemed in earnest. His jokes had a limit. But in the meantime Vasco could not guess what the solution to his problem might be; after all, titles and commissions were not to be picked up in the street.

When he reached the Port Authority, he found Colonel Pedro de Alencar there.

"I never heard anything so foolish, Mr. Vasco."

"It is not that I want to," Vasco answered in confusion. "I try not to think about it, and yet I can't get it out of my mind. I don't want to care, and yet I do."

"Well, I'll fix you up with a title," Georges repeated. "What would you think of the title of master mariner? Do you know what a master mariner is?"

"It's the captain of a merchant vessel, isn't it?"

"That's it. What would you think of 'Captain Vasco Moscoso de Aragão, Master Mariner'?"

"But how?" asked Vasco, turning to the colonel. "How?"

"Very simple. Georges will explain it to you."

The harbor master closed his eyes, leaned back in his swivel chair, and, with a beatific look on his face, began his explanation. In those days the title of master mariner, the post of captain in the merchant marine, was not obtained at a school through regular attendance at classes and annual examinations. It was awarded to chief mates and pilots with long experience, harbor pilots and ships' officers, after a competitive examination held at the Port Authority officers before an examining board made up of officers of the navy. The examination—very difficult, incidentally—consisted in the presentation of a study that was in the nature of a doctoral thesis, in which the candidate proved his competence by describing a sea voyage along a stretch of coast, with full geographical and technical details, from departure from a determined port to arrival at another. In this study the candidate had to resolve a series of navigational problems: on a calm sea, in the midst of a storm, mechanical defects of the ship, threat of shipwreck. Once the thesis was accepted, there came an oral examination on different subjects: navigation by dead reckoning, meteorology, maritime and watercourse law, admiralty law, international maritime law, steam engines and ship's machinery. When the candidate had passed these examinations, he received his license, and could go to sea in command of a ship.

"Simple, isn't it?" Georges asked him, holding a sheet of paper before Vasco's bewildered eyes.

Vasco ran his eyes over the fine but clear print. He learned that the examination in astronomical navigation included the use and correction of the sextant, the use and drawing of charts, orthodomic navigation (by the Great Circle), the use and complete knowledge of the chronometer, the use, theory, and correction of the magnetic compass.

He did not even want to find out what the other subjects were. He laid the paper on the table. He no longer had any doubts. Georges was once more having fun at his expense.

"You promised me..."

"...a title, and I am keeping my word."

"...that you were not going to play any jokes..."

"And what the hell joke am I playing?" retorted the captain indignantly.

"You don't call this a joke? An examination like this... Not to mention the fact that I am not a pilot, nor a chief mate, nor a harbor pilot, nor anything. The only ship I've ever set foot on was one of those traveling the Paraguassu River, to go to Cachoeira. Once I went to Ilhéus, on the *Marahu* of the Bahian Steamship Line, chasing a skirt. I threw up my guts; I never saw anything toss about the way that did, nor smelled such a stench."

"You're right. What I forgot to mention was that it is not necessary to be a pilot, chief mate, or deck officer to take the examination. It is open to everybody. Naturally, on principle, the ones who take it are seamen, and usually after long experience. But a little while back, just to make sure, I studied the provisions of the law under which the examination operates, and it is open to anybody. That's all you need. Besides, I have the rough draft of the application ready; all you have to do is copy and sign it."

He held out another paper. Vasco took it in his hand and stood there.

"All right, I can apply. But how am I going to take the examinations when I don't know the first thing about all this rigmarole; I never saw anything so complicated in my life. Not to mention the thesis. How am I going to be able to write it? I don't even like to write a letter; many's the scolding I got from my grandfather on that account."

"I've taken care of everything. The thesis, a description of a voyage from Porto Alegre to Rio, with calls at Paranagua and Florianopolis, is already being written."

"You're doing it?"

"No, I don't go quite that far. I'm getting old for that sort of thing. Lieutenant Mário is doing you that favor. When it's finished, give him a present if you feel like it...Some little trifle."

"Whatever he wants, not to mention my undying friendship. But what about the oral examinations? I don't know the first thing about all that stuff on the paper."

"Very simple, son. I've thought it all out. We're going to draw up two or three questions on each topic, and at the same time, the answers. We'll give you the questions and the answers. You learn the answers by heart, take the examinations; you will pass with honors, and receive the title you want so much."

Vasco seemed to doubt that the unexpected offer could be true. Georges went on: "Don't forget that the board of examiners is appointed and presided over by me. I am going to name Lieutenant Mário and Lieutenant Garcia, good fellows who are friends of yours. And you will become a captain, signed, sealed, and sworn, and without becoming a danger to mankind, for you will never try to take command of a ship."

"God forbid!"

Georges got up and slapped Vasco on the back.

"And if after all this I ever see you with a long face again, I'll round up a gang of sailors and have them work you over."

"And the day you get your title we're going to stage a first-class celebration. Bigger and better than yesterday's. The kind that leaves you hanging on the ropes."

"I'm going to set the examination date for a month from now," Georges announced.

"Why so far off?" asked Vasco, taking fright.

"Oh, you're in a hurry, are you? Mário needs time to do the written part, and you have to copy it in your handwriting, and learn the answers to the questions for the oral examination, one by one, point by point. You have to have everything at the tip of your tongue. This is the price you have to pay for the title of master mariner, you humbug captain."

"And what if I get mixed up at examination time, or nervous?"

"You're not going to get mixed up and you're not going to get nervous. And now copy the requirements, and then get the hell out of here, for I've got work to do."

"Let's start to make plans for the celebration," suggested the colonel.

Vasco bent over the paper and began to copy it. He was dizzy, it all seemed to him unreal, a crazy dream. There were tears in his eyes, and he had trouble making out the words. There is nothing in the world like friendship; friends are the salt of the earth. He would have liked to tell them so, but he did not know how.

## Of astronomical navigation and international maritime law, an extremely erudite chapter

FOR A MONTH Captain Georges Dias Nadreau guffawed heartily at Vasco's expense, at his nervousness, his concentration on his studies, in this way collecting payment for the favor he was doing him.

The colonel, Jerónimo, and Lidio, Lieutenants Mário and Garcia had their fun, too. Vasco even lost weight, with all the effort he put into learning by heart the complicated answers to the three questions on each subject, all bristling with sextants, winds, ocean currents, tonnage, territorial waters and inland seas, hygrometers, magnetic properties—a mess.

Every afternoon, at the captain's express orders, they subjected the terrified candidate to a test. At first Vasco was confused by the unfamiliar words, for his memory was refractory to those tongue-twisting terms, and Lieutenant Garcia threatened to flunk him. It was a real job to get him to play billiards, poker, visit the girls, for Vasco wanted to spend his nights studying.

Mário and Garcia lived it up during those thirty days. Vasco invited them to lunch every day, paid for their drinks, Portuguese wines of the finest, dinners at the Pension Monte Carlo. Little by little he got the answers in hand, familiarizing himself with the capricious names of the nautical instruments. One day Lieutenant Mário showed him some of the instruments in the offices of the Port Authority, and Vasco went overboard about them. They seemed to him beautiful, wonderful, and he began to love his new profession.

The worst job of all was having to copy in his own handwriting the study prepared by Lieutenant Mário, "his graduation thesis," as he was in the habit of referring to it. Thirty-two pages long, in illegible writing, as though Mário were a doctor and not an officer of the navy, and full of blots. He spent the mornings working on it, locked in the parlor, with orders to the maid not to let anybody in, no matter who.

When the work had been handed in and approved, the day for the oral examination was finally set. It was a solemn ceremony, with the colonel present in uniform, Dr. Jerónimo, and Lieutenant Lidio Marinho. Sailors stood on guard at the door of the room where the examining board, made up of Captain Nadreau and two good-natured lieutenants of the navy, sat solemnly behind a long table covered with instruments and maps. Pale and moved, Vasco was ushered in by a sailor, repeating to himself under his breath one last review of the questions and answers. He heard his name emphatically called out by Georges, he came forward, and seated himself stiffly in the chair in front of the table, his heart going like a trip hammer. But his answers came out effortless and correct, without a single mistake, without even a mispronunciation.

With unanimous approval of the board, his license was conferred upon him, and the name and address of the new master mariner was entered in the register of the Port Authority. Whenever he moved, he was to communicate his new address to the Authority. It was a thick book, bound in green, with the seal of the Republic. On each page there was a name with the date of examination, grade received, age, civil status, address. Few pages had been filled in, only a few names were ahead of his. And nearly all of these held only "rubber stamp licenses," as the certificates of the captains of river vessels were called, for which no written exercise was required, only an oral examination. These licenses were given to the captains of steamships on the São Francisco River, to whom sea travel, the ocean routes, were forbidden. Vasco's title was the real thing, valid for rivers, lakes, seas, authorizing and empowering him to command ships of all registries and flags, on all routes in the five oceans. Complete with international maritime law and the science of astronomical navigation.

"Now," said the colonel, when everything was over and Vasco was holding his license tenderly in his hand, "let's celebrate. Captain Vasco Moscoso de Aragão, lion of the seas, take the wheel and full steam ahead to the whorehouse!"

## *Of how an old sea dog is fabricated, without ship and without sailing*

NEVER IN ALL the history of navigation was the post of master mariner so honored, the title of captain so zealously employed as by Vasco Moscoso de Aragão, with his license in a gold frame on the wall of the parlor, his air of a man whose moral fibre had been tempered in distant seas, his dignity of an experienced sea dog.

He had visiting cards engraved, with his name preceded by his title, and followed by his rank. He called on families whom he had met at parties at the governor's mansion and receptions to which he had been invited, leaving the card of Captain Vasco Moscoso de Aragão, Master Mariner.

He was a stickler about the use of the title, refusing to tolerate the humiliating "Mr." before his name any longer.

"How are you, Mr. Vasco?"

"Excuse me. Captain Vasco, Master Mariner."

"Oh, I didn't know. Pardon me."

"Well, now you know, and be good enough not to forget," he would answer as he handed over the visiting card, of which he made extensive use, especially in the beginning.

.At the brothels and sporting houses, when some woman on the make put her arms around his neck, murmuring in his ear:

"Mr. Aragãozinho..." his reaction was patient but firm.

"My dear, I am not 'Mr. Aragãozinho,' I have a title. I am Captain Aragão of the merchant marine."

Even Carol had to alter her greeting when she met him at the head of the stairs, letting the syllables come tripping from her tongue in a delightful melody: "Captain Aragãozinho, my darling captain..."

The colonel and the harbor master set the example, Captain here, Captain there, over the billiard table, the poker table, drinking beer or uncorking champagne.

Even the governor, who had been advised of the situation and of the new happiness that flooded the breast of his nephew's generous friend, opened his arms wide when he saw him for the first time after he had been awarded his license: "How is my gallant friend, the captain?"

Vasco bowed, deeply touched: "At the service of Your Excellency, Governor."

In the offices of the firm of Moscoso & Company, Ltd., where he now showed up only once or twice a week, as if the mercantile smell of salt codfish and jerked beef offended his nostrils filled with the odor of the outgoing tide, the orders from Menéndez down to Giovanni had been categorical: under no circumstance was the boss's name to be pronounced without prefixing the title of "Captain." When Rafael Menéndez received the order, he bowed his head in agreement, hiding a sly smile. He said that the distinction conferred upon Vasco was a great honor for the whole firm. And he rubbed his eternally moist hands.

Giovanni, surprised and without understanding that sudden sea change in the boss, but finding it well-deserved, told him stories about his days as a sailor, and when Vasco appeared at the business, he spent most of his time with Giovanni, who had to dig deep into his memories.

After the visiting cards, his next concern was his uniforms. His tailor, one of the best in the city, was unable to outfit him, but he gave him the address of a tailor in Baixa do Sapateiro, who specialized in uniforms. The officers of the ships of the Bahian Line ordered theirs from him, and so did the army officers. And in Carnival season he supplied outfits of Russian prince, Italian count, French musketeer, or pirate without a country, to the celebrants.

Never in its history had the tailor's establishment received such a large order from a single customer. It created a veritable hubbub. Vasco wanted at least two uniforms of every kind, summer and winter, service and dress, formal and informal, blue and white, with caps to match, and 14-karat gold braid trim. A veritable trousseau. And he was in a hurry; he absolutely had to have at least one of the dress uniforms in two weeks, for the Second of July parade. The tailor, in a frenzy of enthusiasm, promised that he would work overtime, go without sleep, to have a white uniform ready for the morning parade, and a blue one for the evening reception at the governor's mansion. In return, Vasco promised him a fat bonus for the competent pliers of the needle.

It was an apotheosis that morning of the Second of July when Captain Vasco Moscoso de Aragão, in his white uniform with gold shoulder boards, appeared on the Largo da Soledade—all readied for the parade, with wagons of backlanders, floats bearing the portraits of Maria Quiteria, Labatut, and Joana Angélica, the speakers in their places, Colonel Pedro de Alencar in command of the soldiers standing at attention, Captain Georges Dias Nadreau at the head of the sailors of the Port Authority, the military bands playing marches—and joined the group of civilian authorities waiting for the governor.

With head high, he listened to the speeches, his heart throbbing with patriotism and pride. At Jerónimo's side he marched behind the governor, the colonel, the harbor master to the Largo da Sé, in whose venerable and crowded church the archbishop celebrated a *Te Deum*. For the reception that night he put on his dress uniform, more formal and elegant, though it was hotter than blue blazes. At the whole gathering there was nobody more splendid and noble, of more dignified and distinguished bearing.

Georges came over and congratulated him: "You are absolutely perfect. Vasco da Gama himself would be jealous if he could see you. There's only one thing lacking to complete your glory."

"What's that?" asked Vasco in alarm.

"A decoration, my boy. A handsome decoration."

"But I'm not an army man or a politician. Where am I going to get it?"

"We'll get it. We'll get it. It will cost a little money, but it's worth it."

Jerónimo handled the negotiations with the Portuguese

consul, who owned a pastry shop on the Praça Municipal, impressing upon him the interest of the government in that honor for Captain Vasco Moscoso de Aragão.

"But isn't he that Aragãozinho, of the firm Moscoso & Company which belonged to old José Moscoso, at the foot of Ladeira da Montanha?"

"That very one. Only now he is a captain of the merchant marine."

"I didn't know he had gone to sea..."

"He hasn't, but he's taken the examinations required by law."

"I knew his grandfather well, one of those honest, four-square Portuguese, a good man. But why should His August Majesty decorate the grandson?"

Jerónimo knocked the ash off his cigar, and winked his eye cynically: "For his outstanding maritime exploits."

"Maritime? So far as I know, he's never gone to sea..."

"Listen, Mr. Fernandes, the man is willing to pay. His August and Penniless Majesty is going to decorate our good Aragãozinho in return for a nice packet of contos de reis... And if there were no other reason, remember that he is named Vasco, that he is a captain, the grandson of a Portuguese, practically a relative of Admiral Vasco da Gama... Why the devil argue any more about it? You invent the reason, fix up the decoration, and be quick about it."

Thus it was that the glory of Captain Vasco Moscoso de Aragão was definitively consecrated when, after a few months, and five contos paid in advance, His Majesty Dom Carlos I, King of Portugal and the Algarves, conferred on him the rank of Knight of the Order of Christ, dating back seven hundred years to the days of the Crusades, for his "outstanding contribution to the opening of new sea lanes." With medal and chain. It was something to see. The ceremony was simple and intimate, though it was mentioned in the newspapers and royally celebrated afterwards with cherry brandy and Portuguese wine, in keeping with the time-honored custom.

With title, uniform, and decoration, Vasco Moscoso de Aragão no longer offended the eyes of the harbor master with his long face. His joy was complete and bubbling over; nobody so happy had ever strolled the streets of the old city of Salvador da Bahía.

He now spent a great deal of his time in the antique shops (there were only two in Salvador), looking for maritime objects, nautical instruments. He was willing to pay any price for them. It was in this way that he began his collection of maps, engravings of ships, sextants, compasses, old clocks. Captain Georges brought him back some instruments from a trip to Rio as a gift.

His marine museum was greatly enriched when an English ship was wrecked off the coast of Bahía, not far from the capital. The contents were auctioned off by court order, and the chief bidder was Captain Vasco Moscoso de Aragão. He bought the ship's wheel, a fine pair of binoculars, chronometers, compasses, hygrometers, the ship's clock, a rope ladder, not to mention two cases of whiskey with which to treat his friends.

He never lost that mania for collecting nautical instruments. Several years later, he picked up a telescope from a German adventurer who happened to come through the city. The German had tried to do business with it on the street, charging each customer a thousand reis for a close look at the sky, the moon, and the stars. The venture failed, he had his boardinghouse bill to pay, and the telescope wound up in the house of Barris, from which, moreover, the captain was planning to move.

The favorite object of his growing collection was a replica in miniature of a ship, the *Benedict*, reproducing to the last detail an ocean liner, in a glass case. It was a birthday present from Jerónimo. The journalist had discovered it in the basement of the State House, the case covered with dust, stuck away in a corner as something useless. Vasco went wild over it, he had no words to thank his friend for the gift.

In one of his long conversations with Giovanni, he learned that it was the habit of ship's officers, especially the captain, to smoke a pipe. A captain who did not puff on a pipe was not a captain, according to the authoritative opinion of the old Negro. The next day Vasco appeared before his friends, awkwardly fumbling with an English pipe which was the very devil to smoke, going out every minute. In time he learned to manage it, and he soon had several, of different shapes and materials, briar, china, meerschaum.

Occasionally, in the early afternoon, Vasco would go to visit Captain Georges Dias Nadreau at the Port Authority. He put on his service uniform, his cap on his head, his pipe in his mouth. From the window of the office he eyed the sea, attentively watching the ships docking.

One day in a bar, while he was waiting for the colonel, he was introduced to a gentleman from Pilão Arcado. They struck up a conversation, and the backlander was enchanted with his urban acquaintance.

"So the gentleman is a ship captain? But a real ship, not one of those river boats that are always running around? You must have seen a lot of things. Tell me one thing, sir: have you ever traveled in the vicinity of China and Japan?"

The guileless eyes of the captain rested on the tanned face of the man from Pilão Arcado: "China and Japan? Several times, yes, sir. I know all those parts."

"Then tell me something I have always wanted to know"—and he leaned confidentially across the table—"is it true that the women there are hairless except for their heads, not one hair anywhere else, and that their cunts run crosswise? Somebody told me that."

"That's a lie, they were just pulling your leg. They are like those everywhere, only tighter, a real delight."

"Honestly? What are they like? Have you had many of them?"

"Once in Shanghai I was walking down the street, not going anywhere in particular... In a steep alley I came upon a Chinese girl in tears. Her name was Liu..."

The eyes of the rude backlander lighted up as Captain Vasco Moscoso de Aragão lost himself in the mysteries of Shanghai, in opium dreams, led by Liu, a little Chinese of lacquer and ivory.

The afternoon was falling on Largo da Sé, the vermilion of the setting sun on the black stones of the old church. Taking Liu by the hand, Vasco set out on his voyages.

## Of the passing of time, and changes in the government and the firm, with swindles and a head held high

CAPTAIN VASCO MOSCOSO DE ARAGÃO kept his word; never again did he show himself before Captain Georges Dias Nadreau with a long face. He had his title, he was happy. No sorrow, no difficulty the future might bring could upset his radiant expression, his exuberant happiness. He might be momentarily annoyed or saddened, but his genial disposition quickly reasserted itself, leaving no room for sadness, giving little importance to life's disappointments.

Meanwhile, there was no lack of sadness or disappointments. But a ship's captain, a master mariner, becomes accustomed in the cradle of the deep to the fickleness of the sea and the weather, tempers his character and strengthens his heart, learns to face life's deceptions and adversities with a smile on his lips.

One of the greatest blows, the first to happen, was the transfer of Georges Dias Nadreau, who was promoted and put in command of a destroyer. How was it possible to imagine night life in Bahía, the brothels, the sporting houses, the carousals, the women, the magic of love without the presence of that fair-haired, blue-eyed seaman, contriver of lies, jokes, amusing diversions, always with a Negro or a dark mulatto girl close at hand? When the news got around among the women and the night owls, there was general consternation, tears, and lamentations, and a send-off worthy of its object was prepared.

"Chin up, Captain," said Georges to Vasco when he saw him the night of the farewell party, gloomy and silent. "A sailor never lets sadness get him down."

The next day all of them went to see him off aboard the steamship on which he was going to Rio, and for the first time saw his wife, Gracinha, dressed in deep mourning, her pale face covered by a black veil, her lips a straight line. On being introduced to them, she held out the tips of her chill fingers. It was then that Vasco realized that the words spoken the night before by the former harbor master were not an empty phrase: "A sailor never lets sadness get him down." Those words suddenly took on concrete meaning. He had not let sadness get him down, he had not let himself be defeated.

They went back to town, played a game of billiards, but it was no longer the same. Georges's absence filled the bar, the Pension Monte Carlo. The night was suddenly empty.

Lieutenant Lidio Marinho had got married the year before, and disappeared from circulation for a time. But they all knew that his absence was temporary, that he would be back with them when married life took on normalcy, and so it was. When his duties at the State House were over, he would appear at the billiard table and, most nights, would join them for dinner, and then go to the Pension to dance; at times he shut himself up with one of the girls, for he still caused a flutter in the dovecotes of the sporting houses. A wife was to give him children, keep house, entertain guests. Georges, however, was lost to them for good. He would organize another gang in Rio, navy colleagues, different friends. It was a bad night, but Vasco remembered his words, and saw the depressing figure of Gracinha, and bucked up the others. A sailor never lets sadness get him down.

The new harbor master, Georges's substitute, who might have taken his place in the gang, took months to get there and was a complete washout: standoffish, unsociable, with a horror of sprees, loose women, all circumspection and solemnity. Vasco gave up his visits to the Port Authority.

But he went on visiting the port, to watch the ships dock, to admire their trigness, to identify their flags, to acquire, wherever he could find them, nautical appurtenances and pictures of ships. He still went out every night with Jerónimo and the colonel to play poker and to lose his head over some woman. By this time he was a little past forty, and everybody was in the habit of calling him captain.

The governor's term of office was coming to an end, and it was a melancholy end, for the president of the Republic, influenced by other members of the inner circles of the party, not only vetoed the name of the governor's candidate to succeed him, but almost did him out of a seat in the senate, traditionally reserved for retiring governors. He got the seat, but the election of Jerónimo to congress, and his political career, went down the drain. He was fixed up with a job in the Department of Justice in Rio, attorney or something of the sort. It wasn't a bad job, but his political ambitions were completely frustrated.

With the change of government, Pedro de Alencar left, too. Another colonel was put in command of the 19th Riflemen, a friend of the new head of state. Vasco did not even want to meet him. He was a man who was loyal to his friends, to the memory of that famous gang, and he disappeared from the State House, from the receptions and social gatherings. He still took part in the parades on the Second of July and the Seventh of September, wearing his dress uniform, but not forming part of the government group, just one of the crowd.

He did not want to join another group, become a member of another gang. One who, like him, had belonged to the elite of the city could not mingle again with merchants, clerks, or even young doctors or lawyers. At the sporting houses and cabarets he sat at a table by himself, and the champagne he drank began to take on a bitter taste of melancholy.

Then one day Carol sold the Pension Monte Carlo to an Argentine pander, a disagreeable character who thought of nothing but dollars and cents. Vasco saw her off; she was returning to Garanhuns. Her brother-in-law had died, and her sister needed her help and company. On the pier they recalled the marvelous nights they had had together, and their friends: Jerónimo, who had been her lover; Lieutenant Lidio Marinho, now a captain and stationed in Porto Alegre; Colonel Pedro de Alencar, the peerless drinker; and that unforgettable Captain Georges Dias Nadreau, with his foreign air, his passionate enthusiasm for black wenches, who was such fun. All that was now over for Carol. She was going to help bring up nieces and nephews, a respectable lady, a rich widow in the sedate city where she was born.

She kissed Vasco on both cheeks, and asked with tears in her eyes: "Do you remember the abduction of Dorothy?"

Where was Dorothy now? A backlands colonel had fallen in love with her restless eyes; he was a widower and had taken her off to the ranch. Vasco slept with her the night before she left, and it was a mad night, as though the old magic, the wild passion had been reborn as strong as before. They never heard any more about her, whether she had stayed with the rancher or not. But on Vasco's right arm the name Dorothy and a heart were still tattooed.

"Do you remember the Chinaman who did the tattooing?"

So many memories, so many things to recall on the way to the pier! The ship weighed anchor for Recife, and Carol, plump and tearful, waved goodbye with her handkerchief. "A sailor never lets sadness get him down," even when he is an orphan, deserted on the empty docks of the city.

The years went by; Captain Vasco Moscoso de Aragão gradually disappeared from the brothels, the sporting houses. Nor was he now any longer the head, the boss of the firm of Moscoso & Company, Ltd. The Negro Giovanni died repeating his warning to watch out for Menéndez, that the gringo was no good. But when Vasco decided to take his advice, and really assume control of the business, Menéndez had made himself the real owner of the firm. In those ten years of riotous living Vasco had squandered all he owned and a good bit that he didn't; his debts were tremendous. Long and complicated negotiations followed, with sharp, greedy lawyers. In the end Vasco left the firm, receiving certain properties that brought in a rental, and a number of government bonds that gave him an income on which he could live decently. He sold the house of Barris, bought a smaller one on Largo Dois de Julho, where he installed his nautical instruments, hung his master mariner's license on the parlor wall, the award of the Knight of the Order of Christ, and set the glass case holding the model of the *Benedict* on the center table.

"A sailor never lets sadness get him down," not even when he goes from being a millionaire to having just enough to get by on, when his friends disappear, when he can no longer pluck roses in the garden of love, when he loses his taste for liquor, and gets sleepy before midnight. In the new house, making the acquaintance of neighbors he had never seen before, Captain Vasco Moscoso de Aragão became popular and respected. As he sat in his chair on the sidewalk, they gathered around to listen to him relate his seafaring adventures. He always had a pretty cook to look after him, a carefully chosen young mulatto.

More years went by. The captain's hair turned gray, his cooks were no longer so pretty, the cost of living was going up, but not his income. Nor did the neighbors take him as seriously as before; there were those who said he had never set foot on a ship, that his title of captain was the result of a hoax in the days of José Marcelino's government, and that he had bought the Order of Christ for a fancy price when he was swimming in money and the consulate of Portugal in Bahía was run by a businessman.

Some twenty years after the ceremony at the Port Authority, a worthless character who had opened a gasoline station in the street, and to whom Vasco, always ready to strike up an acquaintance, began to narrate the terrible crossing of the Persian Gulf during a typhoon, interrupted the heroic narration with a jeering laugh: "Don't give me that stuff. Save that baloney for the nitwits. Do you suppose I don't know all about you? Everybody laughs at you behind your back. I've got too much to do, Mr. Captain, to waste my time listening to your yarns."

"A sailor keeps his chin up," but it was hard to start all over again. Where was Georges Dias Nadreau, today undoubtedly an admiral, where were Jerónimo and Colonel Alencar, Lieutenant Lidio and Lieutenant Mário? Dorothy—how good it would be to see your willowy body, your restless eyes, your feverish cheeks... Would Carol still be living in Garanhuns in Pernambuco, calling herself a widow, bringing up grandnieces and nephews? He still went to the water front, rain or shine, to watch the departure and the entrance of the ships, recognizing every flag.

He could no longer walk with head high on Largo Dois de Julho, or on any other street of Salvador da Bahía. He sold the house at a good price, and bought the one in Periperi, a suburb far from the bustle of the city. He took the mulatto Balbina, his cook and bedfellow, his nautical instruments, the ship's wheel, the binoculars, the telescope, his pipes, his framed license, his past upon the decks of ships, ploughing the seas amidst the tempests, and moved.

An old seafarer with head high, his hair blowing in the wind on top of the bluff.

*In which the narrator, a bumbler and always with an eye out for the main chance, falls back on fate*

AS YOU CAN SEE, when a hard-working historian and true investigator begins to delve into chronicles as confused as these, he suddenly comes upon contradictory and conflicting versions of the same facts, each apparently as valid as the other. Whom is one to believe? Of the two versions set forth, that of the captain, a man of indisputable merits, and that of Chico Pacheco, with so many details that can be substantiated, which should be preferred and submitted to the good faith of the reader? How am I to get to the bottom of that well where the truth lies, when it is so cluttered up with stumbling blocks—ship's wheels, loose women—and bring her up, refulgent and naked, to enhance the memory of one of the two adversaries and expose the other to public execration? Whom extol, whom unmask? In all sincerity I must confess that at this point I find myself lost and bewildered.

I sought the advice of Dr. Alberto Siqueira, our eminent, albeit disputed luminary of jurisprudence. Having been a judge for so many years, in the interior and the capital, he should be in a position to discern the truth in all this mixed-up mess. His Honor evaded the issue, saying that it was impossible for him to pass judgment or even give an opinion without first carefully studying the evidence in the case. As though he were hearing the

suit of Chico Pacheco against the state, and not judging a work
of historic research having as its goal the prize offered by the
Public Archives! I was hurt by the treatment my pages had
received, and I told him so. But the self-satisfied magistrate
gruffly replied that my work revealed a lack of the most
elementary notion of what a historical study should be,
beginning with the matter of dates. Nobody could tell when the
events set forth had occurred, the time that had elapsed between
them, the day, month, and year of the birth and death of the
principal participants. Who ever heard of a work of history
without dates? What is History, if not a succession of dates
marking acts and facts?

I swallowed the criticism without saying a word. I had given
no thought to this detail. And so at this juncture I shall clear up
the matter, giving forthwith the most pertinent dates. I know the
date of birth and death of hardly any of them, not even old
Moscoso, nor the governor himself. As for the captain, he died
in this suburb of Periperi in the year 1950 at the age of
eighty-two, and, by a process of subtraction, it becomes
apparent that he was born in the year 1868, and was thirty-odd
years old when he became the intimate friend of those important
personages. The events narrated by Chico Pacheco, real or
fictitious, would have taken place at the beginning of the
century, between the term of office of José Marcelino, which
began in 1904, and the date of the captain's moving to Periperi,
in 1929. What other dates should I list? To speak frankly, I don't
know. Besides, I was never able to remember the dates in history
books, or the names of rivers and volcanoes in geography texts.

Moreover, the blunt ruling of His Honor is due less to an
impartial critical criterion than to a certain ill will he had
developed toward me of late. It began a few days ago. He
stopped treating me with the regard he had formerly shown for
me. He did not invite me to go with him to Dondoca's house in
the afternoon any more and, no matter how much I buttered him
up, praising his opinions and virtue, he remained aloof, eying me
reproachfully. I don't know the reason for this sudden change; it
must be the result of some intrigue, for there is no lack of
troublemakers in Periperi and many of those scoundrels envy
me my intimacy with a jurist who has contributed to journals
published in the south.

I even came to think the worst: His Honor had suspicions, as
yet unconfirmed, of my carryings-on with Dondoca. That would

be a disaster. When I discussed the matter with the sweet lass, my fears grew, for she, too, had noticed a change in the judge. He had become inquisitive, examining the pillowcases and sheets, and was continually demanding vows of fidelity from her.

And now this, as though the difficulties of my work were not enough, the arduous task of re-establishing the complete truth concerning the disputed adventures of the captain! I have here in front of me a pile of notes, the fruit of my investigations. And what happens? If I pick up one of them, I find myself on the high seas, sailing for Asia by way of Oceania, and Dorothy is the unhappy wife of a coarse-fibered millionaire, who leaves him for love of a ship's captain, in whose arms she expires of passion and fever in the dirty port of Makassar. If I pick up another, Dorothy is a prostitute in the Pension Monte Carlo (I have corroborated the fact that such a pension really existed, occupying the first floor of a building where, later on, the *Diario da Bahía* had its editorial offices), changing one lover for another, sleeping with whoever had the price, and who wound up going off with a blacklands colonel. The Swede Johann is a pilot in one set of notes, a businessman in another; Menéndez runs the gamut from shipowner to partner in a business firm, a thoroughly unpleasant character in whatever metamorphosis. What a hell of a mix-up!

I had heard that in the long run time always establishes the truth, but I don't believe it. The more time goes by, the harder it becomes to ascertain the facts, to find convincing proof, the pertinent details. If it was difficult at the time for the inhabitants of Periperi to discover who was telling the truth and who was lying, imagine what it is like now, in the month of January, 1961, thirty-two years after the events. I reached the conclusion that only if fate takes a hand, by one of those chance happenings that defy explanation, can one arrive at the truth. Otherwise, the eternal doubt remains. Was Marie Antoinette frivolous and corrupt, as the defenders of the French Revolution claim, or was she a flower of purity and kindness, as the zealots of Obscurantism and royalty paint her? Who can discover the truth after such a lapse of time? Who can say whether she did or did not sleep with all those counts, including the Scandinavian?

If fate had not intervened at the right moment, I don't know what would have happened in Periperi in that year of 1929 at the end of the winter. For in the face of the amazing story related by Chico Pacheco, the population was divided into two camps. On one side, the supporters of the captain, brandishing the Order of Christ; on the other, his disparagers, brandishing the account of the ex-customs officer. Two parties sprang up, two sects, two columns of hatred. The verbal encounters multiplied; the few who had kept a cool head, like old Marreco, found themselves in hot water all the time. The retired government employees and businessmen, with their rheumatism, their kidney ailments, nearly all of them suffering from stricture of the urethra, spent their time threatening, insulting one another. One day Zequinha Curvelo threw himself on Chico Pacheco, announcing loud and clear his intention of tearing out his foul tongue. As the stationmaster said, the devil had got into the old men.

Not only was the town divided, but the outskirts as well. The partisans of the captain sat on the station benches facing the sea; those of Chico Pacheco, on those facing the street. The beach was taken over by the first; the square by the second. In Plataforma, when Father Justo received the news, he clasped his hands to his head. Now how was he to choose the patron for St. John's festival next year?

In the midst of all this, there was one man who remained calm and serene, smiling his good-natured smile, climbing up on the bluffs to watch through his spyglass the arrival of the ships, preparing his hot grog in the evening, winning at poker, and telling his stories; Captain Vasco Moscoso de Aragão.

When the first rumors of the hullabaloo set off by Chico Pacheco came to his ears, he confided to his close friends: "Pure spite."

And he shrugged his shoulders, prepared to ignore the whole business. But this was not possible, for some of his formerly attentive listeners turned their backs on him, and many of them laughed at his stories. And his staunchest supporters told him he would have to do something to prove beyond the shadow of a doubt the falsity of the story the former customs agent was spreading. Zequinha Curvelo, after he had almost come to blows with Chico Pacheco, opened up his heart to him: "Excuse me, Captain, but you'll have to do something to shut up those slanderers."

"I think you are right. My first idea was not to pay any attention to that despicable tattle. But as there are those who believe it, I have no choice but to take measures..."

That was one of his finest moments: his hand resting on the window, his eyes lost upon the waters, his hair fluttering in the breeze.

"I name you, dear friend, and Rui Pessoa as my seconds to challenge this slanderer to a duel. As I am the one who has been insulted, I have the right to choose weapons. I choose a six-shot revolver, with the right to use all the bullets, at twenty paces. The site will be the beach; the dead man will fall into the sea."

Zequinha Curvelo went wild with enthusiasm and rushed off to carry out his mission. He failed. Chico Pacheco refused even to name seconds. He was not a man who fought duels; that was the most idiotic thing he had ever heard of. Duels were out of fashion, nothing could be more ridiculous. He, Chico Pacheco, had a veritable horror of firearms, he didn't even like to look at them. And that mountebank, who had been running around with officers of the army and the navy, might even have learned how to handle guns, might even be a good shot. He would have no part of such nonsense. If the clown wanted to, let him go to court, sue for defamation of character, and he, Chico Pacheco, would go and prove everything he had said. If he was so brave, let him resort to the law. A duel proved nothing; all the advantage was on the side of the one who was the better shot. No, thank you, no duels.

Zequinha Curvelo answered only one word: "Coward!"

The challenge was delivered in the square where the adversaries of the captain held forth. Chico Pacheco lost ground in the eyes of his admirers. The prospect of a duel was equally pleasing to both groups, promising excitement. However, this advantage of the captain was only momentary. Fundamentally, the doubt lingered. His stories no longer aroused their pristine echo, the enthusiasm they once produced.

Zequinha Curvelo himself one day pointed out to the captain: "The truth is that the fabrications of that skunk have never been denied."

Vasco looked at him with his clear eyes: "If I had to resort to proofs to defend myself from a coward who rejects settling matters on the field of honor, if there are those who hesitate to choose between my word and his, then I prefer to leave at once. I saw a house advertised in the paper on the island of Itaparica. There, at least, I will be surrounded by the sea, as though I were aboard ship, far from calumny and envy."

He raised his head proudly: "One day they will do me justice, they will miss me. But I shall not stoop to refute a coward, a boor."

This was the way things stood, at an impasse, when a new factor entered the case, and the truth was established. It did not depend on the captain or on Chico Pacheco, or Zequinha Curvelo, Adriano Meira, or old José Paulo, alias Marreco, the only one who did not get excited, who kept his head in the midst of the storm. It was fate, destiny, accident—call it what you will.

Would that fate would intervene on my behalf to dispel the growing suspicions of His Honor, Dr. Alberto Siqueira, and prove to him the purity of my relations with Dondoca, which merely reflect the friendship I feel for the illustrious and suspicious legal light. Impossible? Because I have really been putting horns on the old gentleman's head, enjoying his chocolates and his girl? Only on that account? But don't you know that fate is capricious? When it steps in to re-establish the truth, it does so according to its preferences, not on the basis of proofs or documents. Why, then, couldn't it convince the judge of my innocence, even taking into account the service I do His Honor by occupying his place in Dondoca's bed? I leave her in the morning satisfied and happy, in a frame of mind of put up—patiently and smilingly—with the unspeakable dullness of the distinguished representative of the law.

*Which tells how the captain set out
with destination unknown, or to fulfill his destiny, for nobody in this
world escapes his destiny*

ON THAT DAY of uninterrupted rain, with downpours of flood
proportions and a cold, piercing wind from the sea sweeping the
suburb, the sky the color of ashes, the streets filled with puddles,
the captain, too, was in mourning, a black ribbon on his cap, a
mourning band on the sleeve of his wide-collared coat. He
explained to his friends in a grave voice that it was the
anniversary of the death of Dom Carlos I, King of Portugal and
the Algarves, assassinated by hotheaded republicans in 1908,
shortly after His Majesty had recognized the captain's merits
and had honored him with the decoration of the Order of Christ.
Every year on that day he put on mourning, in memory of that
exalted monarch who, from his lofty throne, had seen fit to
recognize and reward the efforts of one who had opened up new
trade routes.

At the station, where the group gathered that day was small,
Zequinha Curvelo, sitting on a bench looking out over the gulf,
was holding forth, throwing into Chico Pacheco's teeth (he was
sitting on the other side of the platform, on a bench facing the
street) that Order of Christ, with medal and chain, an argument
that was absolutely clinching. Only an irresponsible person
could make such a ridiculous and unfounded statement: that a

151

King of Portugal would sell, as though it were salt cod or toothpicks, a decoration of such standing, traffic like a greengrocer with an Order that dated from the days of the Crusades and Knights Templar, so esteemed and sought after that even the republicans had maintained it, and rulers and diplomats, scientists and generals strove to obtain it. Really it was infamous to speak and listen to such bosh; that suburb of Periperi did not deserve the honor of housing in his glorious old age a citizen of such fame and prestige as the captain, the bearer of a distinction which in Bahía only J. J. Seabra possessed: the Order of Christ. In the face of such envy and ingratitude, the captain was thinking of leaving, conferring on some other and more civilized town the privilege of numbering him among its inhabitants.

"What he is doing is running away because he's been unmasked," Chico Pacheco started to answer, "to peddle his cock and bull stories to other customers, the old so and so..."

He did not continue because the ten o'clock train had just pulled in and a mysterious stranger was alighting, someone nobody had ever seen there before, wrapped in a raincoat, opening an umbrella, and asking if any of those gentlemen knew where a certain master mariner, Captain Vasco Moscoso de Aragão, lived. He needed to see him at once, he had an important matter to discuss with him. Friends and enemies, with one accord, prepared to lead him to the house with the windows opening on the sea, in spite of the fact that at that very minute another violent downpour had started. And the leaders of the two groups, Chico and Zequinha, were both dying to know what that important matter was that the stranger had come to talk over with the captain.

The stranger was not closemouthed about his business, and on the way, splashing through one puddle after another, he told them that a ship of the National Company of Coastwise Navigation, one of the big *Itas*, had arrived that rainy morning with its flag at half-mast. On the trip from Rio to Salvador da Bahía, the captain had died. The chief mate had taken over command of the ship, but the law required that at the first port of call, and until the arrival of a captain of the Company, the ship must be commanded by another master mariner, anyone to be found there, whether on vacation or retired. Stupid laws, as though the chief mate could not sail the ship to Belém, where the Company had another captain, a native of Pará, who was spending his vacation in his home state, to whom they had already telegraphed!

He, the stranger, Mr. Americo Antunes, the agent of the Coastwise Line in Bahía, had to solve the problem. As though he didn't have enough to do with the arrangements for the funeral of the dead captain...

"Didn't they throw his body into the sea?" inquired Zequinha.

If only they had, it would have saved him work and headaches. Where was he going to find another captain? Naturally, the records of the Port Authority listed the names and addresses of the master mariners who had received their license from the Authority. Most of them were captains holding a "rubber stamp" certificate, without any experience at sea, serving on side-wheelers plying São Francisco. There was only one captain who had passed the complete examination with an accepted thesis, and that was this Vasco Moscoso de Aragão, whose whereabouts nobody at the Port Authority knew, and who was not to be found at his address on the Largo Dois de Julho. He had finally discovered his present residence and had come to request him to assume command of the *Ita* as far as Belém, the last port on its trip up, where the other captain would be on hand for the return trip. It would be a favor to the Company and the passengers, some of them distinguished, including a federal senator from Rio Grande do Norte, for if he had not discovered this heaven-sent captain, the ship and the passengers would have had to lay over for three or four days till one arrived from Rio de Janeiro. It would have meant a delay for the passengers, and a great loss for the Company.

Chico Pacheco laughed sarcastically: "Well, they're going to have to lay over, for this captain isn't going to take command of any ship. He's not going to stir from here..."

"Don't you believe that," Zequinha Curvelo interrupted. "The captain will be happy to be of service."

"Happy or not," answered Mr. Antunes, "he'll have to do it. He's obliged to by law. Even if he is on vacation or retired."

They reached the door of the captain's house. They saw him in the back parlor, standing by the wide window, looking out at the white-capped sea. Zequinha Curvelo called him, made the introductions, explaining the situation and rubbing his hands: "Now, Captain, here is your chance to squash these snakes."

The adversaries had stayed outside in the rain. Only

Zequinha Curvelo and Emilio Fagundes had crossed the threshold with Antunes. The captain cast a quick glance from one to the other without saying a word. The agent of the Coastwise Line rounded out Zequinha's explanation, saying that the Company would be most grateful to him and without doubt would recompense him in keeping with the favor he was doing it.

"When I retired, I swore never to set foot on the bridge of a ship again. There is a sad story involved in this, of which these friends here know the details."

Zequinha Curvelo found that beginning disturbing: "But under the present circumstances..."

"An oath is an oath, a sailor does not go back on his word."

Mr. Americo Antunes broke in: "Excuse me, Captain, but this is a legal obligation, as you know better than I do. Those are the laws of the sea."

"And of honor besmirched by the envious," added Zequinha.

The captain saw the enemy group in front of his house break up under the driving rain, the more determined taking cover in the lee of the Magalhães sisters' house, the blurred outline of Chico Pacheco backed up against the old maids' door. He turned to his two friends: "Would you allow me to talk alone with Mr. Americo? I want to discuss certain details with him."

He led Antunes into the living room, leaving Zequinha and Emilio in the hall. The conference lasted a little over ten minutes, and they saw the captain return, accompanied by the agent of the Coastwise Line, who kept repeating: "You can rest assured, everything will work out all right."

A handshake and the stranger set out at a run through the rain, for the rumble of the train from Paripe could be heard, and if he did not hurry he would miss it. Chico Pacheco followed at his heels to see what he could find out, but he could not keep up with him, and when he got to the station the train had pulled out.

The captain explained to Zequinha and Emilio: "I asked for a document from the Company, signed by the president, setting forth the reasons why I was breaking my oath."

"You mean to say you are taking over the command?" exulted Zequinha.

"And why wouldn't I, if that is my duty, and they are giving me a statement about my oath? Dorothy will forgive me."

He's going, he's not going, he is a mountebank, he is a great man... The discussion grew, the news spread, dragging the retired employees and businessmen out of their houses and bringing them to the station, in spite of the rain that kept on without a letup. The discussion and the rain went on after the departure of the captain, accompanied by Balbina and wearing his dress uniform, on the two o'clock train that afternoon. Caco Podre carried the suitcases; the captain, the magnificent spyglass in his hand. At the station he shook hands with supporters and adversaries alike; he might have shaken that of Chico Pacheco if the former customs agent had not kept his distance at the end of the platform. When the train arrived, Captain Vasco Moscoso de Aragão embraced Zequinha Curvelo, clasping him to his breast. He did not speak a word. From the door of the coach he raised his hand to his cap in a salute.

"He's taken a powder," crowed Chico Pacheco. "He'll never be back."

"He's going to take command of the ship to Belém," stated Zequinha Curvelo.

"You have to be all kinds of a jackass to believe that. If they don't find another captain, that ship will grow roots in the harbor. What the charlatan is going to do is disappear. Nobody will ever hear of him again."

"Those are lies."

"Then why did he take the maid with him? You just wait, one of these days someone will show up to collect his belongings, bringing the news that the house has been sold. He was already getting ready to run away; this just speeded things up a little."

"The truth will prevail. He who lives will see," answered Zequinha, who had a fondness for high-flown phrases.

At five that afternoon several of them had gathered on the beach in spite of the rain. From there they could see the docks of Bahía, and make out in the murky light the black, majestic bulk of the *Ita* going through the maneuvers of casting off. Smoke was coming out of the smokestack, the whistles would be blowing. The ship was headed toward the bar and disappeared beyond the breakwater.

And the arguments went on harsh and bitter, until the newspaper brought the first news that came in by telegram.

# EPISODE THREE

*A detailed description of the immortal voyage of the captain in command of an* **Ita,** *of the many things that took place aboard ship, romantic love affairs, political discussions, visits to the ports of call, the famous theory of the frustrated, and the winds unleashed in fury*

# EPISODE THREE

*A detailed description of the immortal voyage of the captain in command of an Ita, of the many things that took place aboard ship, romantic love affairs, political discussions, visits to the ports of call, the famous theory of the frustrated, and the winds unleashed in fury*

## Of the captain on the bridge

HE WALKED up the gangplank accompanied by Americo Antunes, the Company agent. A sailor was carrying his two suitcases. A great emotion filled his breast as he set foot on the ship; he could hardly make out the voice of Antunes, who was introducing him to a well-dressed man: "Dr. Homero Cavalcanti, senator from Rio Grande do Norte; Captain Vasco Moscoso de Aragão."

"What luck, Captain, that you should be in Bahía. Otherwise we would have been delayed here, which would be terrible for me. I have important matters I must attend to in Natal."

"The captain was very kind," Antunes observed.

"I'm just doing my duty."

He was introduced to the purser. The passengers gathered around him with curiosity. That had been an eventful trip, with a death on board, the body of the captain laid out for a night and a day in the dance salon transformed into a death chamber, the threat of a layover in Bahía, the gratifying news of the discovery of a retired captain.

Guided by Americo Antunes, he made his way through all the confusion of embarkation, people saying goodbyes, suitcases being carried by stewards, children getting underfoot,

159

the barking of a frightened dog in the arms of a mature, overdressed lady. The Pekinese growled threateningly at the captain, struggling to get free from its mistress's hands. The lady smiled at the captain and said apologetically: "Excuse him, Captain, he does not know how indebted we are to you."

The passengers had learned of his noble gesture, and appreciated it. Vasco felt all puffed up: "My duty, madame."

Not bad-looking. The smell of her perfume enveloped the captain, who asked Americo in a low voice: "Then it is just to say..."

"...just to say..."

They climbed the little stairway leading to the quarterdeck. The sailor walked ahead of them and put the captain's suitcases in his cabin. Vasco pointed to the berth: "Was it there he died?"

"No, he died on the bridge. A heart attack, poor fellow."

The ship's doctor came by. Vasco was introduced to him and he accompanied them to the bridge, where the officers were already waiting, standing at attention.

"Captain Vasco Moscoso de Aragão, who does us the honor and the favor of taking command of the ship as far as Belém."

"Geir Matos, our chief mate."

A fair young chap stepped forward, smiling. Vasco had the impression that he and the agent exchanged a knowing glance, like the wink of an eye. But the chief mate was holding out his hand to him: "It is a great honor to serve under the orders of a man who wears such an important decoration," he said, referring to the medal of the Order of Christ, gleaming on the breast of the captain's uniform.

He was followed by the navigation officers, the chief engineer, the assistant engineer. Then the chief mate, at the head of the others on the bridge, bowed: "We await your orders, Captain."

Vasco looked at Americo Antunes out of the corner of his eye, Antunes nodded his head slightly, as though to encourage him, and the captain said: "As you gentlemen know, my presence here is merely a formality demanded by law. I do not intend to introduce any changes during these few days that I am in command. The ship is in good hands, gentlemen. The chief mate will continue in command. I do not wish to interfere in anything."

"It is apparent, Captain, that you are an old salt, who knows the customs of the sea. We shall not bother you unless some serious problem should come up unexpectedly, making your experienced knowledge necessary, which, I hope, will not be the case."

Americo Antunes wound up the ceremony: "The ship is yours, Captain. And in the name of the Coastwise Line, I wish you a pleasant trip."

He took his leave, it was almost time to weigh anchor. Vasco stood on the bridge, listening to the chief mate issue orders. The gangplank was drawn up, the hoot of the mournful whistle was lost beyond the towers of the churches, handkerchiefs waved goodbye, women were crying in the rain. The ship pushed off slowly in its first maneuvers. Vasco looked in the direction of Periperi. His friends would be there on the beach, Zequinha Curvelo, with arm outstretched, waving goodbye, wishing him luck and a good trip. The captain would have liked to raise the spyglass to his eye, to try to discern them through the rain and the growing distance. But he didn't even dare to move in that solemn hour of the orders for departure.

*Of the captain presiding at the captain's
table on a rough sea, with threats of
internal and intestinal revolution*

THE DINING SALON was not too full at dinner that first night
out. It was raining and blowing, and the ship was bravely
breasting a rough sea, which discouraged the passengers, most
of whom had taken refuge in their staterooms.

Probably Vasco would have preferred to rest in his berth
from the emotions of that busy and decisive day. It would be
safer, too; at times an ominous queasiness rose from his
stomach. However, it was one of the captain's duties to preside
at the meals, at the head of the main table. The chief mate, the
purser, the navigation officers, the doctor took turns at
presiding over the smaller tables. He could not fall short in his
obligations. So, putting on a bold front, he swallowed two
capsules from a bottle he had bought at a drugstore, with the
clerk's absolute guarantee. Perhaps he might meet the lady with
the Pekinese, exchange a smile and a few words with her. The
senator from Rio Grande do Norte, Dr. Homero Cavalcanti,
was already waiting, hungry and impatient.

With the senator on his right, and on his left a congressman
from Paraíba, Dr. Othon Ribeiro, a large landowner and
banker, the captain gave his first order since he had come
aboard: he ordered dinner served. He looked around the room;

162

there were many empty places; the lady with the dog lacked the courage to face the rough sea. What a pity!

The senator and the congressman were talking politics; the presidential campaign was in full swing, and that year of 1929 was one of feverish activity, what with the nomination of Júlio Prestes and Getúlio Vargas, and the formation of the Liberal Alliance, bringing together the governors of Rio Grande do Sul, Minas Gerais, and Paraíba. The congressman from Paraíba prophesied imminent and fatal revolutions against the existing government; he whispered that Siqueira Campos, Carlos Prestes, João Alberto, and Juarez Tavora were in the country, incognito and clandestinely, and were traveling all over Brazil, setting afoot an armed movement.

The senator laughed at such rumors. The country was calm and satisfied, supporting the works program laid out by the eminent Dr. Washington Luiz, which would be continued by his successor, the no less eminent Paulista, Dr. Júlio Prestes. All that agitation was nothing but a tempest in a teapot; it went no further than high-pressure oratory by gaucho orators like João Neves, Batista Luzardo, Oswaldo Aranha. As for the army group, those fly-by-night revolutionists, in the event that they should cross the frontier, come out of their exile on the Plate River, they would be ruthlessly hunted down by the police, tossed into jail. The captain leaned to the right, listening respectfully to the official line of the senator.

"Police . . . jail . . . My dear Senator, do not deceive yourself," answered the congressman. "Your police is no good. Perhaps you had not heard that just the other day Siqueira Campos was seen in São Paulo. The police were fit to be tied; they threw a cordon around the whole block. And while they were doing this he came out of the editorial office of the *Estado de São Paulo*, accompanied by Dr. Júlio de Mesquita, disguised as a priest. He walked right past the police . . . Everybody knows about that."

"Just talk . . . I don't believe a word of it. Those popinjays are in Buenos Aires, quarreling among themselves. They are afraid to set foot in Brazil. They keep sending messages begging for amnesty. Young men without good sense, their heads turned. Which is nothing to be surprised at when even someone like Artur Bernardes fancies himself as a revolutionist. They don't dare . . ."

"They don't dare? With the frontier right there in Rio Grande do Sul?"

"Getúlio Vargas is not crazy; he's not going to get mixed up with those lunatics. And do you think they're going to start a movement to put Getúlio in Catete? If they had any chance of winning, it would not be Getúlio who would become president. It would be Isidoro or Prestes. Don't you agree with me, Captain?"

Vasco preferred not to think, and, above all, not to look at the soup, a nauseating white creamy mess, totally unsuited to the state of the sea that night. He would have to call the chief steward's attention to the matter so such carelessness would not occur again. The ship's menu should always take atmospheric conditions into account. He pushed aside the plate, made a vague gesture of assent to the senator's remark, giving up hope that the lady with the dog might come after all. The congressman went on with what he had been saying after cleaning up—the poor fool!—his plate of soup.

"All right, you go on not believing, stay hitched to the wagon of that pigheaded Washington, and when you come to your senses, it will be too late, the fire will be blazing right under your feet. On my last trip to the north, on an *Ita* just like this, do you know who was on board and got off in Recife? João Alberto, yes, sir. I can tell you, for he is no longer there, I know that for a fact. He was traveling as a salesman for a firm in Rio, but I recognized him at once. All these seafaring people"—and he pointed to the captain—"are with us, with the revolution. They transport the conspirators hidden in their cabins. Moreover, the whole country is with them. Isn't that the truth, Captain?"

A pure, revolting affront, the next course: a slice of fish floating in a tomato and shrimp sauce, accompanied by mashed potatoes in which yellow streaks of butter could be seen. One look at that horror was enough to make the stomach turn over. The captain, to avoid the stare and the dangerous question of the congressman, made a desperate effort and carried a forkful to his bitter mouth. That congressman of Paraíba was, clearly, a scatterbrain, talking about revolutionists and conspiracies and all the while wolfing down pieces of fish, shrimps, the greasy potatoes. Rarely had human nature sunk so low, thought the captain as he viewed that loathsome sight. Indicating with a smack of his lips the excellent quality of the fish, the congressman kept harping on his annoying theme.

"Who knows but what Prestes or Siqueira are right here, on this ship, hidden in the cabin of the doctor or the engineer. Or in that of our brave captain, why not?"

The senator shuddered. In spite of his outward serenity and his faith in the strength of the government, those rumors disturbed him. Hadn't the police themselves told him that Juarez Tavora had passed through Natal shortly before? Plotting with young lieutenants like Juracy Magalhães and agitators like Café Filho? Didn't he know that they had met in the vicinity of the palace? The police only picked up the revolutionist's trail when he had left for Paraíba, where it was public knowledge that the house of José Americo de Almeida was a center of conspiracy. Why didn't that Zé Americo stick to his novel writing? Maybe the congressman was right, and one of those fanatical disturbers of the public order might be aboard the ship. He cast a suspicious eye at the captain, and noticed a strange look on his face.

The congressman, a real alarmist, went on: "One of these days an *Ita* will tie up in Natal, looking completely innocent, and instead of passengers it will discharge a levy of revolutionists. They will march on the State House, bang, bang, bang ... Don't fool yourself, all these people of the Coastwise Line are with the lieutenants. Isn't that so, Captain?"

"I don't belong on the Coastwise roster. I was always in overseas navigation until I retired. I am here because of the unfortunate..."

"Ah, that's right. I had forgotten. It was you who saved the situation. Otherwise, we would have had to lay over until a captain arrived from Rio. Yes, sir, very good! Not that I would mind spending a few days in Bahía. I am not in a hurry like the senator, who needs to get to Natal as soon as he can. I have time and I like Bahía. A nice place, only the Liberal Alliance is weak there, with Vital Soares as candidate for the vice-presidency. But to make up for that, the women are real knockouts."

With an effort, the captain smiled his agreement. The senator, delighted at the new turn the conversation was taking, getting away from the revolutionists who were spoiling his dinner, took advantage of the opening the captain had given them: "Overseas navigation, Captain? Then you must have seen many countries."

"Practically the whole world. I sailed under various flags."

"A nice profession, but isn't it a little monotonous? Days and days at sea, especially on long trips..." mused the senator.

"But you must run into some real babes from time to time. What about it, Captain?" The congressman was giving up the conspirators for women.

The roast chicken looked appetizing. Vasco had eaten hardly anything but bread up to that moment. The trouble was it was hard to cut the chicken with the ship pitching and rolling, and it wouldn't look well for him to eat it with his fingers.

"A captain on duty is a hermit."

"Now, Captain, don't try to give me that..."

"But in port he makes up for it."

"In all those countries you visited, where did you find the best women, the hottest numbers?"

It was not the moment for a conversation of that sort. The chicken was threatening to jump out of his plate, and demanded all his attention and care. Vasco gave up.

"It's hard to say. That depends..."

"Come now, who doesn't know that the English are cold, the French are interested in nothing but money, the Spanish are very passionate. Even I who've not yet been out of Brazil..."

"Yes, it's true, there are differences. In my opinion, the most ardent of all"—he paused and lowered his voice, the senator and congressman leaned over, the better to hear his revelation—"the best of all are the Arabian."

"Passionate?" whispered the senator.

"Regular bonfires!"

"When I was a lad, there was a Turkish woman who kept open house in Campina Grande. What a dish! But you had to pay through the nose. She was not for the mouths of babes, but only for the rich planters," the congressman reminisced.

The fruit salad, with its sweet syrup, almost triggered a catastrophe. The captain had no more than swallowed the first spoonful than it took all his will power to keep it down. There was a commotion in his entrails, a kind of dislike of living, a misanthropy. Fortunately the charming lady had not come to the dining room. He would not have been able to talk with her. Nothing appealed to him; all he wanted was for dinner to come to an end.

"You didn't eat much, Captain," observed the congressman, who had gorged himself.

"I am not feeling too well. Some green hog plums I ate upset me. I don't want to overdo it."

"Can you imagine, I wondered if you might be seasick. Did you ever hear of anything so absurd as a captain being seasick!"

The three of them laughed at the foolish, impossible notion. Vasco decided not to risk the coffee. He waited, controlling himself, until they had all finished, to get up and bring the meal to an end.

The congressman tried to detain him on deck: "Captain, what would you do if you should discover one of those revolutionists hidden in your cabin? Would you hand him over to the police or keep mum about it?"

What would he do? How the hell should he know what he would do in a case like that? He had had nothing to do with politics since the end of José Marcelino's term of office, and the assassination of Dom Carlos I of Portugal and the Algarves. He did not want to hear about revolutionists and revolutions; to hell with Washington, Júlio Prestes, Getúlio. Nothing was going to interfere with his getting to his cabin as quickly as he could. Not even the smiling lady with the dog, if she should show up. He wanted to be alone, with his head resting on a pillow.

"Excuse me, Doctor. I have to take my post on the bridge. I want to see how we're doing."

"You go and then come back, so we can have a chat. I'll be in the library."

Vasco rushed up the stairs. The rain was lashing the quarter-deck. A figure crossed his path as he was making his way to his cabin.

"Good evening, Captain." It was the ship's doctor, smoking a Bahian cigar.

"Are you going up to the bridge to have a pipe? Wouldn't you rather have a cigar?"

He pulled a foul-smelling black one out of his coat pocket.

"Thank you, but I smoke nothing but a pipe..."

"And you are a native-born Bahian?"

"Yes, I am."

"And you don't like cigars? That's a crime," he laughed.

"It's a question of habit. If you will excuse me, I'm going to try to get a little rest."

"You've probably had a hard day."

"Good night, then."

The wind blew the pestilential smoke of the cigar in his nostrils; a higher sea than any that had gone before hit the boat. Vasco rushed toward his cabin. Fortunately, the doctor was going below, for he did not have time to reach the sanctuary of his stateroom. Right there he leaned over the rail, his honor and his life gushing out of him. He had the feeling that his last hour had come; he felt dirty, humiliated, nothing but a rag. He looked timidly around him. Nobody was near. He made it to his cabin, locked the door behind him, and threw himself into his berth, without strength to take off his clothes.

*Of the* Ita *sailing in the sun, a chapter
that is almost folkloric, to be read to
the musical accompaniment of "I Took
An* Ita *Up North" by Dorival Caymmi*

A SUN like that of the Second of July dawned, so brilliant and
warm, with not a cloud in the sky, the sea like a sheet of
burnished steel cut by the haughty prow of the proud *Ita*. When
the captain came out of his bath and found his morning coffee
being served in his cabin, and a solicitous steward smiling at
him, his head came up again, and he drew in the sea air as he had
done in the days of his travels on the Asian and Australian sea
lanes. He put on a white uniform, humming the melody of that
song of the dancer Soraya, which had to do with the sea and
sailors.

Lounges, decks, and corridors were filling up with the
passengers typical of those *Itas*—the *Itabira, Itajiba, Itambe*—
which for so many, many years had been plying up and down the
Brazilian coast from Porto Alegre to Belém do Pará. Before
airplanes were darting across the skies, reducing distance,
shortening time, and stripping travel of all its poetry and charm.
When time was slower and better employed, less effort was put
into the sterile impatience of getting places as soon as possible,
into the urge to live quickly that turns life into a drab adventure
without color or savor, a race, a welter, a mortal weariness.

There were three types of *Ita:* large, medium, and small. They varied somewhat in comfort and speed, but were all equally gay, clean, and pleasant. The trip was a delight; one met people, made friends, flirtations and courtships sprang up, there was no better way for newlyweds to spend their honeymoon; the days aboard ship were a festival.

The large *Itas* called only at the important cities, at the ports of Salvador da Bahía, Recife, Natal, Fortaleza, Belém on the trip north from Rio. The medium ships included Vitória, Maceió, São Luis on their itinerary. The small ones drew out the trip, stopping also at Ilhéus, Aracaju, Cabedelo, Parnaíba, letting off and taking on passengers. The one that had been put under command of Master Mariner Captain Vasco Moscoso de Aragão was one of the largest.

There milled about on it the restless, cheerful humanity typical of the *Itas:* politicians going home to mend their political fences or returning from a quick trip to Rio. That year of presidential elections they kept coming and going, in a feverish activity of hopes and ambitions. Businessmen and manufacturers, returning with the family from a trip to the capital of the Republic, combining business and pleasure. Young ladies and women on their way home from a visit to relatives in Rio or São Paulo; hordes of students returning from the classic trip to the south in the middle of their graduating year, and recalling, with bursts of laughter, details of their sprees, the cabarets, the excursions, the women, sometimes even the scenery. Persons recuperating from an operation who had gone to Rio to find hospital facilities that were unavailable in their own states, and the knowledge and services of doctors of nationwide reputation and exorbitant fees. Old maids hoping that a suitor might emerge from the waves; priests on holiday; friars who were going out to preach the gospel in the jungle; writers from the capital on their way to the northern market with suitcases full of lectures and sonnets; tellers of the Bank of Brazil who had been transferred, and were going to see what their new destination was like. Professional gamblers, taking a different ship each time, changing from an *Ita* to an *Ara*, from an *Ara* to a *Lloyd Brasileiro*, out to fleece the cacao, cotton, *babaçu* palm planters, on their way home from their first and unforgettable visit to Pão de Açucar, Corcovado, Copacabana and Botofogo, the Assyrian, a cabaret in the basement of the Municipal Theater, the Mangue. Traveling salesmen of big firms, with their repertory of stories. And the inspiring presence of prostitutes, relegated as a rule to second class, with their eyes, too, on the planters and businessmen, often showing up in the early morning on the various first-class decks.

It was aboard these *Itas* that there descended from the north and northeast politicians and executives, poets and novelists, the dauntless, impoverished "flatheads"—facing life's outrages with bared breast and indomitable resistance, imagination, and will power, endowed with the gift of impromptu invention and the power of creation, born in an arid land scourged by drought or in the gullies of gigantic rivers swept by devastating floods—the people of Paraná and Bahía, of Pernambuco and Ceará, Alagoas, Maranhão, Sergipe, Piauí, the "pumpkin-eaters" of Rio Grande do Norte. All those who became the theme of folk music in the voice of the poet and bard of the charms of Bahía, along with all the *Itas:*

> *Up north I took on Ita*
> *To come to Rio to live.*
> *Farewell, mother and father,*
> *Farewell, Belém do Pará.*

Those who were returning now, under the command and in the care of Vasco, were the same ones who had embarked years before, on some other *Ita*, seeking in the south fortune, success, power, or just some way of making a living.

Captain Vasco Moscoso de Aragão made his way among them in his impeccable white uniform. He had been up on the bridge, where the navigation officer had informed him that everything was in order, the voyage was proceeding normally, without incident, that they would be docking in Recife the next morning, and would be sailing at five in the afternoon, if this met with his approval.

"As I said, I don't want to make any change, or issue orders when everything is in such capable hands. I'm going to take a stroll."

"Very good, Captain. Your presence will please the passengers, they love to talk with the captain, ask questions about the trip."

He moved about, handing out pleasant "Good mornings" and smiles. He patted the head of a child who was running about on the afterdeck. He lighted his pipe; if the weather stayed like this, the trip would be the reward of a lifetime. Several persons were stretched out in deck chairs. Boys and girls, in noisy animation, were playing games of shuffleboard, ping-pong, and deck tennis.

Poker games were being organized in the lounge. The captain looked about the room and saw only one familiar face, that of the senator. He walked over to where he was sitting.

"Oh, good morning, Captain. How's the trip going? Do you know yet when we'll be reaching Recife?"

"We'll make port by daybreak, God willing. And we'll sail at five in the afternoon."

"That will give me time to have lunch with the governor, and discuss some political problems with him. He lends me an attentive ear; in fact, all the governors of the northeast listen to what I have to say and ask my advice. They know the regard Dr. Washington has for me."

"It is an honor for me to have you aboard, Senator," replied the captain, taking the chair beside the legislator. "An honor and a pleasure."

"Thank you. The one who's getting off in Recife is Othon."

"Who is he?"

"The congressman who was seated at your left. A bright chap, but completely misguided. All tangled up with the Liberal Alliance. He and a group of others are dragging Paríba into that mess—a small state, which depends on the presidency for everything, can you imagine? And, as he knows that they are going to lose the elections, he invents *coup d'états* and revolutions."

"I must confess that I was a little worried yesterday with that talk about plotters aboard."

"A lad with a future that he's ruining. He drinks heavily, too, and he can't see a skirt go by... Since early this morning, he's been hanging around those actors..."

"Which actors?"

"They got on in Rio. A third-rate company which is going to perform in Recife. A small group, four women and four men. The women were not in the dining saloon yesterday. That's why you didn't notice them." Then, pursing his lips: "There they are with Othon. I ask you if that is any way for a congressman to behave—messing around with actresses in plain sight of everyone."

The captain followed his glance. Three girls, two of them wearing slacks, something that was practically unheard of in those days, and the third in a thin, billowy dress, formed a circle around the congressman.

"Where's the fourth?"

"She's an old dame who plays the part of servant. She must be somewhere around, crocheting. She spends the day with the needle in her hand."

Othon had spotted them. The congressman waved, and came toward them, accompanied by the actresses.

"Come over and meet our new captain."

The senator nodded, without getting up from his chair. He did not like to be seen in public, associating with theatrical folk. Vasco stood up and bowed over the girls' hands.

"This is a great pleasure, Captain," smiled the dark one with the curvaceous bosom, who was standing beside Othon.

"Tell me something, Mr. Captain. Is this brute of a ship going to keep rolling the way it did yesterday? I've never been more miserable in my life. It's my first sea trip," said the slender blonde with big eyes.

"I promise perfect weather until the end of the trip. I shall order a sea of roses for you." Not for nothing had the captain spent his time at the dances in the State House and the Pension Monte Carlo, or crossed the seas in command of ocean liners, carrying passengers from Naples and Genoa to the Orient. He knew how to behave with beautiful and charming women.

"The captain is a darling," said the third, with curly hair and dimples.

"Othon . . . Dr. Othon told us that you had traveled all over the world. That you had been awarded medals. Is that true?"

"I've done a good bit of traveling. For forty years."

"Were you ever in Holland?" inquired the one with the dimples, whose name was Regina.

"Yes, ma'am."

"Did you ever meet a family there by the name of Van Fries? They lived—wait a minute, let me see if I can remember—in Sasvangent, something like that."

"Van Fries? I don't seem to recall them. Most of my dealings were with shipowners and people connected with shipping. Were they, by chance, in that line of business?"

"I don't believe so. Theun told me they raised tulips."

"And who was this Theun who raised tulips?" asked the congressman, whose hand was resting familiarly on the girl's arm.

"Someone she was crazy about," explained the thin blonde.

The bosomy dark girl cast a languishing glance at Othon: "A person falls in love, and afterwards suffers for it."

The senator got to his feet. The deck was filling up, and he did not want to be seen taking part in that unseemly conversation.

Regina went on: "He was the prettiest man I ever saw in my life. I was wild about him. He looked a little like you, Captain, only taller..."

"You see, Captain," the congressman laughed, "You're making a conquest..."

"...and younger, of course."

"What can an old man like me expect?"

"Oh, don't take it that way, Captain, I didn't mean to offend you. You're not old. You're still strong and nice-looking."

"The captain could still give a woman a run for her money," added the thin one, who was following the senator out of the lounge with her eyes.

"What did I say, Captain? You're a real heartbreaker," and Othon's fingers slipped down the brunette's rounded thigh. She took his hand and pushed it away, looking around them.

The girls laughed, happy with the morning sun and the calm sea.

"When are you opening in Recife?" asked Vasco.

"Tomorrow night, at the Santa Isabel."

"What a pity I won't be able to take in the show. I'll go to see you on the way back if the ship spends the night in port. I'd like to applaud you."

The barking of a dog cut short the phrase. He looked around and saw the pretty lady, wearing a low-necked, short-sleeved dress, with a scarf tied around her hair, affectionately scolding the Pekinese.

"You'd think she was sweet sixteen, from the way she dresses," remarked the brunette.

"She never lets go of the dog. I never saw such affection; you'd think it was a child."

"It's more than a child," said the congressman.

"What is it, then?" asked the one with the dimples.

"I'll whisper it in your ear."

"In mine," said the brunette.

Othon whispered something, with his mouth close to her ear. She covered up her laugh with her hand, shocked: "How awful! What an impossible man!"

"What did he say? Tell me."

Vasco bowed to the lady with the Pekinese who was the butt of the conversation between the actresses and the congressman. She smiled in return, but then took in the group around the captain, and quickly turned her back. Vasco became worried, he wanted to help her open her deck chair. The blonde was asking him: "Do you think so, too?"

"What's that, Miss?"

"What Dr. Othon is saying."

"I don't know what he's saying. Please excuse me."

He walked quickly away, going over to the lady and taking from her the chair, which she could not manage to open with one hand, the other being taken up by the Pekinese.

"Allow me, madame."

She thanked him.

"So much bother. I am very much obliged."

"Believe me, it is a pleasure. But do sit down."

She sat down, put the dog in her lap, and he bared his teeth at the captain, snarling. Vasco leaned against the rail across from her.

"Quiet, Jasmim. You must show respect for the captain. He acts like that with everybody at first. He's jealous of me. Afterwards, he gets used to them."

Then, in a bantering voice with an edge on it, she said: "Your friends miss you, Captain. See how they are watching us and talking about us."

The captain looked over at the actresses and the congressman, who were laughing. The thin one winked at him.

"They are not friends of mine. I have just been introduced to them."

"They say they are actresses. Third rate, no doubt. They look more like streetwalkers. This has been going on ever since we left Rio, the men buzzing around them like flies. It's a scandal. That Dr. Othon never leaves them for a minute. You'd think there was nobody else on board."

"That's not possible, madame. You must be exaggerating. With you aboard, how can anybody have eyes for another woman?"

"Good Heavens, Captain, you embarrass me."

"Are you getting off in Recife, too?"

"I'm going on to Belém. I live there," and she gave a sigh.

The captain had already looked at her hand and had seen that she did not wear a wedding ring.

"Have you been to Rio on a pleasure trip?"

"I was visiting my sister there. Her husband is an engineer in the Ministry of Aviation."

"Wouldn't you like to live there?"

"It's not possible. The house is full, she has five children. I live with my brother in Belém. He is married, too, but he has only two children."

"And madame . . . ?"

"I?" and she turned her head away, her eyes lost on the horizon. "I never wanted to marry."

A brief silence followed. Vasco felt that he had been tactless, perhaps rude. She remained pensive and melancholy.

"Does your family live in Bahía?" she finally asked.

"I have no family."

"A widower?"

"A bachelor. I never had time to get married, with this life at sea, always aboard ship."

"And you never thought of getting married? Never?"

The Captain held his pipe in his hand while his gaze, too, lost itself in the limitless sky.

"I never had time . . ."

"And was that the only reason? Only because of that?" The lady gave vent to another sigh, as though to make it clear that hers was a graver, more painful reason.

The captain sighed in turn.

"Why recall the past?"

"You, too?" She sighed anew. "It is a sad world."

"Sad for the one who is alone," he answered.

The guffaws and wisecracks of the group gathered around the actresses grew louder. The deck was filling up, the chairs were all occupied. A pair of newlyweds went by, holding hands. The Pekinese yapped at them. The lady declared: "I don't trust men. They are all hypocrites."

She was a piano teacher and her name was Clotilde.

## Of the captain commanding, the lady sighing, the dancer dancing, and the ship sailing on a sea of roses and maidens

THE PROSTITUTES were lolling on the lower deck, doing their nails, reading *Silent Stage* and *CineArt*, combing their hair, basking in the sun like lizards. The students came down from first class, gathered around the women, and wound up engaging them in conversation, fraternizing with them. One of them played the guitar, and he accompanied one of the girls in a popular tune of the day referring to the elections:

> *Oh, Mr. Tonico,*[1]
> *From the land of rich milk,*
> *Better watch your step,*
> *For the Paulista*[2] *is a tough guy.*
> *He reaches for his gun,*
> *Stands steady in the road,*
> *And with all this fooling around*
> *The milk will turn to clabber.*

The captain's glance swept the second-class deck from the bridge. He ought to go down there, chat with those people, who were his passengers, too. He was reluctant to confess to himself his longing to join the pleasant company of the ladies of light

---

1. Antonio Carlos de Andrade, governor of Minas Gerais.
2. Júlio Prestes.

virtue. He had warm memories of them from his early years in the brothels and sporting houses of Bahía, and his adventures in out-of-the-way ports of the Pacific. He knew how to talk to them; conversation with them was no effort. He did not have to weigh his words, as in the case of the first-class passengers, young ladies and women of standing, some of them stuck-up. He came to the conclusion that a ship is a small world where everything is to be found, from the rich and powerful, the politicians and the bankers, to those poor women whose capital was their charm, whose tools were their seductiveness and their bodies. And he was the absolute ruler of that world, the captain, the highest authority on board, whose word was law, whose power was indisputable.

That very morning, when he went up to the bridge before lunch, he had ventured to voice a criticism to the chief steward on the subject of the dinner the night before. If the chief steward would excuse him, that soup, that fish were not dishes to be served when the sea was cutting up. The big foreign liners paid great attention to such details. The chief mate, who was standing by, gave the captain his full support, with an insistence and emphasis that seemed somewhat exaggerated for such a trifling matter.

"You are absolutely right, Captain. It was a deplorable oversight, and should not happen again. It's what I always say: the most important thing about a ship is a captain who knows his business."

"It's not that I want to interfere. But the senator, for example, hardly touched his meal."

The chief steward was listening with a frown, but in view of the firm attitude of the chief mate, he shifted ground, reefed in his sails, and apologized.

"The fact is, Captain, that I forgot to consult the weather bureau before making out the menu. It won't happen again. But, from now on, the best thing will be for me to submit the bill of fare to you for your approval."

"Yes, that would be best," said the chief mate.

"No, gentlemen, that is not necessary. Not at all. I repeat, I do not want to interfere in anything. I am here only to..."

"You are the captain."

He liked that—above all, the irreproachable attitude of the chief mate. An agreeable young chap, that Geir Matos. He would recommend him to the Coastwise Line when he turned in his report.

In those few hours of sailing and association, his popularity among the passengers was established. He talked with this one and that one, informed them of the speed they were making—thirteen miles an hour, nautical miles, naturally—the hour of their arrival in Recife, their departure, and he showed a becoming modesty when they alluded to his feats of seamanship and asked the reason why he had been awarded the decoration. Modest, but without having to be coaxed.

So, in the afternoon, he found himself surrounded in the lounge by a great group waiting to swallow the entertaining account of his adventures. He told them first about a storm in the Bay of Bengal on a freighter of English registry whose crew was made up almost entirely of Lascars. They were enroute from Calcutta to Akyab, skirting the coast of Burma. That was always a dangerous route, whipped by the monsoons, with treacherous currents. Yet, in the many times he had sailed those perilous waters, he had never seen the elements in such fury. Some of the elderly women dropped their knitting or crochet, carried away by the emotion of his tale. How could they keep their attention on their work when the captain was inching his way along the deck, risking his life, in danger of being swept overboard by the mountainous waves, to pull out from beneath the spar of the mast, shivered by a bolt of lightning, the skeleton-thin Indian sailor, with his legs and ribs broken?

The navigation officer stopped to listen to him in respectful silence. He stood leaning against a door, smoking a cigarette; the captain did not even see him, so absorbed was he in his story. The chief engineer was walking by outside, and the navigation officer motioned to him. The two stood there, listening.

When, toward the end of the afternoon, the captain returned to the bridge, he surprised the navigation officer commenting on his adventures with the chief mate, the other officers, and the doctor. He caught only a scrap of a phrase: ". . . he went crawling along the deck like a snake . . ."

The men fell silent when they saw him, and the chief mate spoke up: "Very good, Captain. We were listening to your exploits. One of these nights we'll open up a bottle and have you tell us those glorious tales. We spend our lives sailing up and down this coast, where nothing ever happens. You, sir," he said, pointing a finger at him, "will have to tell us about your voyages, without omitting a detail."

"Mere trifles, not worth repeating. They'll do to entertain the passengers. But for you gentlemen, seamen yourselves . . ."

"We won't let you off so easily, Captain. We insist upon it."

He stood there looking at the prostitutes on the lower deck. The pleasant voice of the mulatto girl floated up to the bridge in the political tune:

> *Mr. Julinho is coming,*
> *Mr. Julinho is coming,*
> *If the man from Minas*
> *Doesn't watch his step,*
> *Mr. Julinho is coming,*
> *Mr. Julinho is coming,*
> *Is coming, but plenty of people*
> *Are going to be crying.*

He tacked about past second class, and went on down to third. There were the passengers returning to the northeast in the same dramatic state of poverty in which they had fled, during the years of drought, to the highly touted lands of the south where there were jobs and money. The hope of bettering their fortunes had one day led those men and women to tramp the trails through the stunted forests, crossing the backlands, the mighty rivers, and the vast plains, bound for São Paulo. Now all they had was the desire to return to their native land, arid and poor, but their own, where they had been born and where they wanted to die. It was a depressing sight and the captain returned to the sentimental melodies and sambas of the second class.

The ladies of light virtue, when they saw him approaching, pulled themselves together, sitting more properly, pulling their dresses down over their knees, and nudging away the students. The mulatto girl stopped singing, and only the guitar kept up its twanging. The singer had a pretty voice, the captain did not want to spoil anybody's fun.

"At ease, everybody. Why did that girl over there stop singing? Please go on, I was enjoying it."

"The captain is a good guy," laughed one of the women, who was getting on in years.

"A good comrade," one of the students spoke up. "The evening before we reach Fortaleza, we're going to serenade him."

"Thank you very much, my friend."

But the girls did not lay aside their air of forced propriety, and the mulatto did not resume her singing. What a pity, thought Vaşco, withdrawing from the group.

In first class, the passengers were beginning to show up after their evening bath—sport shirts and drill pants, cotton dresses replaced by cashmere suits and dinner frocks. He, too, would have to change his uniform, putting on dress blue with his decoration.

But he put this off for a few minutes. For, perfumed, her hair curled to a degree of perfection that must surely have taken up the better part of the afternoon, in a stunning dress, with a silk shawl in her hand, the eyes of a person suffering from a secret sorrow, and without the Pekinese (an encouraging note), Clotilde came gliding along the deck. The captain's heart began to throb. She had already seen him and waved a greeting that was at the same time a summons. He came over to her side.

"A goddess of the sea..."

"Oh, Captain," and she covered her eyes with her shawl, then let it fall and asked in a coy voice: "Wouldn't you like to take a few turns around the deck to work up an appetite?"

"I'd like nothing better. However, I'll have to change to be worthy of your elegance at dinner. But if you'll just wait for me, I'll meet you in a few minutes in the lounge."

"I'll wait, but don't be long, you flatterer."

When he returned, the out-of-tune piano in the lounge was giving all it had to an aria from *La Bohème*. Vasco had a respectful but not a warm admiration for classical music, no real liking. Once, at Colonel Pedro de Alencar's insistence, he had attended an opera brought to the São João Theater by a down-at-the-heels Italian company that had wandered into Bahía at the end of a sorry trip through the opera houses of Latin America. The colonel adored opera; he had a gramophone and a collection of records of arias sung by Caruso. He persuaded Vasco that this was a unique opportunity fate had brought his way to hear baritones and tenors, a marvelous soprano and a no less marvelous contralto in a performance of *La Bohème*, with scenery and everything. He decided to go, disregarding the repeated warnings of Jerónimo and Georges, because it gave him a chance to display his full-dress uniform and the Order of Christ. It turned out to be the worst kind of a bore, real torture, for he was sweating like a butcher. The soprano must have weighed at least 250 pounds, but to make up for it the tenor was as thin as a matchstick. Vasco felt like laughing when the voluminous cackler asked:

*Mi chiamano Mimi*
*Ma perché?*
*Non so.*
*Il mio nome é Lucia.*

Colonel Pedro de Alencar was enjoying himself thoroughly; he knew part of the opera by heart. Stifling with the heat, Vasco cursed the vanity that had made him accept the invitation just to show off his uniform and decoration. When the soprano, with health and pounds to give away, fell, fragile and consumptive, into the arms of the scrawny tenor, who, it was plain, could not hold her up, Vasco burst out laughing, to the great indignation of the colonel, who called him an ignorant ass. Ever since, he had put a respectful distance between himself and what he called "learned" music, undoubtedly worthy of all admiration but too superior for him, beyond his capacity. He now recognized, in the selection coming from the piano, one of those arias which brought back unpleasant memories. If he did not beat a retreat, it was because Clotilde was waiting for him to take a turn around the deck before dinner in her taffeta dress, her hair in coils over her ears, and a world of hope in her swooning voice. He tried to avoid entering the lounge, fearing that protocol would oblige him, as captain, to remain there for a while admiring the pianist. He looked toward the window, turning his back on the corner of the lounge where the piano stood, to avoid a compromising exchange of glances with the performer. Clotilde was not in the lounge. he did not see her. Where could she have gone? The virtuoso seemed to have taken on new impetus, the music grew louder. Where could the lovely lady have got to? He risked a glance in the direction of the piano, and Clotilde smiled at him without lifting her hands from the keyboard, her head bent over, her eyes in ecstasy, the rolls of her hair rising and falling in time to the music. She was a piano teacher, she had told him during their talk that morning, but modesty, known to be the mother of all virtues, had led her to keep silent about her abilities, her artistic gifts, her rank as a pianist capable of playing classical music. He had thought of her as a simple teacher with a beat-up piano, teaching the rudiments of the instrument to young ladies looking for a husband, just enough so they could murder marches, sambas, a fox trot or, at most, a waltz. Nor had he conceived of her going beyond playing dance music at parties in the houses of her friends where there was no orchestra. And there she was, tossing her head, undoing the curls that had taken so much time and work, rolling her eyes as she attacked opera, a real artist. It filled him with pride. He entered the lounge just in time to join the other listeners in the room in a salvo of applause to her gifts as a pianist and, perhaps, to the lowering of the piano lid, signifying that the concert was over.

The captain, bearing down on the applauded and modest performer, who was covering her face with the shawl, held out his hands to her: "But, how beautiful. Such sonority, such perfect execution. What a divine moment!"

"Do you like classical music?"

"Do I like it ... I have a collection of records that I may say without vanity is one of the largest in Bahía and perhaps in all Brazil."

"What about opera?"

"I adore it. Before I retired, whenever I arrived in any port, the first thing I asked was whether there was an opera house ..."

During all this dialogue he had been holding her hands. She suddenly became aware of this, and withdrew them, with a little nervous twitch, a syncopated laugh. He stood, slightly ill at ease, not knowing what to do with his hands, and it was she who picked up the thread of the conversation.

"I never saw a piano as badly out of tune as this one on your ship."

"Is it that bad?"

"Terrible. It's no pleasure to play it."

"I am going to take the necessary measures. I shall send for a tuner in Recife. And now, what about our walk?"

But there was no time. The dinner gong sounded. They walked toward the dining room, discussing *La Bohème*. She was wild about Puccini. He insisted that his admiration and enthusiasm matched hers.

Their stroll about the deck took place after dinner, before the bingo game began in the lounge. They walked with measured step, she playing with her shawl, he puffing on his pipe, talking of Rio, which she adored, of Bahía, which, according to him, was a nice city to live in, of Belém do Pará, where it rained every day at the same hour. From time to time some passenger interrupted them, to greet the captain, or ask him a question. They spoke of Recife, whose aquatic setting had enchanted her on the trip down. Unfortunately, she could not see much of the Pernambucan capital, for it was raining cats and dogs, nor did she have anyone to show her the sights. Tomorrow it would be different, she said with a smile; she would have the captain at her disposal to take her to the bridges and beaches, the avenues and parks.

"The trouble is that I don't know Recife, either."

"What do you mean, you don't know Recife! As ship's captain, you must have gone through it dozens of times."

"That's exactly the point: I've gone through it. But never stopping long enough to really know it, as I wish I did, so I could serve you as guide. When I say I don't know it, what I mean is that I know it superficially. And it's been some years since I was last there. There have been big changes since then."

"Apparently you don't want to accompany me. Perhaps you have a sweetheart there, and you don't want to be seen with me," and she laughed her sharp, nervous laugh again.

The captain stopped and took her by the arm: "Please don't say that. Those days are long since over for me, ever since I retired. I even thought I'd never again look at another woman, but now..."

"What is it?"

A passenger had stopped beside them to inform them: "The bingo game is going to begin. They are only waiting for you, sir."

The lady sighed, Vasco's fingers clasped her arm for a moment, and they proceeded to the lounge. She walked with her eyes fixed on the starry sky and the green water, idly waving her shawl. He had heard the words of the inopportune passenger, but without taking in their meaning, overwhelmed by the perfume that emanated from her, feeling the tremor of her body in the tips of his fingers. Just before they entered the lounge, he had her in his arms, for Clotilde, floating in a dream, had not noticed the drainpipe that crossed the deck, and the stumble threw her against the captain. He held her up and for a fraction of a minute, an eternity of emotion, her bosom was pressed against Vasco's breast, her curls against his cheek, and he even felt the warmth of her barren womb.

They sat down at the table with the senator, who had two bingo cards in front of him, and threw a disapproving glance at the next table, where Congressman Othon and the actresses were calling in loud voices for the game to begin. Sedate ladies, plainly showing their displeasure, turned their backs on the noisy, theatrical group. Children were clamoring for candy and bonbons. All the passengers were assembled in the lounge. A steward came over and the captain bought two cards, one for himself, the other for Clotilde.

"You'll help me find the numbers, won't you, Captain?"

The purser, sitting beside the piano with a bag of numbers, announced the prizes, five in all. The first, for the first person who filled a row crosswise, was a bottle of toilet water. At a sign from the purser, the steward held up the perfume. The next prize, for the first person who filled a row up and down, was a silver key ring, a beauty. The purser made humorous comments about the prizes, arousing laughter and asides from the spectators, while the steward held up the key ring for all to see. The next prize was an ash tray with the seal of the Coastwise Line and a picture of the *Ita* on which they were traveling engraved on it. This was the third prize. The fourth, to whose excellence the purser was calling people's attention, would be awarded for the first card that was completely filled. This was a piece of bric-a-brac in the shape of a china sofa, Louis XV, on which a pair of lovers sat with clasped hands, looking into each other's eyes. That sublime manifestation of petit-bourgeois taste drew "oh's" and "ah's" from men and women, young and old, the senator and Clotilde. All of them longed for it, and the steward, in view of the unanimous enthusiasm, carried it around from table to table, for everybody wanted to see it, beginning with the actresses.

Clotilde sighed: "Oh, if I were only lucky enough to win it."

The final prize, for a winning cross, was a surprise, something even more valuable and beautiful than the marvel just displayed. There it was, on top of the piano, wrapped in tissue paper. A large, square package, possibly a box, that aroused curiosity and comments. The purser asked for everybody's attention, for the game for the first prize was about to begin. He appealed to the children, "those cherubs," for a little quiet. He began to call out the numbers. The toilet water was won by a rancher wearing a goatee and a hop-sacking suit, who said, amidst the handclapping: "I'll take it to the missus back in Crato."

The silver key ring went to a girl about thirteen years old, on the basis of the highest score between her and two other players who had filled their rows at the same time. The ash tray went to the dark actress, who offered it to the congressman under the disapproving glances of certain families and the senator. And then came the exciting moment of the "bull's-eye," the first to fill his card receiving the prize of the sofa with the lovers, "that work of art, that thing of beauty, that *non plus ultra*," to use the words of the purser. There was a complete hush when the calling out of the numbers began.

Clotilde, whose sighs over every prize she failed to win caused the captain anguish, reached the peak of nervousness, got all mixed up with her card, and Vasco had to touch her arm every other minute, calling her attention to a number that had been called and that she had forgotten to cover.

Suddenly she exulted: "I have only one space left to fill."

But no sooner had she said it than a man sitting near the piano called out: "Bingo!"

He was a sportily dressed customer, very talkative, who said he was a capitalist on vacation, taking that trip to make the acquaintance of the cities and scenery of the north, something he had always dreamed of doing and was now carrying out. However, the scenery of the sea did not seem to interest him in the least, for he spent the day and night at the poker table, winning the planters' and businessmen's money. That very afternoon the captain had stopped by to watch the game, and he sensed that this made the man nervous, as though Vasco's presence spoiled his luck, jinxed him. He really did begin to lose, so the captain, who was well acquainted with the game and with players' crochets, tactfully withdrew.

Clotilde was so disappointed she was on the verge of tears: "Just because of one number . . . And I wanted that souvenir so badly . . ."

Vasco comforted her; if the sofa was meant for her, it would still be hers. She was not to be sad.

"But how can it, when that man won it? The hateful beast," and she tapped her heel on the floor, rolled up her eyes.

Vasco had an idea, but he kept it to himself. The purser began to call the numbers for the final prize, the surprise. It was won by the young bride, the one who was always hanging on her husband's arm, the two of them kissing and hugging in every corner of the ship, calling each other pet names, "my little shrimp," "my coconut bug," "my darling kitten," making themselves the butt of malicious smiles and comments. Everyone gathered around her and her husband, to watch her open the package, out of which came a box, and from the box another package, and from the package another box, and more packages and more boxes, until she finally reached a little package, which, when she opened it, held a pacifier. There was an ovation, laughs, wisecracks, the winner smiling in embarrassment, the husband ill at ease.

Dr. Othon spoke up: "Luck knew what it was doing."

And the bosomy brunette added in a low voice: "If they keep on the way they're going, she'll have at least twins."

Throughout the course of the bingo game, the captain had cherished the hope of going back on deck with Clotilde to continue their walk and conversation. He felt romantic and excited. He was about to suggest to her that they leave the lounge, alleging that it was getting warm, and offer her the sea breeze and the stars of the cloudless sky, when a group of young people came over to the table.

"Excuse us, Captain," and turning to Clotilde: "Would madame be kind enough to play something for us so we could dance?"

Clotilde assumed the air of a prima donna.

"I don't like to play dance music. I play only my favorites."

"Oh," pleaded a girl who might have been around eighteen, the flower of the dark beauties of Pernambuco, "it's the last day aboard, at least for me. We wanted to dance a little." A young chap standing beside her smiled at Clotilde, imploring her with his eyes.

"Please play a little, be nice," coaxed another girl, with bronzed skin, loose black hair, a half-breed Indian beauty, with eyes like a flame.

The boys and girls kept pleading, and all that youth, just beginning to live, so eager and so vulnerable, moved the captain and he gave up the stroll he had hoped for, and added his pleas to theirs: "Do play. I would so like to hear you."

"Well, in that case, just to please you, Captain."

She walked over to the piano, escorted by the gay group, adding: "Not for very long. Jasmim is waiting for me."

The first notes had barely sounded when the brunette from Pernambuco was already whirling in the arms of her athletic admirer, whom she had met on the trip, a case of love at first sight. He was on his way home to Fortaleza, where he worked in a bank. He had promised to come to see her in Recife at Christmas time.

The half-breed girl with the smoldering eyes turned to the captain, and made him an amusing bow: "Captain, may I have the honor of this quadrille?"

Vasco got up and took the girl's hand. He was an

accomplished dancer, known as a tripper of the light fantastic
from his days at the Pension Monte Carlo. His fame as a dancer
was still remembered by the sailors who had sailed with him to
the Middle and Far East, the Mediterranean and the North Sea.
There were two styles of dancing: "hot stuff," body against body,
cheek to cheek, the partners exciting one another by this warm
contact. That was the style of the Pension Monte Carlo, the
Yellow Dragon cabaret in Hong Kong, the mysterious
rathskeller, The Blue Nile, in Alexandria. And "society style,"
with the tips of the fingers barely touching the partner's back, a
handbreadth between them, the posture restrained, conversing
with the lady. This was the way they danced at the official
entertainments, at the receptions of the Four Hundred of Bahía,
at the dances on the ocean liners traveling between Europe and
Australia. It was thus he began the dance with the half-breed girl
whose pale beauty was so disturbing. Why did she remind him of
Dorothy when they did not look at all alike? But there was
something in common between the country girl of Feira de
Sant'Ana and that young lady of Belém: the tawny, restless eyes,
the barely contained desire, every gesture a spasm, even the
slightest, the same eagerness and avidity for love. They were, the
two of them, all woman.

And then he felt her against him, her thigh touching his, her
bosom heaving against his breast, her long black hair brushing
his cheek. The girl closed her eyes and bit her lower lip. Vasco
took fright. From the piano, Clotilde was watching them with a
scowl. He tried to put distance between himself and that
starving, maddened body, but she held him tight. He
understood, with a humility he had learned from Dorothy, that
it was not he, Vasco, sixty years old and white-haired, to whom
she clung and gave herself in the dance. It was merely to a man,
regardless of his age, color, refinement, or looks.

Fortunately, the music did not go on for long. Clotilde ended
the piece abruptly, and the couples separated.

Vasco bowed: "Thanks so much, Miss."

"You are a good dancer, Captain. It is I who should thank
you."

He went over to Clotilde at the piano. She remarked tartly:
"So that was why you asked me to play?"

There was no more stroll that night. When finally the young
people let her get up and leave, it was almost midnight, and
Clotilde was worried about her Pekinese, alone in the

stateroom. They arranged to visit Recife together the next day. She was still a little miffed, and called his dancing partner a slut.

Vasco went into the games room. Young fellows were playing "King," and three tables of poker were going. At one of them the *soi-disant* capitalist on a pleasure trip was in his glory, the piece of bric-a-brac he had won on a chair beside him. The other players were businessmen and planters. All three of them were losing. Vasco pulled over a chair, and sat down beside the lucky player.

"Will you allow me?"

"What a question, Captain! With pleasure," answered one of the planters.

"Do you know the game, Captain?" asked the winner.

"Not really. I don't understand it. But I like to watch. Who's winning?"

"Can't you see?" answered another of the losers. "Dr. Stenio. I never saw such luck. He's a born winner."

The aforesaid Dr. Stenio laughed with satisfaction, perhaps at the jest, perhaps because of the captain's confession of his ignorance of poker. Vasco sat on for a while, from time to time asking an idiotic question about the value of the cards and the bets. He watched Stenio deal with great interest.

"Where are you going ashore, Dr. Stenio?"

"In Belém. I'm going to stay there for a few days, and I may go on to Manaus on a Vaticano. I have my return passage on the *Almirante Jaceguay* of the Lloyd." And he answered the bet of one of the planters: "I'll match your 32 and raise you 64."

Around 1:30, one of the players whose losses ran to several contos de reis suggested that they call it a night. Vasco watched as the accounts were totted up, farewells said. One of the planters who was getting off in Recife lamented the fact that he was not going on so he could recoup his losses. Dr. Stenio put his winnings in his pocket, and was on the point of picking up his piece of bric-a-brac and turning in. The captain, however, after telling the other players good night, said to him: "It's still early. Let's have a little talk, Doctor..."

"I'm dead for sleep, Captain. Let's leave it for tomorrow."

"Today and right now. Listen, Mr. Cardsharper, you are not going to Belém. You're going to cut your trip short in Recife."

"But, Captain, what is the meaning of this?"

"Just what I said. Look, my dear fellow, I was born playing poker. I've followed the sea for forty years, and spent twenty of them in command of ships in Asia. I know the whole bag of tricks of shipboard professional gamblers. You get off quietly if you don't want to land in jail..."

"But I've paid my passage..."

"And a good investment it was. You got a fine return on your money. How about it?"

"If those are your orders..." He did not argue, that was one of the rules of the game of his life. He would wait for another ship to take him to Belém.

Vasco got up, picked up the piece of china, and started toward the door.

"Good night."

"But, Captain, excuse me, that thingamajig you're carrying away with you is mine."

"Yours? What?"

"That pretty knickknack. I won it at bingo by pure luck. Without any gypping."

"Without gypping. Could be. But that brings terrible luck at poker, as you've already seen. Better leave it with me."

The gambler left the room, cursing his luck. Why the devil, in a place of the dead captain, did they have to pick an old sea dog, a slyboots, who knew every trick of the cardsharper's trade? He shrugged his shoulders resignedly. He would take a fling at Recife. There were sugar-mill owners there loaded with sugar and crazy about poker. What he did regret was the pretty china sofa with the pair of lovers. He had wanted to take it to Daniela, his wife, as a present. For he was happily married, with four children, two boys and two girls, all of them as cute as bugs. He adored his family, no better husband or father existed.

The captain sighed, picked up the piece of bric-a-brac, and went out into the night air.

## Of the captain sunk in a revery and what he chanced to see in the shadow of a lifeboat

THE CAPTAIN was sunk in a deep revery in those daybreak hours on the deck. He put the china souvenir carefully down beside him; from time to time he tore his eyes away from the stars, which were like infinite pastures where dreams graze, and turned them toward the pair of lovers seated on the porcelain sofa. His whole life had been one of loneliness, a long-drawn-out waiting. On the sea, as he was at this moment, puffing his pipe, alone among the winds and St. Elmo's fire, from one port to another, changing ships and women. His home, a narrow bunk. The day of his last port of call never came, with the family waiting for him on the dock, his wife wasted with longing, his children eager to see the presents he had brought them from distant, exotic lands. He had never had a home of his own in any port; he rested his weary head on the hired pillow of brothels; his burning heart, on the breast of strange women. He was alone in the world, alone with his ship. Alone with his voyages.

And can a man live like that, always alone? The house of Barris was never a home since the death of his father and mother, figures now blurred in his memory. He had grown up in the office and the warehouse, among bales and bills of lading, dried beef and letters to the customers. The love affairs of all adolescents, the timid glance, the shy smile, the farewell waved from a distance, the momentary clasp of a hand, the kiss stolen in the shadow of a doorway, none of this had been his, neither in the office, nor at sea, where as cabin boy he eyed from a distance the beautiful, haughty passengers. When the death of his grandfather set him free, he was close to thirty, and the time for romantic sighs, sweet suffering, and maidens in bloom had passed him by. Alone even among his friends; and when he could really have been one of them, they had left one by one, as had the women who succeeded each other in his bed in the house of Barris. Some had stayed a while longer; Dorothy had left him her name and the heart tattooed on his arm. But they were like fellow passengers aboard a transatlantic liner that sailed on, leaving an endless wake in the waters astern. What did the adventures, the momentary infatuations in the brothels, the dalliance in the sporting houses matter, the surprise love affairs on the voyages, the wild nights in foggy, mysterious ports? Love, a steady love that built a home and a life, that blossomed in children who would carry on his name, the affection of a wife, the voice of a child calling him, a curly little head taking refuge in the fortress of his breast—that he had never had. There was no time for it; he was always at sea, in the bed of Barris and the whorehouses, aboard freighters and steamships. Always alone, in his ship, with his trips, shipwrecks, storms, ocean currents, winds and cyclones.

Now he was like a castaway on this last voyage of his. For he knew it was his last, he would never return to the heaving surface of the deck. He would watch the entrance and departure of the ships from the bluffs of Periperi through his telescope. And always more lonely, more bowed under the weight of his memories, of that reckless life of his, having nobody to share it with, nowhere to rest his head, no other shoulder than that of the grumpy cook, as when in his days of desire he had to unbosom himself in the windowless room of black Rosa in the warehouse at the foot of Ladeira da Montanha.

Ah, yes, the life of a captain aboard his ship is beautiful and enviable, as he was living it now aboard that *Ita*, with so many people depending on him, so many destinies working themselves out under his powerful hand, so much laughter, so many wild hopes, important politicians, rich landowners and manufacturers, the circumspect married ladies with their assured existence, and the branded prostitutes, with their dim prospects and uncertain futures, the young people just beginning to live, the professional gamblers risking their freedom, and all dependent upon him, on his orders as captain.

A captain doesn't even have the right to be guided by his likes or dislikes; he has a duty to fulfill, from which there is no appeal. He had always had a weakness for professional gamblers, who lived by the difficult and risky calling of marked decks, cheating, dealing off the bottom of the pack, by the agility of their hands and minds. He had hobnobbed with several of them during his loose-living years, he could bear witness to the fact that they were generous and loyal, after their own fashion, and knew how to swallow defeat when some trifling accident transformed their perpetual risk into insults, beatings, jail. He had practiced with them, had picked up their tricks in the intimacy of the nights of carousal. If he were not the captain, in command of his ship, with his duty to fulfill, Stenio could clean out all the ranchers, manufacturers, businessmen, sugar millers he liked. He would not care a hoot. He would merely smile, or perhaps even wink an abetting eye at the skillful sharper. But a captain is not the master of his will, of his likes and dislikes. He was under the obligation of protecting his passengers against the perils of the sea and the accidents of the world.

He had taken from him the porcelain sofa with the pink and white lovers holding hands, which Stenio had not stolen, but had won, without cheating. But what good was that work of art to him? Undoubtedly, like the captain, he was a man without hearth or family, without a home port, drifting with the tide. He would leave it in some brothel room, in the hands of the first woman he went to bed with. And Clotilde wanted it so badly . . .

Was there still time? To break his loneliness, to bring the long wait to an end? He was sixty years old, his hair was white, he no longer had the strength that was once his, when he could pick up boxes of dried beef and salt cod, kegs of butter, hold the wheel steady amidst the tempest, a helmsman without rival. But he was still amazingly vigorous for his age, and his heart was that of the boy who had known no boyhood, pure and ready for the great and definitive love of his life. Yes, there was still time. He had a house beside the shore, with green windows that looked out over the sea and that lacked a mistress. In it was a lonely man, with all his life to live, a past to share without having anyone to help him in this task, without an arm to lean upon when later the road grew strait. How much longer could he carry his head high, not give in to sadness, not become a prisoner within the closed walls of his relinquishment? Ah, if she were willing to transfer her genteel person, her music, her piano, her ripe and diffident charms, the coils of her hair and her syncopated laughter to the suburb of Periperi, if she were willing to plant in the disillusioned, bruised heart the shoot of a new love . . . Ah, there would still be time to break down the walls of his encroaching loneliness and bring to flower the gardens of his port of rest at the end of his last and definitive voyage. Besides, the difference in their ages could not be so great. He figured that Clotilde must be around forty-five.

It was only now, when he had met her, that he felt that his whole life had been nothing but loneliness, one long wait.

A stifled sound, like a moan, like someone gasping for breath, was carried to him on the breeze. It came from the other side, from the shadow of the lifeboat. The captain, always on duty, always vigilant, pricked up his ears accustomed to silence and the voice of the sea, and slowly approached. It was then he saw in the shadow of the lifeboat the thin actress and the dignified senator, she stretched out, with her dress up, he coatless, disheveled, panting in that delightful game.

The captain withdrew to think. In strict justice, acting with the inflexible severity he had used in the case of the gambler, he ought to wrench them out of each other's arms, and demand more respectful conduct aboard his ship from a father of his country. But a captain must be flexible, too, avoid scandal, which would give his ship a bad name. Moreover, how could he, a man who had had so many adventures himself, vent his wrath on lovers, even if lovers only for a moment, at the sacred hour of the rites of love? Leaning over the rail again, he remembered that other captain, Georges Dias Nadreau, of the navy. When they came to him with a complaint about a sailor who had been caught in the act with a brown wench in a dark corner of the port, he had just laughed and answered: "Go take your complaint to the bishop. Am I my brother's cod keeper?" And hadn't he himself, Captain Vasco Moscoso de Aragão, one night long ago held in his arms, on the deck of his own ship, the trembling body of Dorothy, ravaged by the fever of love?

Hadn't he been dreaming there, in his revery, of touching the hands of Clotilde, her hair, of whispering passionate phrases in her ear, of crushing her mouth under the light of that flickering star, of taking her body on the deck of his ship?

*Of young people on the bridges and in
the streets of Recife, and an unexpected and fleeting sight*

HE BROUGHT her *mangaba* plums and sapotas in the Rua
Nova, yellow *cajás* and green hog plums on the docks of Rua
Aurora, red Brazil cherries on the Rua do Sossego, coconut milk
on Boa Viagem beach. Clotilde was enchanted by the fruits of
the northeast, the mangoes and the cashews, the full-flavored
pineapple, the star apples, the different kinds of guavas. She
went tripping along, her dignified air cast aside, and the captain
carried her useless parasol. They were like two teen-agers as they
crossed the bridges, the squares, and the streets of Recife,
laughing without knowing why or at what, "two old cut-ups," to
use the expression of an impatient passer-by, almost offended by
the youthful foolery of the captain and the pianist.

The actresses and the congressman from Paraíba had gone
ashore that morning. Also Dr. Stenio, whom the sight of the city
of Count Maurice of Nassau had charmed to the point of
inducing him, so he said, to interrupt his trip and stay there for a
few days to become better acquainted with it. When he stepped
on the gangplank, he cast a reproachful glance at the captain.
Not because he had exposed his tricks at poker; the captain had
been generous about that, he had not handed him over to the
police, and had not said a word about the matter, not even to the

195

plucked ranchers. The reproach had to do exclusively with the china sofa. Where would he find anything as pretty to take as a present to his wife? Several others went ashore, too, for the *Ita* discharged and picked up passengers at each port. Even the brunette, whose family was waiting for her at the dock, got off. As far as she was concerned, the trip had been too short, and right away, as soon as she landed, she introduced the athletic young banker from Ceará to her parents and aunts. In the late afternoon she would come to the pier to tell him goodbye, and her eyes would melancholically follow the wake of the ship.

When the captain, after signing certain papers brought to him by the chief mate, was free and went to look for Clotilde, she was already on the dock with the other passengers. They set out in a large group, to Vasco's visible disappointment. He had hoped to have her to himself that morning and early afternoon, for he had to be back on the ship relatively early, to sign other papers. And he found himself surrounded by the din of whole families, with swarms of children, all asking him the craziest, most absurd questions, as though he were some kind of walking encyclopedia who knew not only the streets, the restaurants, the bars, but also the price of things, including babies' diapers.

He could not follow the example of the newlyweds, who behaved as though they were alone in the Garden of Eden, as though other people did not exist. It was a miracle that they did not stretch out on a park bench, and there, in plain view, pursue their love to its final consequences. Kisses, squeezes, caresses, all sanctioned by State and Church, for they had the benefit of both judge and clergy.

Vasco cursed that first part of their stroll about the city. Especially when Jasmim—the one serious defect he found in Clotilde—jumped out of his mistress's arm to take part, without the faintest chance of success, in the contest being waged in the shady square in the center of the city for the favors of a bitch in heat, a good-sized fox terrier of dubious ancestry. Unless Jasmim was counting on his Oriental lineage, his exotic beauty, to sweep the desired female, three times his size, off her feet, how could he hope to compete with a Boxer showing his teeth, a fox terrier who seemed to have marital rights and was prepared to defend them, and two mongrels? One of these, part Great Dane, who was snarling at the Boxer, was enormous, and the other, with the most rascally air that can be imagined, was a mutt of the first water, with a cynical eye and an ingratiating muzzle. The latter and the fox terrier with the air of a husband were standing by, waiting to see what would come of the fight in the making between the two heavyweight contenders. It would probably end in a draw, leaving them both out of the running, their names scratched from the list of aspirants. Meanwhile, the fox terrier and the smaller mutt sized each other up, getting ready for the second match, which would decide who got the bitch. As for her, she seemed enchanted by that dispute for her favors, the slut.

The situation took a sharp change when Jasmim decided to throw his hat into the ring, presenting his candidacy with a spectacular leap into the midst of the contestants. The four of them turned, snarling at the newcomer. The bitch smiled at him, flattered in her vanity, encouraging him. For a brief moment Vasco had the wild hope that the Boxer and the mutt would tear the Pekinese to pieces, aided and abetted by the fox terrier and the smaller mutt. But it did not work out that way. Those suitors seemed to have plenty of time on their hands, they were in no hurry to fight; all they did was snarl, show their teeth, and give an occasional bark. Moreover, the most aggressive barker was Jasmim.

When Clotilde saw him in the middle of the ring, among the four rough contenders, she almost had a fit. Hysterical little screams came from her lips, she stretched out her arms, gasping: "Jasmim, Jasmim," and then collapsed on a park bench, on the verge of fainting. Turning to the captain, she implored him: "Save the poor little thing, for the love of God!"

Her pleading eyes, her voice, which was that of a person about to have an attack of some sort, spurred Vasco to action. It was a crazy request. How was he going to step into that circle of desire and hate and rescue that plucky little Pekinese, whose bravery verged on foolhardiness? He picked up a fallen branch lying close by, and with Clotilde's heart-rending screeches in his ears, advanced upon the dogs like a knight of the Middle Ages confronting a seven-headed dragon, shooting flames from all of them, with his lance in obedience to the orders of his lady.

His unexpected appearance caused commotion and confusion. The Boxer let down his guard, fell back a step, and the big mutt took advantage of this to fall upon him from behind. Jasmim, feeling himself to be the objective of the captain's maneuvers, dashed forward and knocked over the fox terrier, and the two of them went rolling in the flower beds. And the sharp-witted smaller mutt took advantage of all this to lead the much-wooed bitch away and into a nearby alley, quieter and better suited for love-making. The captain managed to get hold of Jasmim's leash and yank him from between the fox terrier's teeth, who toward the end was looking wildly around for his mate. When he finally picked up her scent and set off toward the alley, it was too late. A litter of mutts was already on the way.

Clotilde did not even thank the captain. She hugged the Pekinese to her bosom, to her face, kissed his bruised muzzle, felt his bones, without showing the slightest interest in the magnificent fight still going on between the Boxer and the spurious Great Dane, now just for the pleasure of fighting, without the bitch as a prize.

But it's an ill wind that blows nobody good. As a result of that exploit, which had aroused the laughter of the other passengers and the malicious curiosity of a group of street urchins, Clotilde decided to take Jasmim back to the ship, for the city was too full of temptations and dangers for the poor innocent. Thanks to this, Vasco was freed from the distasteful and hampering company of his other traveling companions.

As it was almost lunchtime, while they were waiting for the gong to sound, Clotilde busied herself putting iodine on the teeth marks the fox terrier had left on one of Jasmim's legs.

So this was how, that hot afternoon, they came to be strolling the streets like two teen-agers. She had recovered from the morning's canine emotions, and he had risen in her opinion because of the courage he had displayed and the rapidity with which he had heeded her appeal.

After wandering through the streets and squares, they wound up in an ice-cream parlor, where she wanted to taste all the specialties of the house and compare them with the ice cream of Belém, in her opinion the best in the world. Vasco was admiring her appetite, when all of a sudden his heart almost stopped. He happened to look toward the Emperor Bridge (the ice-cream parlor was on the Rua Aurora, from which the noble old bridge could be seen) when, among the passing crowd, he saw a fat woman dressed in black, with a scarf on her head, covering her white hair, leading a child by the hand. He had caught only a fleeting glimpse of her face, but he was certain it was Carol, smiling down at the child like an old and tender grandmother. Vasco forgot the guest at his side, his position as a captain on active duty, the ice cream to be paid for, and ran out the door toward the Rua da Imperatriz, down which the fleeting vision had vanished. But he did not catch up with her, even though he called her name out loud, to the surprise of the passers-by. And then he realized that he had left Clotilde alone in the ice-cream parlor, and hurried back.

She was in a rage. She did not even want to talk to him. He tried to explain things to her, but she had her own version of what had happened. Why hadn't he told her straight out that all along he had been looking for an old flame whose address he had lost. Walking with her along the streets and bridges, but with his thoughts far off, his eyes scanning the face of every woman they passed . . .

"You mustn't think that. It really seemed to me that I saw a person whom I'd not heard about for almost twenty years."

"A woman?"

One day, perhaps, he'd tell her all about it. But this was not the moment.

"A woman, what an idea! A friend, a mate who served with me for ten years on more than one ship. We were intimate friends, like brothers. But he had to give up his career because of the death of a relative in Pernambuco, in Garanhuns, a city in the interior, who left him some property. I never heard of him again."

She must forgive him the emotion he had felt when he saw, in the crowd crossing the bridge, the face of his lost friend. They had been like brothers, so united that if one of them was out of work, the other gave up his job, too.

The more violent lovers' quarrels, the sweeter the reconciliation. They came out of the ice-cream parlor hand in hand, headed for the port. She had wept a little, two tears which he dried with his silk handkerchief with an embroidered anchor in the corner. When he took her hand at the door to help her down the steps of the sidewalk, she did not draw it away afterwards, and they walked like this, in a silence more expressive than words, to the pier where the *Ita* was taking aboard cargo and passengers.

From the bridge the chief mate and the navigation officer watched them approach, hand in hand, with tripping step, their faces reflecting sun and satisfaction.

"Your captain is feeling his oats today," laughed the navigation officer.

Geir Matos, the chief mate, turned to him: "Tell me, did you ever see a captain who played his part so well? So much the captain? Nobody but Americo, that crook, could have turned up a pearl like him."

"A pearl of the sea . . . Of the Japanese Sea, the China Sea, the Oriental routes . . ."

The huge cranes lifted sacks of sugar and the black stevedores stowed them away in the hold.

*In which the narrator once more inter-
rupts the story for no good reason,
but in the greatest distress*

I BEG the reader to forgive me this interruption and the
shortcomings he may have noted in the preceding chapters. If I
am still writing, in spite of everything, it is because the deadline
set by the Public Archives for submitting the original
manuscript (and two carbon copies) expires in a few days. But I
don't even know what I am saying, so how can I pay attention to
style and grammar at a time like this, when the world is
threatening to come down about my ears?

No, I am not referring to the atomic or hydrogen bomb, or to
the cold war, or the grave problems of Berlin, Laos, the Congo,
or Cuba, or a launching pad on the moon from which to rain
destruction on the world. If this happens, we will all go out at the
same time, and misery loves company. I would only like to know
just when this is going to happen so I can get into bed with
Dondoca and die at her side.

I am referring to what happened here in Periperi during these
past days, with the beginning of the new year, the fittingly
celebrated entrance of 1961, which I had greeted with hopes of
glory and gain, thanks to this work of mine, and of tranquil
happiness, in view of the peace and harmony that reigned in the
little house in the Alley of the Three Butterflies where in the

afternoon Dondoca received His Honor and at night your humble servant.

Yes, he discovered everything, and the *dolce vita*—for free—went down the drain. The greatest confusion grips these three souls lashed by the gales of passion and jealousy, by the whirlwind of recriminations and thirst for vengeance. There has already been the devil to pay: screams and curses, insults, accusations, reproaches, excuses, pleas for forgiveness, broken-off relations, the cutting off of allowance and gifts, tears, supplicating glances, and glares of mortal hatred, threats of revenge, and even a beating.

Being a historian who takes his calling seriously, I must bring method to my handling of the story, but I don't know how I am going to do it, for my heart is broken and I have a devilish headache. And Dr. Siqueira must have one, too, for it is his head that is crowned with a spreading set of horns, not mine, and that should be a source of comfort to me, but it isn't. How can I be comforted when there hangs over me the threat of never seeing my Dondoca again, of never crossing her path again, of never again hearing her lilting crystalline laugh, her soft voice begging me to tell her another story about the captain?

It happened all of a sudden, although suspicion was already in the air, in the eyes and the attitude of the judge. I mentioned in an earlier chapter the marked change that had come about in His Honor's relations with me and Dondoca. One day the poor wounded bird found the legal light smelling her sheets to see if he could discover there some strange odor, the sweat of another man. He became gruff and curt in his dealings with me, staring at me steadily and severely, without softening under my praises, laid on with a trowel, as he had done before, to the point of even praising my writing in return. In spite of the fact that, making no small effort, I had very nearly become a complete bootlicker, even going so far as to admire a horrible pair of striped pajamas. His Honor had inaugurated during those days, a Christmas present from his Zeppelin. But, in spite of all this, his nose was still out of joint. We became terribly uneasy, Dondoca and I, and took every precaution, to the point of using one set of sheets and pillowcases in the afternoon and another at night. As for me, I stopped accompanying Dr. Siqueira on his afternoon visits to our loved one. Formerly I had shown up, either with him or after he had got there, to sponge a cup of coffee and chat a while. Then I would discreetly withdraw; after all, he was footing the bills, he had certain rights, and I could not spend the whole afternoon there, cramping his style. Not to mention the time needed for historical research for the work I was writing. But now I stayed out of sight, keeping in the background, going to see him only at night, to chat a while on the sidewalk and to make my daily prudent check up: the movements of the noble cultivator of the law were controlled by the inflexible baton of his worthy spouse, Dona Ernestina, vulgarly nicknamed Zeppelin.

None of this helped. Four days ago, one hot night, just as I had stretched out in the bed, and was beginning to enjoy one of the half-dozen pears the judge had brought back from a trip to Bahía, and Dondoca, in a game she found very amusing and much to her liking, was straddled across my breast as though she were riding horseback, bending over to kiss first my eyes, then my ears, or to nip a bite of fruit from my mouth—in the midst of these pleasantries, at the very minute that I was putting my arms around her to pull her down against me—who should show up in the open door of the room but the eminent Dr. Alberto Siqueira, wearing a broad-brimmed felt hat and dark glasses, laughing like Dracula and saying in a funereal voice: "So it was true!"

So it seemed, at any rate. Although, if he had given me time, I was prepared to argue the matter, for I am a real crackerjack when it is a question of the truth. I learned while I was compiling these memoirs of the captain that it is a very risky thing for anyone to go about proclaiming the truth simply because he finds himself in possession of concrete documentary proofs or on the evidence of his own eyes, which is always overestimated. Why, just the other day, Dona Cacula and Dona Pequana, wife and sister-in-law, respectively, of Tinoco Pedreira, boasted of having seen a flying saucer in this sky over Periperi, with their own two eyes which the earth would one day swallow up. They raised such a hullabaloo that reporters from newspapers in the capital even turned up to interview them, and the pictures of the two old dames, pointing to the sky, appeared in the papers. Afterwards it was proved that it was not a saucer or a round object the color of silver, moving at great speed and with two blazing searchlights. The tide washed up on the beach a huge kite of waterproof paper, which in the sunlight looked like silver, with two red wheels. A kite that had got away, its string cut and its tail pulled off, carried along by the wind, and transformed by the eyes of the two old hags into a flying saucer from Mars or the

Soviet Union, depending on the newspaper's preference.

That was not, however, the moment for such considerations. I must confess that at first I did not take in all the gravity of that apparition, I was so overwhelmed by the dark glasses and the wide-brimmed hat. Glasses and hat designed to hide from any night prowler of Periperi the identity of the judge. That shows you the lengths to which His Honor's premeditation went. It was Dondoca's scream, as she jumped off my breast to the other side of the bed, that aroused me to the full dimension of the drama. I swallowed the piece of pear and could think of nothing to say.

There in the door of the room, his left hand on the latch to keep it open, his right hand pointing to the bed, with index finger raised, his voice choked and tremulous, stood the eminent jurist, the very picture of outraged virtue, of misplaced confidence, of friendship betrayed. In a word, the perfect image of the classic cuckold, of the immortal Othello. I could not but admire him.

However, I could not go on lying there in bed, staring agape at His cuckolded Honor. I got up, put on the bedroom slippers, and heard a cry that came from the depths of the soul, from a broken heart: "Take off my slippers, you scoundrel!"

I stepped out of them and stood there in my bare feet on the cold bricks, and this pettiness on the part of that eminent man was responsible for my catching a cold that I haven't yet been able to shake off. The scene, in which I was both audience and actor, was set like this: at the entrance to the room stood the retired judge, tragic and accusing; on the other side, near the window, with her hands trying to hide her nakedness in perhaps a tardy proof of her modesty and circumspection, Dondoca was sobbing; between the two, the bed, the scene of the crime, still warm, and I, with an idiotic expression, looking at my navel. I think we might have stood there, motionless like that, for hours and days, if Dondoca had not raised her beautiful eyes to the judge and said in a tender voice: "Bertie! Alberto, my lump of sugar..."

Those words produced an indescribable effect. I thought His Honor was going to have a stroke, would drop there as though struck by lightning—can you imagine the scandal!—or would pull out a revolver and fire two shots, one at Dondoca and one at me. He turned red, he turned pale, his body shook as though he were receiving a lashing, he tried to take a step toward Dondoca, and couldn't; he tried to talk, and all he could bring out was a guttural noise, something between a sob and a belch. He stared at the ingenuous girl with the eyes of a wounded and dying animal, turned on me a menacing look charged with hatred, and managed to croak: "Dog! Rhymster!"

I bowed my head, preferring not to answer.

"Snake!"

This was for Dondoca, but she was not reduced to silence, as I was.

"Bertie darling, forgive your pussy cat..."

"Never!" And pulling down the brim of his hat, he spat in my direction, turned his back on us, and left. From the street door he threw into the sitting room the key of the house. We two stood there, naked and stunned.

Dondoca was inconsolable. She had got used to that pampered life, with everything she wanted, house, food, dresses, and candy. I, too, had become accustomed to the judge's slippers and concubine. We did not sleep a wink that night, not because of what you are thinking, but because of the misfortune of which we had been the victims. What lay ahead for Dondoca? To return to the miserable hovel of her parents, to Pedro Torresmo's benders, to helping her mother wash and starch clothes? How could she do that after all this time with painted nails, silks and perfumes, almost nothing to do and lots of petting? To support her, to keep her in the style the judge's bank account made possible, was out of the question for me. My meager salary barely covered my minimum expenses, making it necessary for me to live in this suburb with my parents. In the event that I received the prize offered by the Public Archives—I was encouraged by the fact that the director of the Archives was now that illustrious Dr. Luiz Henrique whose opinion of my earlier work, "a repository of useful information," I have already mentioned—what I could offer her was a present, material for a dress, a pair of slippers, a pair of earrings, maybe a ring. Assuming that some doctor didn't turn up unexpectedly and do me out of the honor and the check. In any case, those twenty thousand cruzeiros would not be enough to keep her for more than a little while.

Dondoca, torn between love and creature comforts, grieved all night long. She wept in my arms, and finally fell asleep on my breast.

The next day things got worse. Pedro Torresmo, who had gone, as was his habit, to put the bite on the judge—money for rum—was turned out of the study where the magistrate wrote his studies of jurisprudence in silence and meditation. It was there he received Dondoca's father, for, as a rule, Dona Ernestina respected his hours given over to thought. Pedro Torresmo arrived trustingly to pay his respects to the distinguished judge and to inquire about the health of the judge's lady. He was informed by a scowling Dr. Siqueira that he was henceforth forbidden to enter that house, that his daughter was a tramp of the lowest order who had abused the trust placed in her. As for money, he could go and ask me for it, for if anybody had the duty of paying for his rum and keeping his daughter, that somebody was I.

"But he hasn't a cent to his name..." answered Pedro Torresmo, giving a perfect description of my financial situation.

That argument cut no ice with His Honor, and he slammed the door in the indignant father's face. The drunk went straight to Dondoca's house, and, affected in his honor and source of supply of rum, gave her a beating of the sort that raises welts, breaking the handle of a new broom on the innocent child's ribs. Another loss at such a darkling moment.

When I showed up there in the afternoon, after ascertaining from a distance that the judge was in his study, trying to cure the pangs of jealousy by studying the penalties in cases of seduction, Dondoca was in a state of utter dejection, her ribs and arms still red from the blows she had received. I was moved to tears, and I looked after that adored body, covering it with kisses and caresses, trying to comfort it. But the main problem remained unsolved: how to pay the bills. The end of the month was at hand, the rent for the house was due, the money for the marketing, the necessities, and the luxuries.

Then all at once things seemed to move toward a solution. After two days had gone by, the distressed mother of Dondoca managed to get an audience with the judge. She told him how repentant her daughter was, how she had been taken in by the blandishments of a character who called himself a poet, who sent her verses, and who had come to see her at her house brought there by the judge himself.

"It was you yourself, sir, who took him to the house..."

(This was not strictly true, but His Honor did not know it.) Dondoca, lonely of nights, was the victim and not the culprit. I had taken her almost by force, but the only one she had thoughts for was her adored Alberto, that ungrateful "Bertie," as she spent her days moaning. If the doctor could only see how the poor thing was suffering, crying all day long, bemoaning her fate, refusing to eat, pining away, and all this because she did not see him any more . . . He ought to go and see her, if only as an act of charity, to prevent the unhappy thing from some act of madness, for she talked of nothing else. She, the mother, was even sleeping there for fear of what she might do, perhaps pour kerosene on her clothes and set fire to herself, dying amidst the flames.

The illustrious pillar of justice was moved, and worried, too. If the little fool were to do something crazy like attempting suicide, it would be impossible to avoid a scandal, gossip, the police, and it would finally come to Dona Ernestina's ears, and he didn't even want to think how the Zeppelin would react . . . "Only out of charity," he said, and returned to the Alley of the Three Butterflies.

The quarrel was made up, true, but I was sacrificed. I was allowed a final interview with Dondoca, but not alone. Pedro Torresmo was in the kitchen, armed with the remains of the broom to safeguard the moral respect and the private property of the judge. Dondoca, with tears streaming down her cheeks, told me that Bertie had forgiven her that one time, but on condition that she never again speak to me. What could she do, the poor unfortunate thing? Worst of all was the stipulation that her mother and father were to come to live with her in a room at the back of the house, watchdogs over the girl's moral integrity and complete fidelity to the judge.

"But you just let a few days go by and we'll find a way, sweetie."

It's easy to say "let a few days go by." When Pedro Torresmo met me on the street, he looked at me with a menacing and baleful eye. The mother announced to the neighbors that she would drive me away with a broomstick if I ever put foot in the Alley of the Three Butterflies. How was I to see Dondoca again?

So here I am, womanless, in the long, slow-moving nights. I never desired or loved anyone as much as that golden mulatto with the greedy lips. I never had so much time on my hands; the hours I formerly devoted to chatting with the judge are no longer occupied, for His Honor reduced to a mere nod his relations with this, his unconditional admirer. Meanwhile, the work moves slowly and laboriously, the phrases come out limping, events get all snarled up in my mind, I can't keep my mind on the captain and his mature beloved, the old maid Clotilde. There is a mature—good and mature—summer visitor on the beach whose eyes follow me. A widow, who has come here for the first time to spend the summer with some nieces. She cannot see me without getting nervous, striking up a conversation, encouraging me—everything but grabbing hold of me. But how can one who has held in his arms the small, terse breasts of Dondoca, her shapely thighs, who has touched her belly that sends out sparks, feel, even out of understandable curiosity, the slightest desire for this ruin who needs only one thing, and that in a hurry: plastic surgery?

How can I arrive at the truth about the captain and his adventures when at this moment what I want to arrive at, bring into the open, make completely clear, is how His Honor found out about my nightly visits to the Alley of the Three Butterflies. I think it must have been through an anonymous letter, one of those suburban mischiefmakers, some Telemaco Dorea, some Otoniel Mendonça, envious of my success in the field of historical writing and of my place in Dondoca's bed. The race of Chico Pacheco has not died out in Peripiri. Ah, but if I ever discover the truth I will not challenge the dirty dog to a duel, as the captain did. I'll knock his teeth down his throat on the first corner.

# Concerning the scientific theory of the frustrated

"THERE GOES the captain, convoying his frustrated lady friend," said the lawyer from Pará, Dr. Firmino Morais, who had literary aspirations and great social prestige. He was on his way home from Rio, where he had been acting as attorney in an appeal to the Federal Supreme Court on behalf of a rubber-exporting company. The trip had netted him a profit of a hundred contos.

There was a large gathering in the lounge. In the center of the group sat the senator, a priest, Father Clímaco, and a lady getting on in years, with white wavy hair, a charming air, who must have been a beauty in her day, and who knew how to grow old with dignity and style. From time to time, her grandchildren came over to lean against her knee, receive a caress, a word, a kiss. The newlyweds formed part of the group, in addition to the two students from Fortaleza, and the half-breed Indian girl, who was sitting beside the agreeable elderly lady, who smiled at her from time to time, admiring her wild beauty. Other men and women were sitting about in the upholstered chairs, happy to be hobnobbing with such illustrious people as the senator, the distinguished lawyer, the priest, and that lady whose family, sons and sons-in-law, were known throughout the whole country. They were watching the captain walking beside Clotilde on the deck.

"You probably have in mind Balzac's women," spoke up one of the students with the self-sufficiency that went his age.

"No. Balzac's women are one thing, and the Frustrated are something very different. Clotilde Maria da Assunçao Fogueira is one of the Frustrated..."

"She has a long name, like the nobility," said the bride.

"Her father was a business agent who made money. Her brother expanded the firm; they're doing very well."

The white-haired lady raised her hand, on which a beautiful ring was enhanced by the delicacy of the finger wearing it; turning toward the lawyer her longish face, she asked, smiling: "Tell me, Dr. Morais, what is the difference between the women of Balzac and the Frustrated?"

"But Dona Domingas, don't you know the theory of the Frustrated? It is a famous one, based on the studies of psychologists and psychiatrists. There are volumes dealing with the subject. I even think that Freud has written a book about it," smiled the lawyer, happy to be the center of attention.

The ship sailed through the calm, green waters, following the white line of the shore. Daredevil fishermen's rafts ventured out on the high seas, passengers standing along the rail watched the diminutive sails in the distance. The captain stopped, pointed to one of the rafts with his finger, and handed the spyglass to Clotilde.

"The difference, Dona Domingas, between them and Balzac's women is a big one. Small details establish great differences." The lawyer had the reputation in Belém of loving paradoxes. Some years before, he had published a small volume entitled *Thoughts and Maxims*, which had been highly praised by the local press, for the "originality of its concepts and the purity of its style, recalling Herculano, Garret, and Camilo," according to a critic of the region. His graduation ring, with its ruby surrounded by diamonds, scintillated against the black binding of the priest's breviary.

"Then let's hear the theory, Doctor. Don't make us have to coax you," said Dona Domingas, settling herself comfortably in her chair, the better to enjoy the boutades of the lawyer, whom she had met on a previous trip.

"The theory, which is highly scientific, as I said, has to do with women who have reached a certain age."

"My age?"

"Your beauty knows no age, Madame. How many girls would be happy to have the charms of this grandmother. Now, Balzac's women as a rule were around thirty. Today, thanks to progress and the art of make-up, at thirty a woman is still young. Take, for example, the wife of Dr. Hélio, that doctor from Natal. Her husband tells me she is thirty-five, and she looks like a girl."

"She's a pretty woman," the senator agreed. "And different..."

"Wasted; the husband is a broken-down old crock," remarked one of the students.

The priest interrupted: "Remember Christian charity, my son."

"And remember the commandment: 'Thou shalt not covet thy neighbor's wife,'" added the lawyer.

"A lady who could not be more virtuous," added the senator, giving the embarrassed student a reproving look. "The husband is a very sick man. The doctor in Rio holds out no hope. And he, being a doctor himself, has no illusions."

"Let's let that poor lady, who deserves pity, alone, and let's hear your theory, Dr. Morais. I am dying of curiosity," said Dona Domingas.

"Well, today we would apply the term 'Balzacian' to a lady in her forties, wouldn't you say, Dona Domingas? When she is highly"—he seemed to be searching for the right word, helping himself with his upraised hand—"highly demanding. The volcanic age."

"Swell," spoke up the student, whose strong point did not seem to be tact.

"Forty?" The senator turned the matter over in his mind with the same solemn, knowing air with which he voted the party line on all government measures.

"Now, the Balzacians have two ways, two means, two methods of sublimating their state when the time comes. The first is by way of grandmotherhood, which is the one Dona Domingas employs to perfection. Bringing to her beauty the dignity due her white hair..."

"That's a somewhat left-handed compliment..."

"Whereas the others, at least the great majority, pass from the state of Balzacian to that of Frustrated. And thus we arrive at the classic definition of the Frustrated, as established by a

Viennese scholar. The Frustrated, Dona Domingas, is the Balzacian when she begins to wither. That is to say, when she has gotten along in her forties, is approaching her fifties, and the container no longer matches the contents."

"What is this all about?" the Indian girl asked, sitting very straight and silent in her chair, her eyes on the lawyer.

"When the exterior no longer matches the inner needs... When the wrinkles begin to turn to sagging folds. The worst of it is that most of the Frustrated don't realize what has happened, and behave like girls or Balzacians. Take Miss Clotilde, for instance... I know her family well, her brother is a friend of mine."

"But you're being unfair to her," remarked Dona Domingas. "She's not yet in that state. Balzacian, but not Frustrated. You who are so well informed in this matter are making a mistake."

"The mistake, and a big one, is yours, my dear friend. You have not yet grasped the rudiments of this branch of science and you are already trying to correct the teacher. I haven't yet had a chance to fully develop the complete theory of the Frustrated. No old maid, Dona Domingas, at any moment belongs in the class of the Balzacians. She goes directly from girl to Frustrated."

The voices of the passengers arguing about scores in the game of shuffleboard reached their ears. The bride, the better to hear, rested her head on her husband's shoulder.

"How's that again?" asked one of the students. "I have seen many a single Balzacian who could be turned to good account. In the Catete pension where a friend of mine lives there is one—what a dish!"

"There is a difference which leaps to the eye, Dona Domingas: the Balzacians, married and at times with a lover..."

"*Vade retro*," spoke up the priest.

"... are happy, satisfied with life. They only really begin to suffer when men no longer look at them with covetous glances."

"That must be sad," said the Indian girl in a low voice.

"And when their social status changes, they descend to the lowest ranks of the Frustrated."

"That theory of yours is not very Christian, Doctor," smiled the priest.

"Scientific, Father."

"The virtuous woman preserves the eternal beauty of the soul," declaimed the senator.

"Let Dr. Morais go on." Dona Domingas imposed silence on the group. That senator was a fool.

"What you say is true, my dear Senator. However, when people look at a woman, they don't look at her soul, but at her legs... But, to continue with the theory of the Frustrated: Father, it is when they begin to hang around the church, decorating the altars, going to confession every day. You know that side of it better than I do. They are embittered, sorry for themselves, troublemakers, slanderers. They belong in the category of the old maids. From the minute they cross the frontier of twenty-eight, and lose the hope of getting married, they immediately join the ranks of the Frustrated, the category of the Great Frustrated."

"What is this about categories?"

"There are categories and subcategories. The specialists who have studied the matter divide the Frustrated into two basic categories: the Great Frustrated, old maids, soured, enemies, as a rule, of the human species; and the Sensitive Frustrated, the category into which the married or widowed Frustrated fall. The suffering of the Sensitive Frustrated comes from the knowledge..."

"Knowledge of what?" inquired the Indian girl.

"...knowledge of what it's all about, Miss Moema. The suffering of the Sensitive Frustrated, Dona Domingas, comes from knowledge and translates itself into yearning."

"Is that a dig? I can assure you that it does not touch me."

"Good Heavens! But you belong to the other class, the class of the beautiful and accomplished grandmothers," and he kissed her still beautiful hand. "In the case of the Great Frustrated, the old maids, their suffering comes from not knowing and translates itself into wanting to find out."

"That must be terrible," murmured the girl, clasping Dona Domingas's hand, as though to ward off the alarming hypothesis.

"Find out what?" Not one single time did the student hit the nail on the head.

"*Vade retro*," said the priest.

"Find out what sin tastes like..."

"The Sensitive Frustrated are, as a rule, tolerant of others' weaknesses, *faux pas*, loose living. They like to help love affairs along, make matches. But one must never trust them too much, for if they get a chance... The Great Frustrated hate pretty women, lovers, brides like you, Dona Maria Amelia. A pregnant woman seems to them something immoral."

"How dreadful," smiled the bride, cuddling close against her husband, pressing his hand.

"Clotilde is one of the Great Frustrated. But another characteristic of the Frustrated, especially the old maids, is not losing hope. And sometimes, though rarely, it so happens that one of the Great Frustrated moves into the class of the Sensitive Frustrated by getting married. That is what Clotilde—nicknamed by some of her piano students Tilly the Swooner—is trying to do."

"The captain is single, so he told me," reflected the priest. "It would be the meeting of two lonely souls, giving each other mutual support in the autumn of life . . ."

"Father, you are a poet. Have you never written verses?"

"Only a few poor efforts in praise of Our Lady and her Son."

"You see how right I was? Now Clotilde Maria da Assunçao Fogueira is a typical case of a Great Frustrated with a Wounded Heart. This is a subdivision, Dona Domingas. One of the most interesting of the subdivisions. It is made up of the Great Frustrated who were on the point of getting married, were engaged, were ready to emerge from the sinful state of spinsterhood . . ."

"What heresy, dear God," the priest lifted his hands.

Miss Moema laughed merrily, Dona Domingas smiled, the senator made a parliamentary gesture, which might as easily have been of approval as of disapproval.

". . . and one day the fiancé vanishes, the engagement is off. That was what happened to Clotilde. It caused a nine days' wonder in Belém. I was around twenty at the time, and she must be about two years older than I am. And I am forty-three."

"You don't look it," Miss Moema ingenuously exclaimed.

"What happened?"

"Tell us about it, Doctor."

"The Fogueira family was made up of the parents and three children, a boy and two girls. Clotilde was the oldest of the three. The brother is rich; he went into business with his father, and when the old man died he expanded the firm very much. The younger sister married an engineer and lives in Rio. Clotilde, accomplished and well educated, was much sought after. She had studied the piano with a Polish lady, the wife of an English rubber exporter. Clotilde really had a gift for music, and her parents were enchanted with the way the daughter ripped melodies from the piano. If she had wanted to marry at that time, she could have, and made a good match. She was not ugly and she had more than enough accomplishments."

"And why didn't she?"

"She was too picky and choosy, too 'uppity.' She wanted a fairy-tale prince. Before she realized it, her younger sister had married and was expecting her first baby. About this time, there showed up in Belém a doctor from São Luis, a chap with a lot of *savoir-faire*. He opened an office, and waited for patients, and while he waited, he courted Clotilde. He won her over with music, he really knew a lot about it. And, besides, by this time she wasn't quite so choosy."

"And today even less. The captain is an old codger."

"He's not so bad. He makes a good appearance..."

"At that time she was around twenty-one or twenty-two, and in those days, when girls married at the age of fifteen or sixteen, she was already an old maid. They became engaged after a month or two of courtship. A short courtship and a long engagement. Maybe he understood music, but he was a washout when it came to medicine. He had a small practice, and did not make enough to keep himself. He had his meals at his fiancée's home, and lived in a boarding house. The engagement dragged on for four or five years."

"Long engagements never work out well..."

"Finally, one day, some friends of his, politicians from Maranhão, fixed him up with a job in Rio, the post of doctor to the Police Department, or something like that."

"And he left and never returned..."

"Take it easy, Senator. I'm telling the story. The marriage was arranged to take place in short order, for he had to leave and take over his job. A fashionable wedding, a well-known family. The newlyweds were supposed to set out for Rio a few days after the ceremony. Now pay attention to this detail, which is important: the same day the wedding was set for, one of these *Itas* left Belém for the south."

Once more they saw through the porthole Vasco and Clotilde strolling slowly, the captain with his pipe, she with her lap dog, he undoubtedly telling her some exciting story, for she was listening attentively. They waited until the two had disappeared in the direction of the prow.

"The marriage was supposed to take place at the bride's

home, both the civil and the religious ceremony, as was the custom in those days. Important people always got married at home. A big celebration, with loads of food and drink. The doctor had had lunch in the house of his future in-laws, and had gone to change his clothes and send his luggage to the hotel where they were going to spend their wedding night. The civil ceremony was set for five o'clock, to be followed immediately by the religious. By four o'clock the house was already full of guests. At half past four the priest, an old friend of the family, arrived. Ten minutes later, the judge and the notary."

"And the groom?"

"Relax. The groom was late, for at ten minutes past five, when Clotilde came down in her wedding dress, he had not yet showed up. The guests gathered around her, admiring her veil and bridal wreath. The groom's tardiness was reaching the almost intolerable limit of half an hour. They sent a messenger to his boardinghouse, and the proprietress told him that the doctor had left with his suitcases, saying he was going to get married. The messenger returned at ten minutes to six. At six, the judge was threatening to leave; the guests, annoyed and annoying, had a dozen theories. At ten past six..."

"This is making me nervous..."

"...the bride's brother went to police headquarters and the first-aid station. It was almost seven when he came back, without any news, but at half past six the judge had left in indignation. When he left, taking the notary with him, Clotilde had her first swoon, the forerunner of those to come. At seven the guests began to leave. They left curious and disappointed, for the dinner and drinks were not served. At half past eight the priest, who had done his best to comfort the bride and her family, but to no avail, deserted. At nine the brother of the bride, who had gone out again at eight to make further inquiries, came back with an incredible piece of news: the wretch had left for Rio on the *Ita*, paying his passage aboard ship, for he arrived just as they were pulling up the gangplank, at five on the dot."

"What a terrible thing..."

"And that was how Clotilde Maria da Assunçao Fogueira became transformed into Tilly the Swooner, entering straight into the subdivision of the Great Frustrated with a Wounded Heart."

"Didn't she ever have another suitor?"

"Never more, Miss Moema. First, because her pride was so

deeply wounded that for a long time she kept away from parties or diversions of all sorts. She locked herself in the house and spent her time at the piano. Then, when she was willing, she didn't find anyone else who was... She lives with her brother, spends part of the time with her sister in Rio, gives piano lessons, looks after her Pekinese—the Great Frustrated always have a dog or a cat—has her swoons, but as you can see, she hasn't given up hope. She's a typical Frustrated."

"It's a sad story," said Dona Domingas. "I feel sorry for her."

"That doctor was not a very exemplary character, to say the least," observed the priest.

"If that had happened in Natal, it would not have gone so easy with him. He'd have been lucky to get off with a good beating," was the senator's considered opinion.

"What about the groom, what happened to him?" asked Miss Moema, smiling and curious.

"He married the daughter of some wealthy and important person in Rio. He kept his Police Department appointment, but he entered high society, what with his father-in-law's money and his wife's beauty. He can be seen every afternoon at the entrance to the Jockey Club, he owns race horses. Today his wife is one of the Sensitive Frustrated. One of the most sensitive, for she has quite a past. From what I have been told, among the brood mares of her husband's stable, she is the most famous..."

"Heavens," exclaimed the priest, while Dona Domingas laughed heartily.

"To the mares of Pharoah I compare thee, oh my friend," recited the lawyer. "That's from the Bible, Father..."

Father Clímaco opened his breviary again: "Verily I say unto you, Doctor, that at times God moves in a mysterious way. Perhaps He was saving her for the captain."

"Except that He gives her to him a little late, Father. Overripe fruit..." He paused for a moment, shaking his head. "No, that's not it. Overripe fruit is an image that can be applied to the Sensitive Frustrated. The Great Frustrated are blighted fruit, fruit which never ripened."

"Blighted fruit. How sad!" Moema murmured.

The group broke up, it was time to get ready for dinner. Once again the captain and Clotilde were strolling, and the two of them were laughing, indifferent to the curious glances. The twilight was beginning to set the sea aglow. The only ones who sat on were the senator and the lawyer, watching with covet~~~

eyes the voluptuous movements of the Indian girl as she walked away. There, thought the lawyer, went a menace, a taunt to every man. For her, any kind of madness was possible: forsaking one's family, wife and children, one's profession, standing, duty. The senator was not thinking. His eyes darkened with a saturnine desire.

*In which slight incidents, apparently
trivial, but all of which contributed
to the final dramatic episodes, are
narrated*

THE PURSER scratched his head in irritation: "I don't know if
there is a piano tuner in Natal...I don't even know if there is a
piano."

Geir Matos laughed: "You are insulting the whole population of a state, showing a lack of respect for the culture of its
capital city. If the senator heard you..."

"But did you ever see the like, Geir? Tuning a piano...The
pianist never considered it necessary. He's been with us for three
years, playing all day long on this miserable piano, and he
always found it perfect. And now this armchair captain turns up
and wants a tuner. Furious because I didn't attend to the matter
in Recife. Giving me a song and dance..."

"And why didn't you get hold of a tuner in Recife? Captain's
orders are orders. See what you can find in Natal."

"Even those of a captain out of a comic opera? Hauling an
old dame around the deck in a ridiculous flirtation?"

"Listen, old man: the captain may be anything you say, but
he was the one who fell to our lot, the only one available in
Bahía. Now, one thing is certain: the old dame, who, moreover,
is a piano teacher and knows what she is talking about, I, the sky
pilot over there, the stoker, any cabin boy, know more about the

piano than that player you speak of. I'd be willing to bet that character had never even played a record on a victrola before he came aboard this ship. When he starts in, it's a regular nightmare. Moreover, a ship doctor and a ship pianist... Take our doctor: if it wasn't for the sick-bay steward, he wouldn't be able to prescribe even an enema."

"You're right. And now, with this captain, this turd of a ship is really fixed up. Not even a Lloyd..."

"But our captain is as dignified as the devil, with that order on his breast, the size of his spyglass... You're a crank, old man. Do as I do: enjoy yourself. I am having the time of my life, and the best is yet to come," and he laughed in anticipation.

"What is it you're cooking up?"

"You go tend to your business, and leave the rest to me. And find a tuner, the best in Natal."

That dialogue on the bridge had come about as the result of a stern rebuke from the captain to the purser with regard to the piano. Why, while they were waiting in Recife, had he not hired a tuner to come and put the ship's piano in decent shape? He had gone ashore expecting his orders to be carried out. And now Miss Clotilde, a professional pianist, a graduate teacher, versed in Chopin, opera arias, difficult pieces, tells him the piano is the same as before, an old tin can. To bang out sambas, dance music, all right. The young folks paid no attention to the fact that it was out of tune; all they were interested in was slithering around the lounge, moving their feet, hugging each other. But what about the real lovers of music like Dona Clotilde? Didn't they have their rights, didn't the Coastwise guarantee them the use of the piano?

"That tough old dame, Captain, is very demanding. Why, on our last trip we had a pianist from São Paulo aboard who even gave a concert. And he didn't complain about the piano."

The captain exploded in indignation: "Purser, you will do me the favor of treating our passengers with respect. Don't use those vulgar expressions. As for that pianist from São Paulo, he was probably some dead-beat running away from his creditors. And see that you get a tuner in Natal, without fail."

Tough old dame... What a lack of respect, what vulgarity! Of course, she wasn't a girl, but she wasn't old, either. She had confessed to him that she was thirty-seven—a little less than the captain had thought. He had calculated her age as around forty-five, making a difference of fifteen years between them, for he had turned sixty, but that wasn't such a big difference. Once in the course of a conversation, when she made a passing reference to her thirty-seven springs, he felt impelled to rejuvenate himself a little, cutting his down to fifty-five. But those were trifling details; five or seven years one way or another didn't mean a thing. What was important, it seemed to him, was that two who yearned had met, two who longed for understanding and love, twin souls willing to take each other's hand and walk side by side, their old wounds healed, in an unending feast of love. The captain was deeply in love, and this state lent him strength and determination. He would tolerate no slackness in the carrying out of his orders.

The voyage continued without any untoward incident, save for a violent political argument on the eve of their arrival in Natal, which involved passengers and ship's officers. It began at dinner, at the table presided over by the assistant navigation officer. Supporters of the Liberal Alliance, on the one hand, and of the government, on the other, praised the respective merits and qualifications of Getúlio Vargas and Júlio Prestes, and their chances at the ballot box or on the field. The assistant navigation officer revealed himself to be a four-square supporter of Getúlio. He was a gaucho, who swore by Flores da Cunha, talked about the troops of Rio Grande do Sul entering Rio de Janeiro on horseback, sword in hand—for the sword is the classic arm of the man of the pampas—to chop off the heads of those rotten, thieving politicians.

Echoes of the debate reached the captain's table, where Clotilde occupied the seat left vacant by the disembarkation of Congressman Othon in Recife. The senator moved uneasily in his chair, as though the gaucho swords, under the command of General João Francisco, as the navigation officer was predicting, were already at his throat. The argument began to spread to the other tables.

Dona Domingas, the mother of a minister and a congressman, replied from the captain's table, opposing to the lances and swords of the cavalry of Rio Grande the carbines and repeating rifles of the *jagunços* of the northeast: "With two or three bands of gunmen we'll put an end to all that nonsense. Lampião can take care of your General João Francisco. Not one uniformed army officer will be needed. Moreover, those Germans and Italians of the south, those gringos, need a good lesson..." Her clear, firm voice, accustomed to giving orders, dominated and reduced the two factions to silence. Even her son, the minister, gave in to her when, laying aside her usual calm, she raised her voice and announced a decision.

"We're as good Brazilians as the best," answered the assistant navigation officer.

The students for the most part were in favor of the Alliance. They quoted phrases from the speeches of the orators campaigning for Getúlio, talking about the regeneration of the country, the reforms that were needed, a new deal.

The senator, who had no desire to get involved in the argument, smiled, pale and superior. He leaned over toward the captain, who was adopting a position of neutrality, busying himself with serving Clotilde, and asked him in a low voice: "Since when has the Coastwise Line, an enterprise subsidized by the government, been hiring agitators?"

"I don't know, Senator. As I had the honor to inform you, I do not belong on the Coastwise roster. I am just doing them a favor, taking command of the ship to Belém."

"That's so, I had forgotten. But, in any case, it does not seem right to me that a ship's officer should be holding a political rally at his table, stirring up the passengers, threatening the public order. After all, I am a senator of the Republic, a member of the government, and that young fellow is preaching revolution, doing away with the senate and the house of congress, the assassination of public officials..."

"There's a lot in what you say, Senator..."

The discussion went on after dinner in the lounge, where the young people were trying to have a farewell dance for those who were getting off at Natal the next day. Seated in a corner, one group was attacking the president of the Republic, complaining about the high cost of elections, elections which were always rigged, and the need for regeneration. The senator left in indignation.

The navigation officer was the most vehement of all. "Those rascals have to go. If they try to steal this coming election, prevent with a stroke of the pen the victory of the candidate of the Liberal Alliance, they will soon suffer the consequences. The people are not willing to tolerate tyranny any longer, support scoundrels in the seats of government. The war trumpets will sound in Rio Grande, calling out all Brazilians. Lances and swords..."

A steward interrupted his brilliant peroration: "The captain would like to see you, sir."

"I'm coming..."

He was crossing the states of Santa Catarina and Paraná; Isidoro and Miguel Costa had already aroused São Paulo, and the navigation officer was entering Rio de Janeiro at the side of Flòres da Cunha and João Francisco. He rose reluctantly in answer to the captain's summons.

"What in the devil does that dope want now?" At that very moment, when Miss Moema had not taken her eyes off him.

"My young friend, I have nothing against your ideas. Everybody is entitled to his opinion. I do not mix in politics any more. I had my fill, here and even abroad. Here, when José Marcelino, of fond memory, of whom I had the honor to be a friend, governed Bahía. In Portugal, on the occasion of the assassination of the king, Dom Carlos. Revolted by the crime, I put myself at the orders of the royal house. But, since then, I have kept aloof from politics. You have your reasons, I am not the one to deny them..."

"This government is leading the nation to the abyss..."

"I am not arguing. You may be right. But you won't take it amiss if I tell you that it does not seem proper to me for a ship's officer to be stirring up the minds of the passengers. I am not reprimanding you, far be it from me. But the senator has been complaining. He even wanted to send an official letter to the Company. I think, my dear young friend, that you should avoid such conversations."

"That senator is one of the worst of the lot. I know several affairs he has been mixed up in that are an outrage. That business of the port of Natal would be enough to put him in jail for life. And what about that girl he employed in the senate? Why, Mario Rodrigues even wrote an article about it a couple of years ago. Didn't you read it?"

"He's a passenger on this ship, and that is all that concerns us. I must request you not to get into such conversations again."

"I am a Brazilian citizen, and I am exercising my rights... I will say what I like and where I like."

Vasco Moscoso de Aragão looked out over the sea before him, and planted himself firmly on the quarter-deck of his ship: "And I am the captain. I am giving you an order. Good night."

The navigation officer walked away stupefied—"that little guy has got his nerve"—without knowing what to do. First he thought of going back to the lounge, but the senator's irritation, the threat of a letter to the Company, made him stop and think the matter over. He went up to the bridge to let off steam.

Vasco came into the lounge, where Clotilde was anxiously looking about for him.

"Wait for me a minute, I'll be right back."

He did not see the senator, so he went to the card room. There sat the member of the august governing body, reading a magazine, with a somber look on his face.

"Senator, won't you come and join us in the lounge? Your absence is making itself felt."

"I am not willing to listen to insults and threats. I am a senator of the Republic."

"You can come with all assurance. I have taken the necessary measures."

"Very well. For you don't know me, I am very hotheaded. If I have to go on listening to the atrocities of that young scoundrel, I am liable to lose control of myself and punch him in the face . . ."

"Don't give the matter another thought. In a ship under my command the crew knows its place. In India they called me 'Iron Hand.'"

He danced with Clotilde until midnight. He described the incident to her in full detail, and then afterwards—one thing leading to another—his part in the fight between the monarchists and republicans in Portugal, moved by his noble sense of gratitude toward King Carlos I. From Portugal he sailed to India, where the cabin boys had nicknamed him "Iron Hand and Heart of Gold," for, though gentle as a breeze and a friend of his crew, in case of disobedience he could be as violent as a hurricane, and implacable iron hand.

*Of betrothal and vows of eternal love,*
*or how the captain dropped anchor in*
*the moonlight in the heart of the*
*Great Frustrated*

THE FIRST word having to do with engagement and marriage was spoken in Natal, timidly, by the captain. The two of them, he and Clotilde, were walking along the beach of Areia Preta, and the beauty of the setting and the charm of the city were so great that they could not help feeling them, and remarking on them with adjectives and exclamations. The *Ita* made only a brief call at that port, and was soon leaving for Fortaleza. With youthful eagerness, they wanted to see everything, and Clotilde uttered squeals of pleasure at the curves of the beach, the white houses, the Fortress of the Three Wise Men, the river gleaming silver in the sun.

"I suppose you've seen so many things, so many beautiful places in the world, that you must be tired of them, they don't attract you any more," she said as she stopped to admire the view of the coconut trees and the sand.

"True, I have seen many things, the whole world. But one doesn't pay much attention to them when one is alone. It isn't even a pleasure..."

"Ah," sighed the Great Frustrated, "that is true. It isn't even a pleasure."

"Pity the one who is alone!"

"Ah!"

"Tell me something: haven't you ever thought that if one day..."

"What?"

"If one day you met a man versed in life's ways and alone... A loving heart... Would you not consider joining your life to his, having a home of your own, being happy?"

"I am afraid. I think I will never be happy..."

She lowered her head, lost in her memories. The captain sought for words, but it was hard. He had never proposed marriage to any woman; his only experience was that waltz he had danced with Madalena Pontes Mendes when he did not even get around to speaking. How was he to do it now?

"If I were to find a young lady to my liking, able to understand an old man..."

"You an old man? Don't say that..."

"I would be capable of..."

"Captain! Captain!"

It was the senator and two other men coming toward them.

"The hateful creature," muttered Clotilde.

"What did you say?"

"That senator. He just went ashore. What does he want now?"

What the senator wanted was to be nice to the captain, whose authority and nautical knowledge had impressed him. He introduced his friends, one a congressman, the other a planter from the interior, outstanding political leaders of the region, members of his party.

"This is Captain Vasco Moscoso de Aragão, a man of wide travel and many adventures. He has been all over the world. A hero."

The two politicians bowed, smiled, admired the hero presented to them by the Honorable Senator.

"Come with me, I want you to see one of Natal's outstanding creations. A thing that exists only here, the only one of its kind in Brazil, something extraordinary. You must see it, Captain. I guarantee that in all your travels you have seen nothing like it."

He took them to visit a school of domestic science, a very well set up institution whose purpose was to prepare the wealthy girls of the state for marriage, equipping them with all the necessary attainments. They went reluctantly, the captain cursing the senator's liking for him—interrupting his conversation with

Clotilde just as he was beginning to come to grips with the matter, to find the right words. Clotilde, with a romantic look in her eyes, an absorbed and faraway air, followed the movement of the drifting clouds.

They hurried back to the ship, for they had spent more time at the school than they had expected to. The principal did not omit a single detail: she showed them everything, explained everything, proud of her school, its teaching, her pupils, their achievements.

"Now tell me, Captain, have you ever seen anything like this in the other places where you've been? Better or even comparable?" She did not wait for an answer, but went on: "There's nothing like it in the world. Even the Swiss—the Swiss, sir—recognize this. We've already had letters from Switzerland, asking for information about the school. From Switzerland, yes, sir."

"It is a remarkable, a very remarkable institution," agreed the captain, dejected at having lost that unique opportunity, that propitious moment when Clotilde was moved by the beauty of the beach.

But that night, after dinner and a brief pause in the lounge, where she tried out the piano, which had been tuned by a competent tuner of Natal, Clotilde asked him if he would not like to take a turn around the deck.

"There's a full moon," she said with that syncopated laugh of hers.

Vasco's heart gave a leap. This was the chance he had been longing for. They went up to the upper deck, which was deserted.

The huge moon, of blood and gold, was rising the sea.

"Just look," she said, walking over to the rail.

The moon was emerging from the waters where it slept and rested, preparing to set out on its review of sweethearts and lovers, on the beaches and in the streets, on the wharfs of Bahia, in distant ports and on the decks of the ships. The thick oil of the moonlight spread over the green northeastern waters, and the northeast winds, the land breeze of Pernambuco, the north-wester of Ceará, came from south and north to greet the moon with gentle swirls of breeze. Through the moonlight sailed the *Ita* on that magic night when the captain, standing behind Clotilde, took her hands in his, and spoke in a loving, shy voice: "Clotilde! Ah, naughty Clotilde..."

"Me, naughty?" She trembled and her voice was no more than a murmur. "Why do you say that, Captain?"

"Don't you see, don't you understand, don't you feel?"

"I've lost my faith in men..."

"I did not believe in women, either... But now I believe in you, I am dying of love..."

"I have lost faith and I am afraid..."

But she did not withdraw her hands from his, and she was leaning against him and could feel his breath. Without anybody knowing how it happened—one of the mysteries of the sea on a night of full moon—she rested her head on the captain's broad shoulder, adorned with shoulder boards and anchor. He put his arm around her waist, she trembled and sighed. He drew her toward him, and their lips met in a prolonged kiss with years of thirst to quench, of young hearts with an old hunger to satisfy.

"Oh," she sighed when, though still in his arms, she could breathe. "My God, what have I done. How shameful... And now what is going to happen?"

"We're going to get married, if you will have me."

Then she told him her unhappy experience, the reason for her melancholy single unblessedness. One day she had loved a man, had given him her virgin heart, had innocently bestowed on him her complete confidence. He was a doctor who was very rich, very famous, who had come to Belém from Rio. He had an enormous number of patients, he could hardly look after them all. The best match in Belém, and crazy about her. A great lover of music, he even played the piano a little. They played duets together, their souls joined in the music. Clotilde interspersed her story with sighs. They became engaged, swore eternal love, and set the day for their marriage. She was seventeen at the time, a shy, ingenuous provincial girl. She gave her heart to the doctor, trusting in his uprightness and his love...

What could have happened? Vasco asked himself in alarm. Beyond a doubt, one of those nights when they were playing duets, and perhaps the family was out, he had taken advantage of her childish innocence, seduced her and had then run away. Leaving her with her shame and her betrayal. But she had nothing to worry about. He would not respect her the less on that account. On the contrary. It would only stimulate his burning love, reinforce his decision to offer her his hand in marriage.

Trusting in his uprightness and his love... But men are false, nearly all of them. Just imagine what happened on the eve of their wedding...She could hardly bear to talk about it. It was like opening an old wound, she could still feel the ache in her heart. She learned that in Rio he had led astray a poor girl, a seamstress. The unfortunate young thing had had a child, and he sent her money every month. When the poor creature learned about his engagement and approaching marriage, she wrote Clotilde a letter, telling her everything and placing her fate and that of the child in her hands. What could she do? It was like tearing her heart out, but she broke her engagement to the doctor, and ordered him to return to Rio and marry the mother of his child. He obeyed her, and today he is a famous doctor in Rio, wealthy and important, a member of the Jockey Club. The seamstress was transformed into a great lady. As for her, she had sworn that she would never marry, would never open her heart to any man, never look at a man again. But on this trip...

The captain was touched by such nobility of soul, such generosity. He was not worthy of her, not even to kiss the hem of her dress. But as love lifts up a human being, he raised himself to her eyes, her face, her insatiable mouth, covering them with kisses in the moonlight.

Then he, in turn, told her the reason for his solitary existence, why he had never married. Her name was Dorothy, he wore her name and a heart tattooed on his arm.

"Tattooed? You mean it will never disappear?"

"Never. It was done by a Chinese, a master at the art, in Singapore."

"You mean that you haven't forgotten her, that you're still running after her?"

"She died." A moment of tragic silence followed. Dorothy stood there in the moonlight, her slender body, her feverish longing for love. She died before they could marry, on the very eve. She had just gotten her divorce, the husband had finally agreed to set her free...

"Ah! So she was married!"

Yes, she was married when he met and loved her aboard the *Benedict*, a big liner on the Europe-Australia run. It was a passion almost as sudden and overwhelming as that he now felt aboard the *Ita* for Clotilde. She was traveling with her husband, but what do convention and laws mean in the face of love? He left the ship, she her husband, they went ashore in a remote Asiatic port, to wait for the husband's decision...

"The hussy! A married woman!"

No, Clotilde must not be unjust, or think ill of her. Because there was nothing between them, nothing happened. Dorothy told her husband all and ran away only because that selfish creature did not want to give her a divorce. They had not gone beyond a few chaste kisses. She stayed in the house of a saintly missionary, Sister Carol, waiting. Only after the divorce and remarriage would they belong to each other. Dorothy herself had insisted on this. She finally received her decree, the documents for their marriage were being drawn up, when fever, that terrible Asiatic fever, to which he was immune, finished her off in three days. Her, and his career. He nearly lost his mind, he swore never again to set foot on a ship, and if now he was in command of the *Ita* as far as Belém, it was because the law so ordered, he could not fail in his solemnly sworn duty, after his brilliant examination when he received the license of captain. That was why he had never married; he had locked his heart and thrown away the key. But, on this trip . . .

She asked for time to think it over. Before they reached Belém, she would give him her answer; she was still confused and fearful. Besides, he would have to secure the assent of her brother in Pará. And of Jasmim, she added smiling.

The ship glided through the moonlit night, sea and sky drenched with silver and gold. On the deck beside the rail, the captain and Clotilde exchanged vows of love. They laughed for no reason, they sighed, they spoke disconnected words, stealing kisses, squeezing hands. Until they heard footsteps on the stairs, and withdrew to the shadow of one of the lifeboats. Another couple was coming on deck. First they made out the figure of Dr. Firmino Morais, the lawyer from Pará. He looked around carefully, finished ascending the stairs, then gave a sign to the person behind him. It was Moema, the Indian girl, who then appeared, and right there they fell into each other's arms and began kissing with the most unseemly fury and haste.

"The shameless creature," murmured Clotilde. "And he a married man!"

"Love," replied the Captain, "knows no laws, it is like a tempest."

He took her by the hand, and led her away in the opposite direction, and they rejoined the other passengers in the lounge. Clotilde asked him to keep their vows pledged in the moonlight a secret. She wanted to get married without guests, without an announcement, without a celebration, just she, Vasco, her brother, and her sister-in-law. And, if it was to be, they should do it all quickly, she would not accept an engagement and delay...

"Just the time to prepare the papers."

He wanted to return with her to Peripéri, with the wife he had found on the sea, the one for whom he had waited so long, on the bridge of ships, illuminated steamships, dark freighters, on remote and lonely routes. In a last ray of moonlight she saw her loneliness dissipated forever, her long wait come to an end.

*A somewhat silly and very happy chapter, with the privilege of visiting the engines, the hold, and sending an S.O.S.*

THE CAPTAIN was happy. The Great Frustrated was happy. The two of them laughing in out-of-the-way nooks of the ship, exchanging tender glances and shy smiles, squeezing hands when nobody could see them, murmuring sweet nothings, both coming to life again in stolen kisses and plans.

She was romantic and had suffered a great deal. Suffering had made her demanding and distrustful, her romantic nature adored mystery. Because of all this, she had not even told the captain her full name. She was just Clotilde. Nor details about her family, aside from the vague information that she had a brother, married and with two children, in Belém, and a sister with five, married to an engineer in Rio. Moreover, she forbade him to make inquiries about her of the passengers from Pará. She wanted to test his love.

"I'll introduce you to my brother on the pier in Belém. He'll be there waiting for me."

"But, Clo..."

He had known a Clo more than twenty years before, a blonde with a smooth milky white body, he could no longer remember whether in Iceland, among icebergs and fiords, or in Carol's house or Sabina's. That Clo of ice and geyser and this virginal

232

Clotilde had something in common; perhaps their full breasts, perhaps a childish way of talking and behaving. When he called Clotilde "Clo," he could not help recalling those nights of the past, that unforgettable white flesh.

". . . you must bear in mind that I can't go ashore with you, my love. I'll have to wait and sign the papers. It is the last port of call, the end of the trip, I'll be a prisoner aboard . . ."

She adored mystery.

"When we get ready to go ashore, I'll give you a paper with my full name and my address. I've already written it, it is here," and she pointed to the neck of her dress. In the warmth of her bosom she carried the paper that was the key that opened the door to her family, to the captain's new home. "I'll be waiting for you at home, you can come to dinner with my brother and my sister-in-law. I'm going to tell the cook to prepare scalloped crabs on the half shell. It is much better that way. I'll have time to talk to my brother . . ."

"But why all this mystery, this secrecy?"

"I want to test your feelings for me. Know that you love me for myself and not for my family."

"But don't you know already?"

"I am making the test . . ."

Patience. If that was the way she wanted it, that was the way it would have to be. To tell the truth, it didn't matter. He was not going to marry her name or her relatives. She was right. However, he could not keep from speculating about that secrecy. Clo undoubtedly belonged to some distinguished, cautious family out of the top drawer of Pará society, rich and with claims to nobility, like that of Madalena Pontes Mendes. Moreover, at the beginning of the trip, when he had hardly noticed her, he had heard one of the passengers remark about the excellent financial position of Clo's brother. They were probably millionaires, reflected the captain, the owners of tracts of land as big as countries, with whole forests of rubber trees, islands in the Amazon, Indians, cougars, and snakes twenty yards long. Who knows, perhaps all that mystery was the doubt she had as to whether her brother might oppose the marriage of such a rich heiress to a simple ship captain, a retired master mariner. They might think he was an adventurer, a smooth operator, trying to get his hands on his wife's fortune.

On the other hand, if she was so rich, why did she give piano lessons? To keep from being bored, no doubt, to pass the time, and because of her love of music. The first chance he had, he let her know that his income was not merely his retirement pay. He owned a house, and a good one, in Periperi, one of the most elegant beaches in Salvador, a large number of government bonds, more than enough to assure him—and her—a long comfortable life.

Clo held out her hands to him: "Even if you were as poor as Job's turkey."

In those days the ships did not tie up in Fortaleza, as there were no docks there. It was a sight to see the passengers disembark, jumping, from the ladder let down over the side, into the little sailboats. Screams from the ladies, laughs, hesitation, and the rowers with muscular breasts and bronzed skin, steadying their boats beside the ladder. The lawyer from Pará, standing in the prow of one of the boats, was making a display of strength, with his legs widespread. He took Moema, who was standing on the last rung of the ladder, by the waist, lifting her in the air and then setting her trembling body down beside him. For a moment the two of them stood there in the prow of the boat, which was rising and falling with the movement of the waves, beautiful and strong, whipped by the wind. The captain could not emulate him; not that he lacked the strength or inclination, but the smiling Clotilde was too heavy to take such risks with, and besides it wouldn't look right.

Earlier, when he was standing on the bridge, Dona Domingas came to say goodbye, and to thank him for all his attentions: "You have been the perfect captain, sir, it was a pleasure to travel with you." She held out her beautiful hand on which the ring glittered. She complimented the chief mate, the officers, adding: "You gentlemen are fortunate to serve under so able an officer as Captain Vasco."

"One day they will do him justice," answered the chief mate, a somewhat ambiguous phrase, undoubtedly due to the difficulties of handling the ship at that moment.

The athletic young bank clerk also came to say goodbye. He had spent the last days of the trip writing letters to the girl in Pernambuco. In Natal he had stuffed the letter box full.

"A very distinguished young lady," said the captain, as he embraced the love-stricken youth.

On the trip from the boat to shore they laughed a lot. The oars splashed the passengers with water, and Clotilde, to avoid getting wet, pressed up close to the captain. They went to see the city after the beach of Iracema, where Clotilde bought lace "for some new nightgowns," as she explained, blushing and hiding her face in her scarf. With the result that Vasco, in a sudden explosion of desire—seeing the other Clo with her breasts showing through the lacy nightgown—kissed her wildly in front of the fishermen and the lacemakers. When they came back from the city, she wanted to pray in a church. With contrite head bowed low, she knelt in prayer. The captain took advantage of this interruption to disappear. When she had finished her prayers and looked about for him and could find no trace of him, she felt her heart stop beating. Tears rose to her eyes as, with growing uneasiness, she looked all around for him. Finally she saw him, coming quickly toward her. Her voice sounded harsh: "Where did you go? You left me here . . ."

But he took her by the arm, made her go back to the empty nave, leading her under the light of a stained-glass window, and took out of his pocket a little box containing the two engagement rings he had just bought. Thus they sealed their betrothal in that hour in the silence of the church. But he did not kiss her until they were outside, for she would not permit it in the church, accusing him of being an atheist and a heretic. He was merely happy, the captain.

On the next to the last day of the voyage—they would be arriving in Belém the following day at three in the afternoon, and there the *Ita* would spend the night, not setting out on its return trip until the late afternoon of the next day—a whim of the Great Frustrated caused uproar and confusion aboard ship. Clotilde announced her wish to see the inside of the ship, to go down to the engine room, the hold, acquaint herself with its inner workings. Hadn't ships been Vasco's home for forty years? It was a romantic and understandable desire, natural in a betrothed, longing to make hers everything that had to do with her future husband. This was the way she explained it to him, and, with a kiss, he promised it to her.

What was apparent was that the captain, carried away by his passion, had lost sight of the difficulties of the undertaking. Not because of the signs on secret doors saying "No Admission." Naturally, this did not hold good in the case of the captain and a guest of his. But how was it that he, an old seaman, did not think of the dangerous stairways, the exiguous attire of the stokers? And so, twenty-four hours before the completion of the trip, he took his beloved by the hand, and set out for the belly of the ship.

He opened a small, forbidden door, and below them lay the abyss, and that iron stairway, narrow and perpendicular, hanging vertical above the abyss. Clo let out a little scream: "Ay!" but he had begun the descent, holding out his hand to her. Why the two of them did not break their necks is a mystery that goes to prove, if proof were needed, that there is a god who watches over lovers.

The chief engineer's jaw dropped; his explanations were laconic. There was a commotion in the engine room. Stokers and oilers, practically naked, became flustered at the sudden appearance of that lady in their midst. The second engineer clapped his hands to his head. Clotilde, in a frenzy of excitement, wanted to throw a shovelful of coal into the glowing furnace. She was suffocating with the heat. The captain helped her, saying that this brought back his days as cabin boy, when he sometimes went down to work with the stokers.

They went to the hold packed with cargo. The purser, who had been quickly sent for, came down with a face the color of suet. What would happen if it should occur to that crazy captain to schedule a visit of the passengers to the interior of the ship? With him, anything was possible. But the captain barely greeted him, paying no attention whatever to him. The purser went up to the bridge, and said to the chief mate: "Your captain is taking that old dame all through the ship. They have been in the engine and boiler rooms. I am assuming no responsibility..."

"Since when hasn't a captain the right to show a passenger over the ship? Especially one he's in love with. Let him alone..."

"They're going to fall down a ladder and kill themselves..."

"That will make two captains we have buried on this trip. A record."

They had barely concluded their conversation when Vasco and Clotilde appeared on the bridge. The chief mate and the purser could not hold back their laughter. Her face and arms were black with coal dust, his white uniform was a sight to behold.

"I have been taking Miss Clotilde on a tour of the ship. I am going to take her to the radio room."

"Wouldn't you like to show her the control room?"

"Afterwards, perhaps."

The purser went down the stairs, clenching his hands. Vasco headed for the radio operator's room. The radio operator, who was lying down, resting, got to his feet when he saw the captain.

"Is it from here that you send out the S.O.S. when the ship is in danger?"

"Right from here, Madame."

What if she should ask him to send out a dramatic S.O.S., thought Vasco. But the idea amused rather than frightened him; he thought it would be a droll farce.

On the way he showed her his cabin, the captain's home. She looked in, putting her head through the door, but without entering. On the table there was a photograph of a handsome woman with silver hair, a smile on her lips, and two boys standing beside her, one about fifteen, and the other somewhat older.

"Who is that?" asked Clotilde suspiciously.

"The wife and children of the captain who died."

As they were going down the stairs, she said to him: "What I would really like would be to marry a captain..."

"And what am I?"

"Yes, I know... But to marry him and live aboard ship. To go with him everywhere on his ship, see the whole world, city after city."

"It is forbidden to have one's wife aboard. Did you ever think about the dangers? Day after day at sea on a freighter, with a crew of rough men—didn't you see the stokers?—and the wife of the captain on board... Did you think about that?"

"They made a picture with a plot like that, about a captain who sailed with his wife. It was very good, but I missed it."

The captain smiled. One day, when they were living in the house with the green shutters looking out over the sea in Peripheri, in their quiet evenings at home, she knitting, he smoking his pipe, he would tell her what had happened to him once off the coast of Turkey when a silly and impassioned Mohammedan girl had stowed away in his bunk and he did not discover her until the ship was on the high seas. He would tell her many stories, S.O.S.'s, distress signals, dangers he had run in opium and smuggling ports. He had an exciting life to hand over to her, to unbosom to her, to share with her. The next day he was to be introduced to her family, he would dine at her house, and officially ask for her hand.

# Of the complete and augural knowledge of the science of seamanship

ON THE MORNING of that day of the last lap of the voyage, when the muddy waters of the Amazon River had already penetrated the ocean and the sound of its tidal bore could be heard in the distance, Captain Vasco Moscoso de Aragão, for the first time in his long and active life, committed a theft. Afterwards, to be sure, he behaved with the greatest correctness, tamping down his intense curiosity, honoring to the letter his promise to be discreet.

The theft took place in the lounge, which was empty at that early hour when the captain began his inspection of the ship. He had taken a liking to that *Ita*. Nothing worth mentioning had happened on the trip; there was no danger of shipwreck, nor did the crew mutiny, nor any serious navigational problem arise, with the needle going crazy, the sextant off the beam. He hadn't even discovered any revolutionists aboard, as the congressman from Paraíba had said would be the case. But he had maintained discipline, sailed his ship safely, and found on it the woman of his life. He would go back to Periperi with her, to live there among his friends, his head higher than ever, for who could now doubt his title and his achievements? It was at that moment that the idea of stealing crossed his mind. He loved that *Ita*, he wanted to have among the nautical instruments on the big table in his living room a souvenir of that last voyage of his as captain. When he went home it would be as a passenger, an honored passenger, to be sure, who would be treated as an ocean-going captain deserved, to whom the Company owed all consideration, but the fate of the ship, the crew, the passengers would not be in his hands. A simple souvenir, some trifle, to remind him of the happy days aboard. One of those ash trays, for example, with the seal of the Coastwise Line and a picture of the *Ita* engraved on it. One of those that had been given as a prize at the bingo game, like others to be found on the smoking tables. Vasco looked all around, but he did not see anybody. The ash tray disappeared in the right-hand pocket of his jacket. And as one has only to acquire the habit, another went into the left-hand pocket. This was not a sudden attack of kleptomania, but the memory of that good and loyal Zequinha Curvelo. What better present could he take him, what better token of friendship?

After carrying out the theft with such speed and dexterity, the captain felt not the least remorse. The National Company of Coastwise Navigation was rich; two ash trays meant nothing to its budget one way or the other. He would not have thought of stealing them if they had been for sale on the ship. He had inquired about this from the purser and had learned that the last one of the shipment they had received had been put aside as the bingo prize. What did arouse a twinge of remorse was that somewhat forced gift of bric-a-brac from that crooked Dr. Stenio. However, that was not stealing, and it had pleased Clotilde so much. She had told him the very night before, when they were taking their farewell look at the moon and the sea, that she had realized his love for her at the very moment that he brought her the china sofa with the romantic pair of lovers seated on it.

All these things were in his mind as he was making his way to the quarter-deck, where he ran into the lawyer from Pará, Dr. Firmino Morais. The attorney was leaning against the rail, sunk in deep meditation. He turned when he heard the captain's footsteps, greeted him, and they fell into a conversation. The usually affable passenger seemed worried and uneasy. He latched on to the captain as though he needed somebody to keep him from thinking, from being left alone with his problems and cares. He fell into step with him.

"So, Captain, today we will be in Belém do Grão Pará."

"At three this afternoon, Dr. Morais." He looked at his watch, it was seven o'clock. "In eight hours."

"It was a good trip, pleasant."

"Calm, the calmest of any I have ever been in command of."

"Calm?" the lawyer asked himself. "Was it?"

"Wasn't it? We didn't run into any storms, hurricanes."

"Maybe there were other storms... In the souls of the passengers, Captain."

Would that be an allusion to his love affair with Clotilde? With malice behind it, trying to insinuate possible sexual intimacies, unseemly behavior like that of the lawyer with the girl Moema?

"As for me, Doctor, I have always behaved with the utmost propriety. And if I have been moved by any feeling, it has been decent and pure, with the most honorable intentions."

Could that be a reference on the part of the captain to his philandering with Moema, the walks on deck in the moonlight, their conversations alone on the quarter-deck, their going off from the rest of the passengers in Fortaleza? The lawyer could not hope that his intimacy with the girl, that forbidden idyll, had not aroused malicious comments. And now what would happen when they reached Belém? He knew that to give up seeing her was out of the question for him. That mad, wanton virgin had got deep under his skin, he could think of nothing, see nothing but her face, he wanted nothing in the world except to take her for his own, at least once. Even if he then had to kill her and kill himself not to suffer shame and remorse, the tears of his wife, the horror of his daughter, who was almost a young lady. Why didn't this captain take the wheel of his ship, change course, and head for the open sea, without fixed destination, in a voyage that would never end?

He was in such despair that he felt the need to behave meanly, as though to avenge himself for the dilemma on whose horns he found himself. He'd be willing to bet that Tilly the Swooner, the Great Frustrated with the Broken Heart (it was while he was holding forth on his favorite theory that the affair with Moema had begun), had told the captain nothing about that ridiculous business of being left at the altar. He would tell him about it, and perhaps that might lighten his heavy heart.

"And what feelings that were not honorable could your breast harbor, Captain? I presume you are going to get married.

And you are going to marry very well, into a family worthy of the highest esteem. I am a friend of Clotilde's brother, he is . . ."

The Captain cut him short: "Please do not go on." Not that he would not have liked to know those details Clo had so jealously guarded, but he had promised, and a promise is sacred. "I don't want to hear a single word about Clo's family. Nor about her . . ."

"But, why? What I was going to tell you is all to her credit."

"I appreciate that. But I took an oath, and I don't want to break it."

And to avoid further indiscretion on the part of the lawyer, he alleged that there were many things he had to do, and left him alone on the threshold of his miserable despair.

There was now considerable movement on deck. Clotilde appeared, leading Jasmim. The equatorial heat defied the sea breeze. The captain went over to his lady with the clear conscience of one who had lived up to his glorious past.

It was a nervous day. The passengers were nervous, packing their suitcases, looking at their watches in their impatience to arrive. Those final hours were the slowest of the trip. Clotilde was nervous, thinking how to tell her brother about her engagement, how to explain the ring on her finger. The captain was nervous, not quite knowing how to confront that important family of Pará, those aristocrats, "worthy of the highest esteem," as he had heard the lawyer say. The hours dragged, the heat mounted.

At the lunch table, at the request of the rest of the passengers, Dr. Firmino Morais proposed a brief toast to the captain for the successful trip and his courtesies to all of them. Vasco was touched and he thanked them, wishing them all, boys and girls, ladies and gentlemen, much happiness. He clinked his glass against that of Clotilde. At that, the beautiful Moema got up from her table, came over to the captain's, and kissed him on the cheek.

They were coming close to shore now, and in a little while the city of Belém loomed up in the distance. Vasco clasped Clo's hand, went up to the bridge.

With the spyglass to his eye, he looked the city over, the houses covered with Portuguese tiles, the picturesque turmoil of the Ver-o-Peso market, the "Port of Pará" pier where the *Ita* would be tying up. The ship's officers were all on the bridge, even the purser. The chief mate was giving orders. The ship was

241

heading in. Vasco's eyes lingered on the flags of the freighters and steamships already at anchor. Everything seemed to indicate that the *Ita* would be berthing alongside an English freighter; farther along, there was a small ship of the Lloyd Brasileiro, a yacht from French Guiana, and a number of side-wheelers. Blonde sailors saluted from the English ship. The captain thought his mission was accomplished, for the engines were running slower and slower, almost at a stop. The ship had reached its destination. All he had left to do was to sign some papers, and then he could go down the gangplank, overtake Clotilde, receive from her hands that note with her full name and address, perfumed from contact with her virginal and impassioned bosom. Papers which the representative of the Company, standing on the dock, was holding in his hand. Among all those people waiting for the passengers, which one would be the brother of Clotilde? Vasco tried to guess his identity among that crowd shouting to the ship, waving impatiently. Porters were offering their services, each pointing to the number on his breast. Everything was going fine, thought the captain. It was at that very moment, when a smile of perfect satisfaction played upon his lips, that the voice of the chief mate, surrounded by all the ship's officers, including the purser, echoed in his ears: "Captain!"

"What is it?"

"Well, Captain, we have come to the end of our voyage."

"Fortunately, everything has gone well."

"Fortunately. Now all you have to do, sir, is to give the final orders." He stepped solemnly in front of him, raising his voice: "Captain, with how many hawsers shall we tie up the ship at the dock?"

"How's that?"

"With how many hawsers shall we tie up the ship in Belém, Captain?" he repeated even more solemnly.

"But I already told you, my friend, that I did not want to become involved in anything. I do not want to give any orders. I came here to help out in an emergency, but the ship is in good hands."

"Excuse me, Captain, but it must have slipped the mind of an old sailor like yourself, so familiar with all the laws governing nautical matters, that this is our last port of call, and that at the last port it is incumbent upon the captain, and the captain alone, to decide the number of hawsers with which the ship shall be tied to the pier."

"The last port. You are right, it had slipped my mind . . . The hawsers . . ."

In Salvador da Bahía, just before the ship sailed, it had seemed to him that he noticed an exchange of glances between the chief mate and that Americo Antunes, the agent of the Coastwise Line in Bahía, who, nevertheless, had sworn and promised him . . .

"Captain, we are waiting. We and the passengers. The engines are running at less than half-speed. With how many hawsers shall we tie up the ship?"

Vasco looked at him with his clear eyes: "With how many hawsers?" The prophetic gift that inspires poets lighted up his brow, there could be no possible mistake. "With how many?"

He paused for a moment, and then said, in his captain's voice, accustomed to giving orders: "With all of them!"

The ship's officers exchanged looks of surprise, taken aback for a moment. That was not the answer they had expected. The truth of the matter was that they had not expected any answer, but embarrassment, confusion, exposure. But after a second of perplexity, the chief mate smiled—now the joke would be complete—raised the megaphone to his mouth and transmitted to the crew the astounding order: "Captain's orders: tie up the ship with all hawsers!"

The other officers took in the situation, and restrained their smiles. The purser went running down the stairs: he had to prevent the passengers' getting impatient, explain what was happening.

The crew began to scurry about, the curtain rose on that spectacle staged by the *Ita* which was to attract so many people to the dock, with the officers and crews of all the other ships, including the side-wheelers, looking on.

Standing before the captain, the chief mate asked again: "How many sheet anchors, Captain?"

"All of them!"

"How many bower anchors, Captain?"

"All of them!"

"Captain's orders: all the sheet and bower anchors!"

There was bedlam aboard the ship, with the anchors dropping over the side amidst an infernal uproar. The purser was going around among the first-class passengers, explaining to them one by one what was happening.

"How many spring lines, Captain?"

"All of them!"

The sailors uncoiled the cables, tossing them to the longshoremen on the dock, who fastened them to the heavy iron bollards.

"How many head lines, Captain?"

"All of them!"

"Captain's orders: all the head lines!"

"How many stern lines, Captain?"

"All of them!"

Hawsers, steel cables, lines were stretched taut, definitively mooring the ship to the pier. As though it were not already there by deep roots, as though sheet anchor, bower anchor, were not more than sufficient guarantee against the worst storms and the most brutal typhoons—storms and typhoons which no meteorological service predicted, nor the most weatherwise eye of the oldest seaman foresaw. The forecast called for fair, calm weather, with a light offsea breeze.

A burst of Homeric laughter arose from the docks, as well as from the first class of the ship. The chief mate went on: "What about the kedge, Captain?"

"That, too." He heard the mounting laughter, he understood the trick that had been played on him, but he was like a man possessed, he could not stop.

The sound of that laughter reached the bridge, a universal laughter.

"Secured with cable or chain?"

"Both!"

"Captain's orders: drop the kedge anchor and make it fast with cable and chain!"

The chief mate bowed to him: "Thank you, Captain, that takes care of the mooring."

Vasco Moscoso de Aragão's head drooped, crestfallen. It was the general jeering, the laughter that overflowed the docks, reached the city, made people come running to see the sight of an *Ita* moored to the piers of Belém as though the day of the Last Judgment were at hand, and the world was going to end in typhoon and tempest.

Crestfallen, he made his way past the officers, who were gasping with laughter, to his cabin, where he already had his bags packed in his eagerness to overtake Clotilde. He picked them up. Who was there in Bahía to whom he could send a telegram, asking him to sell his house in Peripери and buy that of Itaparica? He had no friends in the capital; all of his old gang were gone, and he couldn't ask Zequinha Curvelo to look after a thing of that sort. Nor even appear before him, look him in the face. The shouts of laughter, forming one colossal guffaw, filled the cabin.

He went down to the first-class deck, all the starch out of him, and got there just in time to hear the purser, bursting with laughter, explain to Clotilde: "...It's just as I'm saying, Madame..."

She had a piece of paper in her hand. Their eyes met, she gave Vasco a withering glance, and tore the paper, still warm from her bosom, on which she had written his name and address, into scraps. The passengers pointed to him, laughing, looking at him out of the corner of their eyes. Clotilde, turning her back on him, went down the stairs to find her relatives. But from the first step she sent him another withering glance, pulled the engagement ring from her finger, and threw it at him. It rolled along the deck and fell with a clink against the metal rail. Vasco's sight became blurred, and he had to hold on to the rail. Haltingly, he made his way to the stairs, when an arm took hold of his to steady him: "Aren't you feeling well, Captain?"

It was Moema, the only one in all that crowd on the ship and the docks who was not laughing.

"It's nothing..."

He did not even thank her, his voice was gone, his joy of living was gone, his crest had fallen. He was almost at the stairs when again he was interrupted, this time by the representative of the Coastwise, with the papers he had to sign. He scrawled his name on them, for his sense of duty did not desert him.

"I have a room reserved for you, sir, in the Grand Hotel. The ship will be sailing tomorrow afternoon at five, and I have reserved a first-class stateroom for you." He was making a great effort to hold back his laughter.

Vasco did not answer. He began to descend the gangplank along with the last passengers. In that strange place, sailors, officers of the docked ships, customs officials, ship chandlers, and many, many persons who had come from the city were marveling at the *Ita* made fast to the pier with all its cables, hawsers, and anchors. It would stay like that until sailing time the next day. The whole city would have a chance to come to the dock to view a sight never seen before.

The target of pointing fingers, accompanied by the unending laughter, Vasco went over to a porter: "Could you tell me where I'll find a cheap boardinghouse?"

"There's Dona Amparo's place, but it's a little way off..."

"Could you tell me how to get there?"

"If you like, I'll carry your suitcase, and show you. You pay me what you like."

From the bridge the chief mate and the officers watched the captain disappear around a corner, his shoulders bent, his step faltering, like a shipwrecked sailor, suddenly an old man. The laughter on the dockside continued.

# In which the truth is brought up from the bottom of the well by the fury of the unleashed winds

IT WAS around five in the afternoon when Vasco reached the boardinghouse of Dona Amparo, a friendly, snaggle-toothed woman from the backlands. She gave him a room with a hammock and her immediate liking, for Vasco reminded her of a helpful acquaintance from Acre. She asked him if he was sick. The heat was suffocating; Vasco sat down in the hammock to think things over. Sick? No, he was empty, drained, he could not even bring order into his thoughts, into the problems confronting him: his return to Bahia, the sale of the house in Periperi, the purchase of the other on the island of Itaparica. The street lay silent under the weight of the sultry afternoon, but there still rang in his ears the sound of the howls of laughter. He would never stop hearing them; they echoed in his breast. It was a sharp pain, sharp and everlasting. Captain Georges Dias Nadreau, this time there was no way out. Something had snapped in the old sailor, he would never again raise his head. Bowed under the weight of sadness, he was the laughingstock of the city.

When Dona Amparo came to call him for dinner, she found him in the same position, stretched out in the hammock. He had not even taken off his coat.

No, he did not care for any dinner.

Dona Amparo was a woman whom life had taught many things, as her boarders and neighbors could testify. It did not seem to her that he was suffering from a bodily ailment. She diagnosed it unhesitatingly and exactly. That was sorrow, and of the bad kind. Perhaps the death of an only son. Perhaps, and more probably, his wife's running away. Married to a young woman, no doubt, he had come home and found nothing but a note; she had gone off, taking with her the furniture and the happiness of the poor man. Dona Amparo knew of several similar cases.

Wouldn't he at least like a drink, to restore his strength and fight the heat? For the heat and a runaway wife, there was nothing like a glass of rum. How about it? He accepted with a nod of his head. She brought the bottle quickly; a swig would not suffice for his needs.

Vasco had been a famous elbow-bender in his day. In recent years, however, he had limited his drinking to that hot grog prepared with such care in his house in Periperi. Now he raised the bottle to his mouth, as he had done when he was young, and drank greedily and without pause. He still preserved something of his old resistance, and was able to stand up and go to the dining room in search of more rum. The boarders, rubber-gatherers from the interior, looked at him curiously.

After he had gone into the hall with the fresh bottle, Dona Amparo explained: "Poor fellow. It's a sad case. A man like him, getting on in years, and with uniform and everything, and his wife, a tramp, ran away with a corporal, a bum. Look at the shape he's in . . . This is a sad and deceiving world."

Vasco slept, a deep, dreamless sleep, under the influence of the rum and the heat. He could barely manage to take off his shoes and his coat. He was half asleep when he took his last swallow.

As a result, he was the only person in all Belém do Grão Pará that night who did not feel the supreme terror, the chill of death, the sensation that the inexorable end was at hand. For when Dona Amparo and the rest of the boarders ran out of the door, aroused from sleep and calling on God, they did not even remember that he existed. There were few who in that desperate hour remembered father or mother, wife or children.

For that night, suddenly and unexpectedly, without any warning, making the experts of the Meteorological Service look like monkeys, flouting all the weather forecasts, astounding the old experienced seamen, a storm broke over the port and city of Belém such as no one had ever seen before, a hurricane unlike any in the memory of the oldest inhabitant, the worst storm on record in those equatorial waters.

All the winds had joined forces, furious, unleashed. They came in a rage, whistling with hate, headlong, merciless. From the four quarters of the earth they came in a vengeful typhoon, eager to destroy everything, as though to say "Sleep no more."

There came the burning simoom with the fiery tongue of the desert, whipping up the sands into a hideous wall. The monsoons came from the Indian Ocean, where the captain had done so much of his traveling, joining hands to rip the houses from their foundations, and send them whirling through the air like dead leaves. Black harmattan arrived from Africa, whistling his song of death, spinning wildly, and tore ships from their moorings, slamming them against the piers, smashing their masts and funnels. The trade winds sank ferryboats, sail boats, and rafts. The mistral fell upon the yacht from French Guiana and, as a macabre joke, dragged it out to sea, tore off its sails, yanked off its rudder, flinging it up on the island of Marajó, where the terrified turtles were invading the villages. The deadly cold that descended on the city came from the steppes of Siberia on the white wings of the icy winter winds. These came from afar, and were about half an hour late, but when they arrived it was the end of the world. The northeasters—the terral and the Aracatí—occupied themselves with the English vessel and the Lloyd ship, tearing them loose from their inadequate moorings, and smashed them against each other to the sound of shattered hulls. The Aracatí sent the Lloyd out to sea, shorn of masts, deck housings, quarterdeck. The terral, fiercely chauvinistic, concentrated its fury on the English freighter, running its tongue of sharpened steel, its tongue of northeastern death, over the throat of the blonde sailors. With a whirlwind, terral wrecked the freighter beside the docks, leaving it there as a remembrance and a warning.

With the winds came the rains from nearby, from the Equator, where they slept in the damp forests, bringing all the stagnant waters full of malaria, typhus, smallpox. They came and turned the city into thousands of rivers, creeks, brooks, gullies. The Amazon began to rise, to eat away the land with its hungry, watery teeth, manufacturing islands and corpses. The bore's scream grew so loud that its horrendous noise spanned miles and miles and was heard on the coasts of Africa, in the city of Dakar, and in remote villages where the trembling savages recognized the war cry of Xangó.

The inhabitants of the city left their houses, the thunder roared, the electric lights were replaced by flashes of lightning, which were so numerous, coming one on the heels of the other, that everything could be seen, the collapsing houses, the carriages and automobiles dragged along on the water, the side-wheelers drifting down the river without anyone at the helm, running aground on the new islands formed by earth torn from the bluffs. The people ran about the streets in frenzied despair, the looters and murderers got to work, men and women knelt, saying improvised prayers, a priest quickly tried to organize a procession, the churches were full to overflowing. It was a scene from the Last Judgment. And the ships which had been tied up at the docks were lifted by the hands of the winds from the four quarters of the compass, torn loose from their moorings, and left at the mercy of the storm. The rains fell, the poor wept, and the rich gnashed their teeth.

The storm lasted only two hours. One more hour, and the city of Belém, with its Portuguese tiles and its antiquated charm, would have disappeared from the map.

The city of Belém would have disappeared, swallowed up by the flood, carried away by the typhoon, but the *Ita* would have remained tied up at its pier, with all the moorings ordered by Captain Vasco Moscoso de Aragão, Master Mariner, the only one of all the old sea dogs capable of foreseeing the storm, and of taking the necessary measures to protect his vessel against it. There it lay, steady at the pier, unmoving and unmovable.

As suddenly and unexpectedly as it came, the tempest departed. The air became clear and serene, and the truth then covered the firmament.

When their terror had passed, the poor began to count their dead and missing; the rich, their losses. The dead were few, the missing many, but the losses ran into the millions. There was danger of epidemics in the city, whose sewage system had been destroyed. The docks of "Port of Pará" were a heap of debris. Undismayed, amidst the surrounding destruction, the *Ita*, with its proud prow, rode at anchor, saved by the foresight of its captain.

Late that morning, when the agent of the Coastwise Line, the ship's officers, the people finally arrived at Dona Amparo's boarding house, which they had had so much trouble finding, Vasco was still sleeping, oblivious to everything that had happened. The people who had laughed, and then wept the night before, were now cheering in the sun-drenched morning. Dona Amparo, recovered from her terror, knocked at Vasco's door. He woke up, but when he heard the voices of the crowd, he thought they were so mean that they had found him out and come there to insult him.

But they pounded so hard at his door, called his name so many times, that he finally opened it and stood facing them, unshaved, in his stocking feet, his pants all wrinkled, his tongue thick from the rum. Before him stood the chief mate, and the hall was crowded with people.

By that time the national telegraph and cable had transmitted to the whole country and the five continents the news of the devastating cataclysm and of the genius of Captain Vasco Moscoso de Aragão, the only one to foresee the storm and save his ship. Telegrams which were published in the headlines of the newspapers of Bahía for days afterwards, avidly read in Periperi, and memorized by Zequinha Curvelo. As well as those which described the homage paid the invincible master mariner by the Coastwise Line: the moving celebration on board the *Ita* which he had saved and on which he returned in triumph to Salvador da Bahía. There he was awarded a scroll and a solid gold medal commemorating his feat. From the bridge he looked out upon the sea: his head once more erect, modest, smiling.

## Concerning the moral of this story and everyday morality

AND NOW I have come into port at the end of my labors, of this investigation into such a controversial tale. What can I add? The news of the arrival of the captain on the docks of Bahía, with a band of musicians waiting for him, a representative of the governor, the harbor master, and Americo Antunes in a frenzy of happiness? His pictures in the papers, the speech he was asked to make over the radio while still aboard ship? His triumphant landing in Periperi, on the two o'clock train, to the sound of fireworks and hurrahs, and how his friends carried him on their shoulders to the house with the windows looking out on the sea? The enemies of yesterday were now his most enthusiastic admirers, with the exception of Chico Pacheco, who preferred to move away; the town could not hold the two of them, he with his lawsuit, the captain with his glory. Describe the emotion of Zequinha Curvelo when he was handed the ash tray with the picture of the *Ita* emblazoned on it? The questions thrown at the captain, all at the same time? The demand that he tell everything, down to the last detail, without omitting a single one? The conversation that night in the big room with the telescope, when he recalled Clotilde? It was a lyrical moment.

"So pretty she was... And with all those young men on

board, her eyes fell on me, and she was swept away...She wasn't more than twenty; I called her Clo in the moonlight, on the quarter-deck. She had long hair and a bronzed skin, one of those girls with Indian blood from Amazonia. She came to ask me to dance with her, can you imagine! She was at the dock to tell me goodbye when we left."

As you can see, once more it becomes difficult to arrive at the truth, strip it of the veils of fantasy. In the last analysis, whom did the captain love, to whom did he propose that night on the deck under the full moon? To Clotilde, the Great Frustrated, getting on in years and given to swoons, or to the rustic, wanton Moema, whose hand had steadied his arm in that hour of trial, Moema, impatient to reach her dramatic destiny? As far as I am concerned, I do not know and I have given up trying.

One thing, however, does seem to me certain and worth noting: if fate was on the captain's side, and favored him, its help in breaking off his engagement to Clotilde should not be overlooked. Can you imagine the Great Frustrated in Peripери, making life in that suburb a hell, playing sonatas and arias on the piano, making of the grand old age of the master mariner a daily round of nagging, restrictions, swoons, sulks? He would never have lived out his eighty-two years, honored and happy, if the engagement and marriage had gone through, that disastrous idea of towing her in.

Now, I have nothing more to tell, my task is ended. I am going to send this work—and no small effort and suffering it has cost me—to the jury named by the director of the Public Archives. If I should win the prize, I will buy Dondoca a new dress and a flower vase; something of that sort is needed in the cheerful parlor of the little house in the Alley of the Three Butterflies.

Don't be shocked, and let me tell you the latest developments on this front of my struggle for existence. His Honor came around, and the three of us now live in perfect understanding and peace. It so happened that Dona Ernestina, the stout and worthy wife of the illustrious jurist, discovered (an anonymous letter, beyond the shadow of a doubt) that nocturnal sally of Dr. Siqueira's to Dondoca's house. Neither the dark glasses nor the broad-brimmed hat had protected him. The Zeppelin went into a fury, it was like the storm at Belém. There was nothing for the retired judge to do but lie, and lie he did, like a trooper. He had gone to that questionable house, true. But he had done so to fulfill a duty and help a friend. The duty was to avoid a scandal in Periperi; the friend who needed help was this modest provincial historian. Didn't she, Ernestina, know that the father of that deplorable girl, Pedro Torresmo, had sworn to invade the house where his daughter and her lover cohabited? Word had reached him of these threats, and, worried about the life and reputation of the young man in question, he had gone there, violating his nature and his moral principles, to warn him. It was a noble decision, of which he was not ashamed.

But the Zeppelin demanded proof, and His Honor was obliged to grovel at my feet, asking my forgiveness, begging me to share once more with him the bed and the charms of Dondoca, with me assuming, however, before the agitated matron, his wife, full responsibility for the girl. I agreed to do it—as a favor to him, I pointed out—not letting my delight, the rejoicing that filled my breast show. For I was almost on the point of letting myself fall into the arms of the Sensitive Frustrated, that overripe vacationing widow whose profile I sketched in an earlier part of this narration. So great was my need. But it was in Dondoca's arms that I satisfied my hunger.

Since then, we have been living in the best of all possible worlds, three kindred souls, His Honor, Dondoca, and I, talking, laughing, making the most of life as long as the heads of government allow us to, all the time threatening one another with guided missiles and hydrogen bombs. One day, by accident, one of those bombs is going to go off, and then we'll all pay the piper.

Returning, however, to the captain and his adventures, the sole object, I repeat, of my feeble efforts, I confess that I have reached the end of his story sunk in confusion and doubt.

Will my readers now, with their learning and their experience, tell me what is the truth, the whole truth? What is the moral to be drawn from this at times indecent and coarse tale? Does truth lie in the everyday events, the daily incidents, in the pettiness and vulgarity most people's lives are compounded of, or does the truth have its abode in the dream it is given us to dream to flee our sad human condition? How does man rise above his journey through this life: by the day-to-day scheming and intrigue, or by the untrammeled dream that knows neither frontiers nor limitations? What led Vasco da Gama and Columbus to the deck of the caravels? What guided the hands of the scientists who launched the sputniks, creating new stars and a new moon in the heaven of this suburb of the universe? Where is the truth, please tell me—in the tiny reality of each of us, or in the immense human dream? Who leads it about the world, lighting up man's path, His Honor, the judge, or the poverty-stricken poet? Chico Pacheco, with his whited sepulcher integrity, or Captain Vasco Moscoso de Aragão, Master Mariner?

RIO DE JANEIRO
*January 1961*